GW00863450

The Rector's Husband

Keith Mullins

For Pui Kei, Jess and Toni

1

There is a tramp on our doorstep.

"She's not here," I say.

Clouded grey eyes stare up at me.

"Ambrose, isn't it?"

The familiarity irritates me. "It is."

He gives me a leery grin. My doorway is becoming infused with the reek of alcohol and decay and ancient, crusty sweat.

"Can you spare a bit of cash? Because she always..."

"No," I interrupt. "She doesn't."

How about some food then?"

"No."

He looks shocked.

"What do you mean, no?"

"I mean no. Now, why don't you just fuck off and leave me in peace?"

He backs away, curling his matted hair around a finger. A nervous habit. He is probably less than my age, but looks twenty years older.

"You can't talk to me like that!"

I take a step down towards him. "I can talk to you how I want. So just do as you're told, and get the hell off my doorstep."

I watch as he shambles off down the path, my fingers itching to wrap themselves around his bloated pink neck. But it would be very stupid to kill someone in my own front garden, just because they annoyed me.

I was lucky to get away with it the last time.

*

My name is Ambrose Hillier and I work in the HR department of our local council. I am there to serve our different stakeholders – the corrupt management, the indolent, incompetent employees, and of course our paymasters, the insanely ideological politicians. The other stakeholders, the voters and council tax payers, are someone else's concern. Or perhaps no one's, I do not know.

I was born in Illinois, and I am still an American citizen. But my parents moved here when I was a child and culturally I am now British. I even speak the language.

My wife - my beautiful, perfect Helen - is the Rector of the parish of St Nicholas, High End. Accordingly we live in the magnificent, if slightly leaky and draughty, Victorian Rectory, which also has a large and delightful garden, much loved by the local residents. We are happy. Or at least, we were happy. But things have changed.

Despite it being by far the most architecturally interesting building left in our depressing inner London

2

borough, the church authorities are trying to have our beloved Rectory demolished. Their plan is to replace it with a dreary, soulless block of flats. As you might expect, both Helen and I are appalled by this prospect.

Unfortunately, she is not really able to do much to prevent it, other than inspire the community to write copious amounts of letters to the council. I, however, am in a slightly stronger position. For example, I have access to the personnel files of all the planning officials. It is therefore down to me to prevent this outrage.

We have no children, which is a great sadness. Our only daughter was stillborn, and after that Helen was told she could have no more. Such an event would have shaken most women's faith - she had always been religious, unlike me - but for Helen the loss only seemed to strengthen it. She threw herself into her church activities, and a few years later was ordained, one of the first women priests in the Church of England. I cannot tell you how proud I am of her.

Oh, and I enjoy cycling, though not in London. Only the country.

So that is us – a totally typical twenty first century family unit. Completely normal.

Mostly, anyway.

*

I am sitting on the sofa doing a Sudoku when she returns. It is a Killer. They are my favourites. Chamber music plays. Locatelli. Very relaxing.

I hear the slam of the heavy front door and a few moments later she enters the room. Helen - my wife,

3

my love.

She is still wearing her dog collar and looks exhausted. She lowers herself into an armchair and pulls the stiff white band away from her throat with a satisfied sigh. It is a symbolic gesture – work is over at last.

I get to my feet. "You look like you could do with a drink. Gin and tonic?"

She turns and gives me a tired smile. "And they say there are no such things as angels."

I go to the kitchen to prepare the drink. A good slug of gin, two ice cubes, and a slice of fresh lemon. Not too much tonic.

Her eyes are closed. Streaks of grey are appearing in her dark hair and I kiss her on the brow.

I see her take the glass, take a gulp, then another, slower one.

"Mmm," she says.

I return to my seat. "Tough day?" I ask.

A shadow seems to pass across her face, like when an aircraft flies in front of the sun.

"I spent most of the afternoon with Abigail Jones. Her son, Darren, has just been diagnosed with leukaemia."

This is bad. I do not like Abigail Jones – she is one of those women who whines a lot and always seems to have a cold – but leukemia is not something you would wish on anyone or their family.

But I am more concerned at the effect such news will have on Helen. Anything to do with children, and she is in pieces. Not obviously, not to other people. But I can tell.

I watch her closely. "Are you okay?"

She shrugs. "I'm fine. I just feel so – helpless, you know? I mean, what can I say?"

She gets to her feet and starts pacing the room restlessly.

"It's times like this I wonder... Why does God do these things? I know all the pat answers, of course I do, but I can tell you, they sound pretty hollow when you're talking to a woman who may be about to watch her child die right in front of her eyes."

I stand and go to her, putting my arm around her and gently guiding her to the sofa. I seat her, still with my arm around her and pull her head onto my shoulder.

"You do what you can, that's all you can do. And the world's a better place for it. For you."

She lifts her eyes to meet mine, her expression serious.

"What would I do without you? You're such a rock to me."

Her gaze drops, and her hand reaches for mine. I feel her grasp before she continues.

"You know, people always go on about virtue, and good works and so on. But I sometimes think the really good people are the invisible ones, the ones behind the scenes."

Then she looks up again, and gives a smile so radiant that I feel I must faint with love for her.

"Like you, Ambrose. You're such a better person than me. Sometimes I think you really must be an angel."

I smile back. "I'm not sure everyone would agree with that."

5

"Well everyone is wrong then. I mean, look at you."

She leans back and eyes me up, her expression mischievous.

"You even look like an angel. How the hell did I manage to pull the best-looking man in our year?"

At the risk of sounding immodest, I have been told this before (the bit about being good-looking, that is. Not the angel thing). Certainly the old biddies who make up the bulk of Helen's congregation appear to think so. Nor are they afraid to tell me so, though I would rather that they did not.

"Perhaps because you were the best-looking girl in the year?" I reply.

"Yeah, right," she says.

She returns her head to my shoulder. "I don't know what I'd do if I lost you," she says.

I lean forward and plant a kiss on the top of her head.

"You never will," I say. "You never will."

*

Later, when we are lying in bed, I remember to tell her about the tramp.
"By the way, there was a tramp looking for you earlier."

She peers over her glasses at me in a reproving way. "I think you mean a homeless person."

This is a longstanding joke between us. I say something un-PC, she pretends to disapprove. She is only pretending because she thinks I don't mean it, though she does still slightly disapprove because in her view I should not even be joking about such things.

6

What she does not know is that I am not joking.

She continues. "Was it someone that we know? One of the regulars?"

This tells you everything you need to know about Helen. There is a large colony of these 'homeless persons' about half a mile away, under the railway arches. To most of us locals they are, depending on our political leanings, a pest, a nuisance, an unfortunate blot on the neighbourhood, or an unacceptable indictment of the values of contemporary society. But in each case it is a collective judgement. None of us attempts to differentiate between the various members of the colony.

Only Helen does that. Only Helen has regular tramps.

"I don't think so. I didn't recognise him."

"What did he want?"

"I don't know. He just asked to see you. When I told him you weren't there he went away. But I thought you ought to know."

She leans across in the dark and pecks me on the cheek. "Quite right. But it shouldn't matter if I'm not there. You can always give them some food yourself, you know."

"Of course."

After a while her breathing turns heavy and regular and I know she is asleep. I continue to lie there, thinking again about the tramp.

If there is one thing that gets my blood boiling it's the way people take advantage of Helen, and their presumption is that she is always available for them and their petty concerns. I hate what the job does to her anyway – the pain that is inflicted on her by the bereavement of others, the responsibility she feels for the lonely and hopeless. But all that goes with the territory, and I know that her job is her life, just as she is mine, and that I will always play second fiddle to that. It used to hurt but now I accept the situation - though I sometimes wonder whether that is one of the reasons I have become as I am. Not that I am blaming her, of course.

But the people. The unthinking, careless, claustrophobic mob, who press around her and drain her of her energy and her spirit.

I detest them.

*

I think back to the first tramp. Not unlike this one – drunk, noxious, disrespectful – but even more so. Vile. An utterly pointless parasite on the face of the planet.

I recall the conversation word for word.

"Can I see the Reverend?"

"No."

A surprised lurch back, unsteady from the alcohol. *"Is she out? When'll she be back?"*

"She's ill. She's in bed. She can't see anyone." A lurch forward this time, grabbing me for support. I recoil at the stench but do not react. As I have said, I'm naturally a very calm person.

But then he makes his big, his ultimate mistake.

"In bed, eh," he says. He winks at me obscenely. "I wouldn't mind being in bed with the lady Reverend. Keep me warm, that would. But I bet you keep that pussy all for yourself."

8

He laughs uproariously and turns, staggering down the path towards the gate.

But a fog has descended over me. That this scum should speak, even think in such terms about my Helen.

I throw myself at him. He hits the ground, I roll him over and then my hands are round his neck, pounding his head against the paving stones.

"Don't – you – dare ever speak about her like that. Do you hear me?"

He struggles but is no match for me. And when the fog clears he is no longer struggling.

And then the panic set in.

But I have always been good in a crisis and I kept my head. I had not been seen – the garden is shielded from the street by thick trees. I dumped the body behind the wall, then 'discovered' it on my way to work the next morning. Of course, I was questioned by the police, but what motive did I, the Rector's husband, have for murdering a harmless old tramp? It gradually became accepted that the culprit was another member of the homeless community (as described solemnly by the police spokesman on the television news) with some sort of a grudge, or local thugs, of which we have no shortage. To the best of my knowledge the case has never been closed, but it has long ago ceased to be active. Practically no one remembers now that Martin Kevin Elliott died a premature, violent death in our garden.

Though I do. It is not the sort of thing that you forget.

But over time the horror of it all, the shock of knowing that I had committed the ultimate taboo, that has faded. I have come to terms with my act of summary retribution. Did he deserve to die? Perhaps not. I realise now he was so drunk that in all likelihood he had no idea what he was saying. But even so, I think it is possible to view what I did as a Public Service. The tramp was useless. He contributed absolutely nothing to society - and I rid the world of him. You could even argue it was an act of kindness to put him out of the misery of his meaningless existence.

The strangest part came later though, much later. When I came to realise that, somewhere between the rage and the fear, I had actually quite enjoyed the killing of Martin Kevin Elliot.

But as I said, that was later. In fact, it was not until I killed for the second time.

2

At work I have an Issue.

A man named Forbes enters my office. Graham Forbes. He is some sort of section head in the accounts department. He looks anxious. But then many of my visitors do.

"Do you have a moment?" he asks.

I gesture him towards the chair in front of my desk.

"I've got a problem with two of my staff," he continues. "They're having a sort of feud."

I regard him with disfavour. He is prematurely balding, but what is left of his dark brown hair is in need of both a cut and a wash. As, I suspect, is his cream, open-necked shirt – the wash, that is.

But worse, he is clearly one of those people who expect me to do their job for them. He is a line manager. He does nothing useful, like sweep the streets, or deliver food to the elderly. His sole responsibility is to manage people, probably no more than half a dozen.

Which by the sound of it, he does not do very well.

I decide to test him.

"Are you asking me for advice on how to deal with it, or to actually sort it out for you?" I ask.

He shifts uncomfortably in his chair. "Well, it would be great if you could deal with it yourself. I've obviously tried talking to them both, but..."

"Indeed."

I make a mental note to take a look at Graham Forbes' own performance. We are always under pressure to reduce headcount.

I pick up my Cross pen (a birthday present from Helen) and prepare to take notes.

"Okay," I say. "Talk me through it. What are their names?"

"Hilary Jones and Amra Fazal."

"And what's the feud about?"

"Hilary says Amra speaks too loudly on the telephone. And Amra has accused Hilary of racism."

I look up from my pad. "That's it?"

Again he squirms.

"I think there may be also some problem over a boy. They know each other outside work."

"Is Jones racist?" Because this really would be serious. Annoying behaviour is one thing, incompetence even. But contravention of the council's Diversity Code is an altogether different kettle of fish. If that is not an unduly species-ist way of putting it.

He shrugs. "How should I know?"

Because you're their line manager, and are supposed to know about your employees, you cretin, I am tempted to say. But his own shortcomings must wait for the time being.

"You've spoken to them both, though?"

He nods. "They're both adamant they're right, and neither will back down. I don't know what to do – they're both good workers. I can't afford to lose either of them. But they've both said to me, 'it's her or me'."

I ignore his bleating, all except the last sentence, which I am most pleased to hear. It will make my task much easier.

"Okay," I say. "Give me your notes, and send the two of them to me individually. I'll see Jones first, in," I consult my watch. "Half an hour."

*

Hilary Jones sits in front of me, arms crossed, lips compressed, eyes fixed on mine in unblinking defiance. Her blonde hair is pulled back in a tight ponytail, and I see the dark roots beneath.

I give her a reassuring smile. "I want to talk to you about your complaint. About Amra Fazal's behaviour."

"Yeah? Bloody cow. Yacking away all day. It does me head in."

"Indeed. And you've spoken to her about this?"

"Course I have! All I got was a mouthful. And she called me a racist!

"Are you a racist?"

Eyes widen in indignation. "Course I'm not! I got mates that's black, asian, whatever. It's just her."

"And what does Mr Forbes have to say on the matter?"

A snort of derision. "Him! Nothing. Just whimpers on about having to work together, give and take, blah

13

blah blah. Bloody useless, he is."

I make a note of this last comment for future use. "And what was your response to that?"

"I told him. She's got to go, I said. It's her or me."

I allow my eyebrows to rise ever so slightly. "Really? So you were offering to resign?"

The girl, who has been beginning to relax under my benign gaze, suddenly freezes. "Resign? No way! Who said anything about resigning?"

"You did. 'It's her or me' translates in my mind as, 'fire her or I resign'. Wouldn't you agree?" I consult the file in front of me, though I know already the answer. "One month's notice you're on, is that right?"

"Now look here!" There is fear in her eyes. This pleases me. "That's not what I meant. I just meant he had to – you know – sort her out."

I lean back in my chair.

"Does the word 'cuts' mean anything to you, Hilary?"

She stares. "Yeah, I suppose."

"The council has to reduce the number of people it employs. So resignations are very welcome at present. No redundancy payments, you see. Now, are you resigning or not?"

"No! Of course I'm not resigning!"

"Fine." I lean forward and scrawl some meaningless notes on my pad. "You will receive a written warning. I suggest you go back to your office, get on with your job, and stop wasting everyone's time."

"Written warning? What the hell for?"

"For unprofessional behaviour." I look up at her.

14

She is pink with resentment but I also read defeat in her eyes. "If I were you I'd make sure that no more is heard about this matter."

*

A short while and a similar conversation with Amra Fazal later, and my Issue is resolved. Personnel management the old-fashioned way.

I turn my attention to Graham Forbes.

*

It is raining hard by the time I leave to go home.

As I prepare to pull out of the car park onto the main road I have to brake suddenly to avoid a young woman who steps out in front of me. This would normally irritate me but she has no umbrella and is getting drenched so I make allowances.

I recognise her as Jane somebody, who works in Planning. As soon as I realise this an idea forms in my mind and I roll down the window and call to her.

"Jane? It is Jane, isn't it? Are you okay? You're getting soaked."

She wipes her spectacles on her sleeve and peers into the car.

"Oh, Mr Hillier – it's you." There is respect in her voice, which I like. "No, I left my brolly at home this morning. But it's all right – it's only a short walk to the bus stop."

"Nonsense! Hop in and I'll give you a lift. Where are you heading?"

She hesitates for a moment, then pulls open the door and squeezes in.

Jane somebody is not a small girl.

"This is really kind of you," she says. "I just need a

15

number 516 – I live over towards Marsh Green."

"Oh, not far then," I say as I ease out into the traffic. "Tell you what, the bus is going to be heaving tonight – I'll take you the whole way."

"Oh no, Mr Hillier, I couldn't let you do that." She sounds shocked. A plain girl, she is probably not often offered lifts home by her colleagues. Certainly not ones so much more senior than her. "The bus will be fine, honestly."

"No arguments – we're already on our way."

We drive in silence for a minute or so. Jane somebody has no small talk and I do not want to appear pushy.

After what I believe to be a decent interval I speak.

"So," I say. "How's life in Planning?"

She shrugs. "Oh, you know. Same old, same old."

I adopt a rueful expression. "Actually, I don't, you know. We're pretty cut off over in HR. We don't get to hear much of what's going on, let alone the gossip. It's a pity, really – I think you feel much more involved in an organisation if you're working with other departments, but - well, it is what it is."

I glance at her to gauge her reaction. She looks intrigued, even a little puzzled. Clearly this is not something she has thought about before. I press on.

"Believe it or not, I think we all get a bit lonely there." Pretending to sense scepticism I continue. "No, seriously. I mean, think about it. All you guys, every so often you'll go down the pub together, right?" She nods, though I doubt that she is often invited out for drinks by her colleagues either. "And there you'll bump into people from Housing, or Environment, or whatever, and you'll have a chat, compare notes, that sort of thing. But us – well, we just don't."

This is in fact true. At least as far as I am concerned, I believe some of my colleagues in HR may socialise after office hours. But I do not. I prefer to keep my private life private. And I always like to get home to Helen as quickly as I can.

I shut up now, leaving the conversation hanging, allowing time for Jane somebody's limited social skills to find a response.

Eventually she speaks. "You could do, you know," she says. "Come down the pub, I mean. I'm sure everyone would be pleased to see you."

I laugh. "Maybe I will one day."

Then I smack the steering wheel with both hands as if suddenly struck by a great thought.

"Now here's a crazy idea." I say, turning to her. I ignore her startled expression and give what I believe to be a twinkling smile. "I don't want you to take this the wrong way or anything, I'm a happily married man - in fact my wife is a priest, for Christ's sake – but why don't we start now?"

She looks bemused. "Start what?"

"The pub thing! Why don't we stop at a pub on the way, and I'll buy you a drink, and we can talk about stuff. You know, break me in gently to the whole thing. Instead of a bar full of idiots from Housing, just you and me. How about it?"

Now that I am putting my plan into action the whole thing sounds utterly ludicrous. Any normal young woman would at this point ask if she could get

17

out of the car, then run away as fast as her heels allowed her. But perhaps I have been fortunate in my choice of Jane somebody. It is possible that she herself has few friends, and therefore the proposal to improve the social life of a random older colleague sounds perhaps less deranged than it would do to others.

"I'm not sure..." she says.

"Oh, go on," I say. "You'll be doing me a favour. And I give you my word – I have nothing dodgy in mind, I promise you."

The car is stopped at a red light at this point and we are looking at each other. She seems reassured by my words but there is also something else in her expression. I wonder if perhaps a part of her is a little disappointed that I am not, after all, interested in her fleshly charms.

Then she smiles. For a moment she appears almost pretty.

"All right, then," she says.

*

I choose a nondescript pub on one of those nowhere roads that crisscross London, joining up the bits that actually have names. I do not want to risk running into anyone I know. It is sandwiched between a launderette and a Chinese takeaway, and is called the Halfway House.

I buy a pint of lager for myself and a large chardonnay for Jane somebody then we sit down at a table to talk. I do not wish to appear to be pumping her so for the duration of the first drink I let her talk about her home and her family, details so tedious that I forget them as soon as I hear them. She begins to relax in my company.

I wait until the second round until moving the conversation onto matters that interest me.

"So how long have you been in Planning?" I ask.

She considers for a moment. "Just under four years."

"And you work with Tom Bates, is that right?"

Tom Bates is one of the Planning Officers. I have no idea whether she works with him or not, but it is a start.

"Not so much, no. More with Alan Grant." Another of the Planning Officers.

"Oh, of course. I don't know Alan that well. Good bloke to work with?"

She wrinkles her nose promisingly.

"He's all right I suppose. Keeps himself to himself."

Less promising, I think, but then she continues.

"Not like Tom Bates. No one could accuse him of doing that."

"How do you mean?"

She gives me what I believe my grandparents would have described as an arch look.

"Well, the story is... No, I really shouldn't."

"Go on – you can't stop there."

"No, it's not fair."

I cannot tell whether she is merely waiting for whatever nugget she is in possession of to be teased out of her or whether she really has thought better of it. I decide to play it safe.

"What about the other girls? Are they a decent bunch?"

She shrugs. "There's only me and Louise in our area. She's okay, but..."

"But?" I prompt.

She puts her head on one side. "Well, let's just say, she prefers male company."

"Ah," I say.

Her tone has become waspish and I feel my pulse quicken. There is surely something for me here.

"So she gets on with Tom and Alan okay?"

She has raised her glass to her lips to drink but replaces it on the table at my question.

"Oh, come on," she says. She leans towards me and her hair, still wet from the rain falls across her face. She brushes it aside. "You must have heard about them. Even locked away in HR, you can't have missed that one."

"I told you, we hear nothing. We're like the three wise monkeys."

This confuses her, and for a moment I worry that I have spoilt the moment. But then she flicks her head, as if to clear it, and continues.

"Right. We had this offsite a few months ago. Bloody waste of time it was if you ask me, but anyway. We were up in this hotel near Heathrow, two days it was, so we stayed overnight. In the evening there was a dinner, and some stupid games, supposed to make us bond."

"And did it? Make you bond, I mean?"

The corner of her mouth twitches in a sly smile. "That's one way of putting it."

"Meaning?"

"For *some people* it seemed to work very well

20

indeed."

She leans right across the table now, so that our noses are almost touching. She smells of wet hair, like a dog.

"Tom and Louise," she says in a stage whisper. "She spent the night in his room. So I'm told, anyway – obviously I didn't see it firsthand. But Andy McRae, he had the room next door, and he heard them." She raises her brows significantly, just in case I am under any misapprehension about exactly what Andy McRae heard.

"Wow," I say. "But I suppose these things happen. And they're both adults."

She looks affronted at my apparent lack of interest.

"They do, but they shouldn't, especially not when one party is the other party's line manager. I'd have thought you being in HR would have been pretty hot about things like that."

Indeed I would be. And in fact I will be, when I speak to Tom Bates about the matter in the morning.

Can it really have been this easy? My absurd hunch paying off, and for the price of a couple of drinks Jane somebody delivering me the ammunition I need to have this wretched planning application stopped in its tracks?

It would appear so.

But there is no reason for her to know any of this.

I adopt a chastened look. "Oh – right," I say. "I hadn't realised that was the case. No, that's not good."

I look at my watch. "God, is that the time? I'm going to have to dash.

I've got a whist evening to attend. I bet that's the weirdest excuse you've heard in a long while."

She does indeed look surprised. "Whist evening? I wouldn't have..."

Her voice tails away.

"Wouldn't have what?"

She now looks confused. "Well, it's just... You seem a bit too cool for that sort of thing. You know. It's what old people do, isn't it?"

It is pleasing that someone as young as Jane somebody considers me cool and youthful.

I flash her a smile. "It's a church thing. Drink up, and I'll drop you home."

*

The short journey to the modest house that Jane somebody shares with her parents and her younger brother is conducted in silence. It is not until I am drawing into the curb that she speaks.

"I hope I haven't got them into trouble. Tom and Louise, I mean. Only I wouldn't like..."

I feign surprise. "Trouble? What, because I'm HR you mean? Goodness, no, you don't need to worry about that. I've forgotten it already." I grin at her. "Scouts' honour."

She stares at me for a moment. "That's all right then."

She opens the car door. "Thanks for the lift."

"You're welcome."

I am already impatient to be on my way. But then I have a thought. The information that Jane somebody has given me tonight is priceless. But supposing at some later date I need more from her?

22

An insurance policy can do no harm. After all, I do not have to call on it.

I continue. "This was fun, though, wasn't it? Can we do it again sometime?"

She pauses in the act of shutting the door and turns back to me.

She smiles.

"Sure," she says. "Why not?"

3

There really is a whist evening at the church.

I am not what you would call a regular worshipper at St Nicholas High End. I have my job and Helen has hers, and although it is never discussed, I do not share her faith. But I attend about once a month, enough to appear respectable.

There is a tacit agreement however that I attend all the social functions. These are without exception horrendous, but with marriage comes duties. The worst is the Harvest Supper and Barn Dance, at which I am expected to do country dancing, which I loathe.

The whist evenings are slightly less wretched. At least I do not get simpered at and flirted with. Even so, I am frequently tempted to write a cheque (from my own pocket) in lieu of the paltry contribution such events make to the vast demands of the church restoration fund, and spend the evening at home.

But I do not, because that is not what Rectors' husbands do.

*

I find Helen in the kitchen, putting away crockery.

"You're late," she says. But it is an observation rather than an accusation.

The phone rings. "I'd better get that," I say.

I go to the study and pick up the receiver.

"Can I speak to Barry Frith, please?" A male voice. Adenoidal Scottish accent.

"Sorry, no one of that name here. You must have the wrong number."

"Is that 02071483255?"

"Yes, but there's no one of that name here. You have the wrong number."

A pause. "How long have you lived there?"

"Long enough. As far as I'm concerned, no one of that name has ever lived here. Now, good..."

"You see, I represent the Southern and General Finance Corporation, and Mr Frith is behind with his payments. It's urgent that we get in touch with him."

I cannot believe this Caledonian moron has the nerve to phone me up and interrupt me and in not so many words accuse me of protecting his wayward debtor. If Helen were not in the next room I would let him know exactly what I think of this. However, I keep my tone firm but mild.

"It may be urgent but it's also your problem, not mine. Now, goodbye."

I return to the kitchen. Helen turns to me curiously. "Who was that?"

"Just a wrong number."

She has already changed for the evening, and is wearing a tight black polo necked jumper and a pair of designer jeans. She looks stunning.

25

I kiss her and gently squeeze her backside. "You look nice," I say.

"Thank you," she replies. Then she sniffs. "Is that beer I smell?"

"I had to have a drink with someone after work. You know, informal chat, that sort of thing. Just boring HR stuff."

She replaces the last plate in the cupboard and shuts the door. "Anyone I know?"

"Shouldn't think so. A girl called Jane. Works in Planning."

"A girl, eh?" She puts a hand on her hip. "Should I be jealous?"

I regard my beautiful wife standing in front of me, then think back to Jane somebody, with her heavy features and shapeless body.

"Probably not."

She goes into the hall and starts putting on her coat. "Still. Planning. Might be useful with this wretched thing about the Rectory."

"True," I say. "I hadn't thought of that."

*

There is a side gate between the Rectory garden and the churchyard, and from there a path that leads to the back of the church and the vestry entrance. This is the route we take.

As we enter the vestry I feel, as I always do, a frisson, something between a thrill and a shudder. For it was here, fourteen months ago, that a man died. Derek Harkness, the church's verger, was brutally clubbed to death with a large pewter candlestick. It caused a great stir at the time, as you can imagine, particularly so soon after the incident with the tramp in our garden. The motive was assumed to be theft, as the previous day's collection money, some three hundred pounds, was found to be missing. But the killer was never caught.

Helen sails ahead of me, seemingly oblivious to the ghosts in this small room. But then she is here practically every day. I linger for a moment longer, and remember.

Like the tramp, it was an accident. Or at least unpremeditated. This is not to say that I had not thought about strangling Derek Harkness, on a number of occasions. But that was simply a normal human reaction to an intensely irritating person. I am sure many other people must have felt the same way about him. It was just that I did something about it.

After the tramp I did not imagine that I would kill again. It had been a shock, a frightening one, and I knew I was lucky to have got away with it. But it was over. No harm done, or not much anyway. Just one of those unfortunate incidents, never to be repeated. But things never turn out as you expect.

Derek Harkness could not be described as a stupid person. He had a certain low cunning, almost entirely devoted to annoying other people as far as I could see. But there was definitely something missing. In the playground when I was a boy we had many other names for his type, but they are mostly banned from use now. Blacklisted, we might have said once, except that is banned too.

He had strong views on many matters. One of these was the role of women, and women priests in particular. He could never come to terms with having a female Rector. He never took on Helen directly, but he was always making little digs about her to everyone else. And about me – including to my face – for what he saw as my failure to manage properly a woman that was my responsibility.

Why Helen put up with him at all is a mystery, explicable only by the fact that she is a saint. I, however, am not a saint (though there was a Saint Ambrose).

That night I was looking for Helen. I cannot remember why, but it must have been important. She was not in the house or the church so I tried the vestry.

She was not there either. But Derek Harkness was.

He is lolling in Helen's desk chair.

The top of his head is completely hairless, a shiny pink dome. Perhaps to compensate, what hair does remain has been trained into a long, straggly ponytail. Jeans and tee-shirt, both soiled. He looks like a washed-up roadie for a has-been rock band. A loser.

He is reading the sports pages of some tabloid.

"Have you seen Helen?"I ask.

He glances up, then returns his attention to his newspaper. "No."

"I need to talk to her. Have you any idea where she might be?"

Another brief glance in my direction, this time accompanied by a sneer.

"What, you think she tells me what she's up to

when she doesn't tell her husband? If you can call him that."

I take a step further into the room. "And what's that supposed to mean?"

I now get his full attention, that is to say a wide smirk. "It means we all know who wears the trousers in the Rectory."

I take another step forward. I am now less than a yard from him. "You really are a nasty little retard, aren't you?" I say. "Why Helen doesn't just chuck you out on to the street where you belong I can't imagine."

A vein starts to throb in his temple. I am pleased to see that I have got to him.

"Perhaps her ladyship likes to have a real man around. Perhaps that's what she wants really – someone to show her who's boss."

"Yeah, right. You? A real man? Don't make me laugh."

He licks his lips and gazes up at me. "That's what they all want, you know, She's no different. A whore in a dog collar. It's an abomination."

And that is his mistake. Just like the tramp, he has crossed the line.

There is a pair of old pewter candlesticks sitting on the shelf behind the desk. They are a relic from the old days, when the church looked like a church and not the TV room in an old people's home. Not valuable enough to sell, they just sit and gather dust.

I do not even think.

I pick up the nearest of the pair and I slam the heavy base down on the top of Derek Harkness's head. Again and again, until it is no longer pink and shiny but

red and grey and white and jagged. Then I fall back
against the door frame and stare at what I have done.

The room is much the same as it was then, except that there are no longer any pewter candlesticks on the shelf.

I follow my wife through into the church proper.

*

A woman is hovering by the doorway.

"There you are. We were waiting for you."

It is Joyce Burnside, one of the two church wardens. Tonight she is completely beige – beige trousers, beige cardigan, even her face and hair seem beige. I assume it is deliberate.

A flustered look appears on Helen's face. "Sorry, Joyce. Ambrose got held up at work."

I glance at the clock. It says twenty past seven. The whist evening is due to start at seven thirty. So we are not late and I do not think that Helen should be apologising to this woman.

I do not like Joyce Burnside. She is a bully. Everybody is frightened of her because she has been a member of St Nicholas, High End for over fifty years (it is impossible not to know this fact) and a church warden for four different Rectors (also impossible not to know) and has become accustomed to getting her own way. She disapproves of me because I do not attend church. But I am not afraid of her.

She is also probably a lesbian, though I do not really care about that.

She sees me looking at the clock and her beige lips purse. Then she turns and walks away without another word.

I look around the church. There are about thirty people there, mostly regular members of the congregation. Because I am the Rector's husband they will remember my name, and I will have to pretend to remember theirs. It is not easy, being the Rector's husband.

The chairs have been removed from their usual rows and rearranged in groups of four, each around a small table. A buffet has been set up on trestle tables against a wall and I go over to inspect it. Sausage rolls, a rice salad, cold sausages, another rice salad. Normal church buffet food.

I take a glass of white wine from a young woman with many spots who I believe to be named Fran. I taste it. It is room temperature.

"Ambrose!"

I turn to see the other church warden, Maud Jones, advancing towards me, arms outstretched. She is a cheerful black woman of about my age. I like her, though I wish she did not wear so much perfume. I have been told that she is to be my partner for the whist tonight.

Her arms close around me in a tight hug and I hold my breath. "How is my darling handsome boy then?"

I am still holding my breath so I wait until I am released before replying.

"I'm very well, thank you Maud," I say. I take a gulp of warm wine in an attempt to banish the scent of violets, though I already suspect it will linger on my clothes for days. "And you?"

"Oh, can't complain, can't complain."

31

"That's good. And the boys?"

"Yes, them too." Then she sighs. "As much as I can tell, them being stuck in their rooms all the time playing those computer games of theirs. But at least I know they're not getting into trouble that way."

"True," I say.

Then her expression brightens. "Your ears must have been burning the other day. We were talking about you in the PCC."

This is news to me.

"Really?" I say. "How come?"

"We were discussing this planning application, and someone suggested that you might be able to help. You being so high up in the council."

I laugh. "I wish. It doesn't work that way though. My department has nothing to do with planning recommendations. And it's the politicians who make the final decision, anyway."

"Ah, the politicians." She shakes her head. "We're for it this time, then. But it's..."

"Right, everybody!"

We all turn to see Joyce Burnside, standing on the dais. She addresses us in the manner of a primary school headmistress, with much imperious finger waving.

"It's now seven thirty, so everyone take their seats. There's a plan on the board over there, and even numbered pairs move after every..."

The whist evening is underway.

*

Later that night, the whist evening finally over

(Maud Jones and I came second), I lie awake and fantasize about Joyce Burnside.

Nothing sexual, I hasten to add. That would be weird. Just the feel of my fingers around her neck, or the look of surprise on her face as some heavy object descends on her skull. Watching the light fade from her eyes, hearing her last breath. Her expression as she realises that it is all over.

The days and weeks after the death of Derek Harkness were the most stressful of my life. I had no regrets about what I had done. He was a nasty little man, no loss to anyone. And clearing up afterwards was no more difficult than it had been with the tramp. I took the collection money, and dumped it later that evening near the homeless colony. (A nice touch, I thought). Then all I had to do was wipe the candlestick clean and go home and pretend I'd been there all the time. It didn't matter about my fingerprints on things like the door handle, because I often visited Helen in the vestry.

But the attitude of the police was very different this time. Because we all knew Derek Harkness, we were all questioned at much greater length. Especially me, the Rectory being so close to the scene of the crime. Probing questions, invasive and intrusive. I had to pretend to care about him, even more than I had to pretend to care about the tramp. It was all very exhausting and unpleasant.

So I made a Rule: Never Again.

Never Again. I carried that thought with me daily. I would never go through an experience like that again.

For a while I felt secure, at peace even. But then I

found myself experiencing an emotion I did not expect.

Regret.

This puzzled me. What exactly was I regretting?

I am a naturally analytical person. I am interested in the workings of the human mind, understanding what motivates people, what makes them who they are. It is what makes me good at my job.

This is what I concluded about myself.

It is all about control. I like to be in control. The killing of Derek Harkness – and that of Martin Kevin Elliott as well, for that matter – had two distinct phases. The first, which covered the killing itself and the immediate aftermath, was when I was in control of events. The second, starting with the discovery of the body and encompassing the police investigation, was when I was not.

The second phase was stressful and unpleasant. This is the part I do not wish to repeat. It was the first phase, especially the moment itself, the moment where I had absolute control over the life and death of another person, that was the subject of my regret. I did not like the thought that I would never experience that feeling again.

This was an important realisation for me. I am not easily shocked, but I confess that it took me some while to accept this new aspect of myself. Killing people is frowned upon in our society, and to admit, even to yourself, that you take pleasure in doing it, is a big deal. Even if (as I believe) the despatch of both Martin Kevin Elliott and Derek Harkness was a Public Service, and that the world is a better place without them. But the facts were the facts. I got a kick out of killing.

Equally, however, the Rule was the Rule. Yes, I had killed two people, yes, it was an interesting thing to have done. But I was now finished with all that. It was over. Even though I may have enjoyed it (or perhaps especially because of that) I decided it was something that I should not dwell on. It was better forgotten.

And, though I say it myself, I have been very good. It is now fourteen whole months since I have killed someone.

But things change. Sometimes a single event, or even a series of otherwise disconnected occurrences, can make a person re-evaluate everything that has gone before. Experience can recalibrate you, give you a new perspective. What had seemed black you now realise was white all along. You understand that you have been focussing too much on the means, and ignoring the end.

I think something like that has happened to me.

It is all very well having Rules. But, as the old saying goes, Rules are meant to be broken.

So maybe one day I will have the pleasure of watching Joyce Burnside die.

4

The next morning I call Tom Bates.

"Tom? It's Ambrose Hillier from HR."

"Hi," he says. "What can I do for you?"

His tone is guarded. I am used to this. Few people are pleased to pick up the phone and find HR on the other end of it. Especially in the current climate.

"I need to have a quick word with you. In private. Would you mind popping over to my office?"

"What? Can't it wait? Only..."

"No. It can't wait. I need to see you now."

There is silence for a moment.

"What's this about?"

"It's a bit sensitive. I can't really tell you over the phone. Oh, and it might be better if you didn't tell anyone where you were going."

As I intended, the element of intrigue proves irresistible for Tom Bates. His curiosity overcomes his annoyance.

"Right. Okay. I'll be straight over then."

*

In less than two minutes Tom Bates is standing in my office doorway.

"Let's go into one of the interview rooms," I say. "It's a bit more private in there."

He follows me into one of the small, airless rooms, and sits obediently when instructed by me. There is as yet only mild anxiety in his expression. Though that will change soon.

I observe him. His face is familiar to me, as are many of those that toil in this building, but I do not know him as a person. He has a strong, confident jaw line, a prominent chin, and grey hair cut slightly long for my taste and swept back in a broad parting. It is easy to see how Tom Bates charms the ladies.

I give him one of my most disarming smiles.

"Thanks for coming over, Tom. As you probably know, we're having to look at headcount across the board," I say. He nods gravely. "So we're looking at everyone one by one, at their performance, how they're seen and so on, and I was particularly struck by this person." I gesture towards the file on the table in front of me. "Louise O'Hare."

His eyes shoot open at my words. "Louise? You can't be thinking of getting rid of her? I mean..."

"No, no," I interrupt. "Perhaps I phrased myself badly. I mean I was struck by her appraisal, written, I believe by you. It's very glowing."

He shrugs. "Yes, well. She's a very good girl."

I raise my eyebrows. "We don't refer to our female colleagues as 'girls' over here, Tom. Louise is a woman, wouldn't you say?"

A nervous smile. "Yes, of course."

37

"I mean, you have firsthand experience of her as a woman, haven't you?"

The smile remains fixed. "If you want to put it like that."

This is fun.

"So what would you say Louise's two most outstanding features were?"

He frowns at me, and starts picking a tooth, a classic sign of nerves. And bad manners. "I'm not quite sure what you mean."

I also frown. "I think it's a simple enough question."

He shrugs again. "Okay, well – she's very talented, got a good aptitude for the work, and also has a very positive attitude around the office. That what you want?"

I ignore the fact that this is three features and nod. "Absolutely. Excellent. And this positive attitude, does that go down well with everyone in the office? Or does she just go down well with you?"

He is now staring at me with the expression of a man who has just swallowed a dodgy prawn.

"What exactly are you getting at?"

I pick up the file. I open it and give a sorrowful shake of the head.

"What I'm getting at, Tom, is that you, as a line manager, wrote a highly favourable appraisal for a member of staff with whom you were conducting sexual relations."

He tries bluster. "That's nonsense. Who told you...?"

"You were seen, and heard, by a witness.

Shagging. Heathrow, your offsite. So cut the crap."

Tom Bates appears to shrink before my eyes.

"So what happens now?" he asks.

His tone is subdued. He is beaten.

It is a pity. I was enjoying the game.

I shake my head. "This is a serious matter, Tom," I say. "You know our code of conduct, and this blasts a hole right through it. So I have two options. I could either instigate a full disciplinary hearing against you, with, I think, the obvious outcome. I'm guessing in the current climate the Chief Exec would jump at the chance of firing someone of your seniority without compensation."

His expression is grim. "And the second option?"

"Or, you could undertake some community service, designated by me."

He stares.

"Community service?" he repeats after a moment. "What, you mean like picking up litter, or painting old people's houses?"

"Something like that. Only I was thinking of something more suited to a man of your qualifications. You are going to save, for the community, a vital resource of buildings and open space."

"I don't know what you're talking about. How...?

"Simple," I interrupt. "There is an application in your department to knock down the Rectory, and destroy the garden, of St Nicholas High End. The intention is to replace them with a repulsive block of flats. You are going to ensure that doesn't happen."

I watch as realisation sinks in.

"Hillier, right. Yeah, I've seen your name on one of

39

the objections. And you want me to scupper it?" He leans forward and shakes his head. "You know I can't do that."

I shrug, and start to stand up. "Fine. Option one it is then."

"Hold on, hold on."

His expression is now panicked. I sit down again and wait.

"Look, I didn't mean that. It's just not that simple."

"Actually, it is. This is a precious resource for the community, an open green space in an overbuilt area. What could be simpler than saying it should be preserved?"

"But there's also a housing shortage, and..."

I raise my hand to stop him. "Tom, you are not hearing me. I'm not here to debate the rights and wrongs with you. I'm telling you what the answer is. And I'm helping you out by giving you the justification. That is it. End of story. Is it that difficult to understand?"

He frowns and looks down at his hands, which are tightly clenched on the table in front of him.

"No, I understand what you say," he says carefully. "But I'm afraid you're not hearing me. It really isn't that simple. I simply can't do what you ask."

I give an exaggerated sigh. "Okay, Tom. Tell me why it's not that simple."

He rolls his eyes, as if I have asked a particularly idiotic question. This irritates me immensely, and I am seized by the desire to drag him across the desk and pound his stupid pretty face onto its surface.

But I do not. In the office I am always professional.

"For Christ's sake," he says. "It's not even my case. It's Alan's. And I know he's in favour of the application. So how the hell am I going to get it blocked?"

"You can use those powers of persuasion of yours," I say. "They worked well enough on Louise O'Hare, didn't they?"

He throws me a disgusted look.

"Have you ever met Alan?"

"No, I haven't had that pleasure."

"Right, well. If his mind's made up he's as likely to listen to me as you are to fly to the moon."

I stare at him.

"So that's it?" I say. "That's your answer? Sorry, you'll have to talk to Alan?"

He shrugs. "Pretty well."

I lean forward and speak very slowly and quietly.

"I can ruin you," I say. "I can get you fired from here with no compensation. I can make sure you never work in local government again. Is that what you want? And think very, very carefully before you answer."

I see his Adam's apple bob as he swallows. Beads of sweat have broken out on his forehead.

"I'll do my best," he says. "I'll try. But I'm telling you, it won't work. We just don't have that sort of relationship. Please. You've got to believe me."

His eyes moisten. And as I look at the pathetic mess sitting in front of me I realise that beneath the preening good looks lies nothing but weakness. If I were Alan Grant I would not listen to him either.

I sit back so suddenly that he jumps.

"Just fuck off," I say.

He gets to his feet but then hovers in the doorway.

"What happens now?" he asks.

"I don't know," I say, as much to myself as to him. "I really don't know."

5

This evening I am meeting my old friend from university, James.

Most of our friends are like us. Forty something liberal professionals, all in the public sector or 'caring' jobs of some sort (HR counts as caring for these purposes, which I often think is odd). We all read the Guardian, although secretly I prefer the Times as it has better Sudokus. We all have similar views, similar politics, and similar concerns, or in my case, pretend to do so (it is simpler that way), though as Helen and I are childless, I do not have to (pretend to) worry about schools as much, except in the broader sense. And we meet regularly for supper (dinner is too bourgeois) to discuss these matters. In fact we are going to Ben and Naomi's next week.

James is not like us. After university he went to work for an American bank. There he became what is called a bond trader, and made a great deal of money. He then fell out with the bank (he said they were not paying him enough, I was never sure if that was a joke) and set up his own business, also trading bonds, although he sometimes talks about currencies as well, so he might do both. He lives in a huge penthouse overlooking the river in Chelsea, and has no wife but a string of girlfriends, sometimes overlapping, all called things like Ekaterina or Ivana and, I believe once, a Qiuyue.

Our other friends all disapprove of James. Their favourite adjective to describe his lifestyle and his wealth is 'obscene'.

It is therefore required that I also disapprove of him. But actually I find him much more interesting than them.

We are meeting at a private club in Mayfair. James is a member. It sounds very grand, but it is really just a bar with high prices and not very many customers. It is a pleasant place for a drink though.

He is already there when I arrive, drinking what looks like a gin and tonic and reading the Standard. He sees me and folds the paper away.

"Ambrose, me old mucker, good to see you. What'll you have mate?"

James often speaks like this, despite having gone to Charterhouse. I think it is something to do with being a trader.

I gesture towards his glass. "One of those would work well."

He mimes an order to the pretty blonde girl behind the bar, then sits back and smiles broadly.

James always smiles a lot.

"So," he says. "How's life with you? You still managing to dodge George Osborne's swingeing axe okay?"

I think of the planning application and my earlier abortive conversation with Tom Bates, and how I now know that I have somehow to find a way of exerting pressure on Alan Grant, a man I have never even met. But these are not matters to discuss with James.

I give a shrug. "You know how it goes. The worse things get, the more work there is for HR. I'm not sure I've ever been busier."

He raises his eyebrows. "Really? Must be a bit of culture shock for you, after decades of public sector cosseting."

I adopt a hurt expression. "Excuse me. You do realise you're talking to a dedicated public servant?"

He laughs. "How could I forget? Such a waste, though. You'd have been great in the City."

He has never said this to me before and I am intrigued. I had always thought that if I did not work in HR I would have liked to be a philosopher. But the City would have been interesting as well.

"You really think so?"

"Sure! You'd have been fantastic in one of those clever backroom roles – research or corporate finance or something."

"What about doing what you do?"

He shakes his head. "Not so sure about that, to be honest. You need a bit more of the old killer instinct to be a trader, you know what I mean? You're probably too nice."

For an instant an image of Derek Harkness's shattered skull flashes across my mind.

"That's a shame," I say.

"Anyway. Probably just as well you're keeping yourself busy, eh?"

I nod. "You certainly don't want to look underemployed at the moment, that's for sure."

His mouth twitches in a strange half smile.

"Indeed."

*

My drink arrives and James flirts with the waitress. It sounds like the continuation of a conversation from earlier in the evening, or perhaps another occasion altogether. She responds well to his jokes and his smile and I wonder for a moment if he is actually interested in the girl or whether it is simply habit. I never know with James.

I tune out and look around the room. It is busy tonight, perhaps because it is Friday. The other customers are all like James – well-dressed, rich and confident looking. I should feel out of place, but for some reason I am never bothered by that sort of thing.

I hear different languages, different accents. London is now a very diverse city, I think. But then I correct myself. My neighbourhood is diverse, which is an Issue. This is cosmopolitan, which is Interesting and Glamorous.

The waitress departs and James turns his attention back to me.

"Nice girl," he says.

I glance towards the bar, where the waitress is now propped on her elbows. Her bottom, barely covered by her black skirt, is pushed out towards us. It is a nice bottom, if nothing else.

"If you like that sort of thing," I say.

46

He smiles again, then the smile fades.

"I don't know Ambrose," he says. "I reckon you're well off out of it. The City, I mean."

This surprises me. James has, in my experience, never shown self-doubt, either about the fabulously affluent parallel universe he inhabits, or his ability to prosper within it. This is a marked contrast to the liberal hand-wringing and angst of our other friends, and while I am aware that I ought to deplore this attitude, it is difficult not to admire it.

I look at him more closely. Now that he is not smiling there are deep lines in his forehead, and I notice for the first time heavy grey bands beneath his eyes.

"Things not going so well, then?" I ask.

He shakes his head. "Last year was great, but this... We've been totally carried out on the dollar. I should have cut but like an idiot I doubled up. And we got the yield curve wrong and then to cap it all we did the other side of the bargain using the yen!"

I nod sympathetically. I do not understand what he is talking about but I can tell from his expression that it is not good.

"These things can turn round, though, can't they?" I say. "I mean, I don't know anything about it but from what I read everything is so much more volatile these days..."

He smiles, but this time, now that I am watching him I can tell that it does not mean he is happy.

"Yeah," he says. "You're right. It'll be okay."

He downs the rest of his drink in a gulp. "Anyway, enough of all that bollocks. Where do you want to

47

eat?"

*

James wants sushi. Personally I prefer my fish to be cooked but I am happy to fall in.   Over dinner I ask him again about his business. He is more James-like this time, laughing off what he said earlier and explaining that he had a bad day. I am pleased about this – I do not want James to fail. He is my guilty pleasure.

I also like the idea that I could have done well in the City, even if not in the same way as him. There is always a part of me that wonders what it would be like to be an amoral, grasping parasite.

After we have asked for the bill he rubs his hands together.

"Right," he says. "Where next?"

I had assumed that 'next' would be home. But if James really has had a bad day, and wants to go on partying, it would seem ill-mannered to refuse.

"I don't know," I say. "What do you suggest?"

He thinks for a moment.

"Samarkand's just around the corner. Awesome girls, there. Absolutely stunning."

"Girls?"

There have been awkward situations in the past, where James seems set on what he calls a takeaway. In contrast I, however tempting the array of flesh on offer, never have any desire to do anything other than go back to Helen (without removing my trousers on the way).

He laughs. "Not that sort of girls. Nice, normal girls – models, actresses and so on."

48

This is what is considered normal in James's world.

"Fine," I say.

*

There is a gaggle of people waiting outside the club. But the shaven-headed bouncer recognises James and smiles.

"Evening Mr Weston," he says. He pulls aside the red velvet rope.

The club is quieter than some that James has taken me to before, which pleases me. I do not like having to shout to make myself heard the whole time. Perhaps I am getting old.

James orders a bottle of Bollinger and we lean on the bar, looking round the room. It is still early (by club standards). Only about twenty people are here, some standing in groups or sitting, talking, but mostly just eying each other up. No one is dancing yet.

James points out a man on his own at the end of the bar, slim, in his thirties. He is smartly dressed in a navy suit and white shirt (though with one or two too many buttons undone for my taste).

"See him?" I nod and he continues. "That's Andre. He's the resident dealer. Coke, mainly, but other stuff if you need it."

I observe the man with interest. While like any right-thinking citizen I deplore the cynical exploitation of the drugs industry and the misery and destruction it causes, it is difficult not to be impressed by all the varied things (and people) that James knows.

"You don't, though, do you?" I ask.

He shoots me a glance. "What, drugs? Nah." Then

he grins and takes a swig of his champagne. "Not often, anyway."

Two young women, one blonde and one brunette, wander in and settle at the bar next to us. Both are pretty in that quirky, modern way, and both unhealthily skinny. I wonder if they are some of the models that James was talking about.

The blonde fumbles in her handbag while the brunette glances around the bar, her eyes darting about, never resting anywhere for a second. Eventually they meet mine, at which she pauses, and gives a quick smile.

I feel a sharp nudge in the ribs. "There we are, Ambrose, the old magic's still there."

Before I can reply he has turned his attention to the girls.

"Good evening ladies, can we tempt you to join us for a drink?" He gives a theatrical bow in the direction of our ice bucket.

The women exchange a quick glance, then the blonde answers for both.

"Why not? Thanks very much."

James beckons to the barman for two extra glasses. "I'm James, and this is Ambrose, by the way," he says. "And you are..?"

"I'm Ella," says the blonde. "And this is Carla. We're both models."

The brunette is staring at me curiously. "Ambrose," she repeats. "That's unusual. Where did you find it?"

I am momentarily confused by her phraseology. Then I remember that in their world many people choose names that they think will make them seem more interesting.

"Oh, I don't know," I say. "It just came to me, and it seemed, just, right, you know?"

She nods, and I see James give an approving smile. He likes me to role play when we are out on these occasions. For example, I am never allowed to say I am in local government because that is very uncool. Instead he usually describes me as a 'fixer', whatever that is.

"Shall we sit down?" he suggests.

We take a table. The conversation seems to naturally segment, with James chatting to Ella and me to Carla. I hear about Carla's hopes for her modelling career, while I speak in very general terms (as I have no idea how a fixer would actually spend their time) of my imaginary life, sprinkled with references to LA and New York and Cannes (which I also have to invent).

It is an amusing way of passing the time, and it allows me fantasise about what it would be like to be, in reality, the person I am pretending to be. Coming to places like this, drinking champagne whenever I want, taking a different anorexic home every night (at least the dinner dates would be cheap), occasionally buying illicit substances from Andre. I think I would be good at it. Certainly Ambrose the fixer seems to be a hit with Carla.

After a while Ella leans across and whispers something to Carla. Carla nods and they both get to their feet, giggling.

"If you'll excuse us for a moment," says Ella.

They disappear in the direction of the cloakrooms,

still giggling. On two occasions Carla glances over her shoulder at me.

James watches them go with a satisfied smile. "Think you're in there, mate," he says.

I glance at my watch. It is half past eleven. "I think you're right," I say. "But I'd better be going. Some of us have to work in the morning."

He turns and stares at me for a while before speaking. "Ambrose, did anyone ever tell you how weird you are? I mean, you go to all the trouble to chat up a beautiful girl, getting her all up for it, and then you just suddenly say, 'right, I'm off'. It's not natural."

I shrug as I get to my feet. "You go fishing, don't you? And you enjoy it, even though you sometimes have to throw them back? It's the same thing."

He is still shaking his head as I clap him on the shoulder.

"I'm a married man, remember? Anyway, it's been fun. Say good bye for me, will you?"

*

My journey home on the night bus is disturbed by a group of youths, foul-mouthed and bestial in their drunkenness. I imagine myself following them when they leave the bus and giving them what they deserve, but I do not do this. I recognise my bravado as also being induced by alcohol, and I am not a vigilante. In addition there are four of them (and one of me) and they probably all carry knives.

I think back over my evening. I do enjoy these visits to James's world. I enjoy the unaccustomed luxury, the play-acting, all the might-have-beens.

Equally, though, I am also always happy to return

home, to see Helen again. A night in the bony clutches of Carla would, I am sure, be very entertaining. But I have no interest in putting this theory to the test.

Not while I have my wife.

*

It is gone midnight before I arrive back at the Rectory. I am feeling a little flat. Maybe it is that I have had a little too much to drink, or maybe it is the youths on the bus. Perhaps it is simply tiredness. I have not been sleeping well recently, worrying about our home. Then when I wake, it is always with a sense of unease, of something precious slipping away from me.

Perhaps I really am just getting old.

The living room is in darkness, but to my surprise I find Helen sitting on the sofa. The plans for the redevelopment of the Rectory are where I had left them earlier, spread out on the low table in front of her. Also on the table I see a bottle of Cotes du Rhone and a glass, both empty.

I switch on the light.

"Everything all right, my love?" I ask.

She looks up at me and it is as if I have been punched in the stomach. Her eyes are red and there are dark streaks running down her cheeks.

My darling wife has been crying.

"There was a meeting about the Children's Party," she says. "Planning all the entertainments, the food, who's doing what and so on. It's only a few weeks away now. Then it suddenly hit me. This might be the last time."

The annual Children's Party is the highlight of the church's social calendar. It is held in the Rectory

53

garden, with tents and stalls put up all over the huge lawn. There are games and refreshments, clowns and musicians. All the children in the parish are invited, and we always get a good turnout. Half of them probably never get to see a proper patch of grass any other time. Helen loves it. The church's chance to make a real contribution to the community, she calls it.

"This bloody planning application," she continues. "It's just vandalism, Ambrose. Absolute vandalism."

My concern increases. Helen never swears.

I sit beside her and put my arm around her shoulder. "It's not a done deal, you know," I say. "The council have got to approve it yet, and you've done a marvellous job of mobilising the congregation and the residents' associations. They're going to get a hell of a lot of letters against."

She gives a tired smile. "I know, but do you really think they're going to make a difference? Honestly? You know how these things work. Once these big institutions decide on something the little person doesn't stand a chance."

I have nothing to say. Because of course she is right.

"You see?" She sighs and lays her head on my shoulder. "Oh, what are we going to do, Ambrose? I can't bear it."

We sit in silence for a while and I think.

To me, the Rectory is a pleasant building with an unusually large garden, but that is all. Buildings are erected, and they are demolished (unless they fall down first). It would not shatter my world if this one ceases to exist.

But it is not about me. It is about Helen. And Helen is different. She is very attached to this house, and especially the garden. It is her home, of course. But of more concern to her is its importance to the local community. It is a heritage that should never be lost, she has said. Right now, even the prospect of its destruction is enough to cause her real distress. How she will react if these plans go ahead is not something that I can contemplate.

There is no question about it. These plans must be stopped.

How I am to do this now that my efforts with Tom Bates seem likely to come to nothing, I do not know. But one thing is clear. My campaign needs to be radically intensified. My wife's happiness is at stake.

First thing Monday morning, I shall go into action. Properly.

My gaze alights on the photograph of Helen that stands on a table in the corner of the room. It is my favourite picture of her.

It is a large photograph, about a foot high, and was taken a few years ago when we were on holiday in Corfu. She is standing on a rocky outcrop on a beach, a colourful sarong tied around her waist. Her hair is blowing in the unseen wind and her face is tanned and relaxed. She is laughing.

She looks beautiful.

I look back down at the woman settled against me. And I know that there is nothing I would not do to return that carefree expression to her face.

Absolutely nothing.

"We'll beat this, Helen. You've going to have to trust me. But we're going to beat it."

6

Saturdays are a strange time in our house. If Helen is not taken up with her priestly duties we do normal family things. Shopping, reading the papers, maybe going out for a pub lunch. Often though she will have a wedding, sometimes more than one, in which case I will be left to entertain myself.

So I have recently taken to loading my bicycle into the back of our new Skoda estate and heading off to the countryside. This was Helen's idea, actually. I do not do a great deal of exercise. I detest gyms, and I cannot believe that running around the polluted streets of our neighbourhood is good for you. But I love the exhilaration, the tautness in the muscles, that sense of sweaty achievement you feel after a long, hard bike ride. Something to do with endorphins, I believe.

Today there is just the one wedding that Helen has to attend. I was hoping to go to the Chilterns, which is very suitable for my style of cycling, but it is pouring with rain. So instead I shall stay in and do some Sudokus.

It occurs to me that it is also a shame for the happy couple.

*

After Helen has gone I settle down on the sofa with the newspaper and a cup of coffee, but I find I cannot concentrate. I keep thinking about my previous trip to the Chilterns. It was only a few weeks ago but after what happened that day – well, it seems longer.

It all started ordinarily enough. It had been a difficult time for me, and what with one thing and another I was feeling very stressed and angry with the world. I headed out of London for some hard riding. But by the time I returned home I had had my Revelation. Or as Helen might say, my Road to Damascus moment. (That is if I talked to her about such things, which I do not).

I close my eyes and remember.

I am sitting, leaning against a tree. I am having my lunch, a small picnic I have brought for the purpose, and reading my newspaper. I have wheeled the bike a little way down a side path and pull it a few yards where there is a patch of more open ground, and I can enjoy the sunshine.

It is busy today. It is good walking weather, and there is scarcely a moment when there are not at least two different parties visible on the path. Many of the walkers nod or smile in my direction as they pass. I do not wish to encourage this behaviour so I avoid eye contact, concentrating instead on my newspaper. But equally I do not wish to appear overly unfriendly.

I have finished my sandwich and am thinking of

moving on when a man approaches me.

"What the hell do you think you're doing?" he asks.

Addressed directly in this manner, I have no option but to respond, and I look up.

The man is about sixty, dressed in a green waxed jacket and a tweed cap. He has a prominent nose, a weak chin and a small, petulant mouth.

I think of various sarcastic answers but do not wish to cause myself unnecessary aggro.

"I was just finishing my lunch," I say. I give him a disarming smile.

"I can see that. What I want to know is, why you're doing it on my land. This isn't bloody Hyde Park, you know."

He speaks in a penetrating upper-class bark, and I stare at him with dislike. I have tried to be pleasant but he is simply being rude. "As far as I'm aware this is Forestry Commission land." I say.

The man glares down at me. "You left the Forestry Commission Land half a mile back. You are now on the Dundridge estate. There's a Right of Way, but it says specifically that walkers are not to leave the path. Didn't you see the signs?"

I begin to get annoyed with the man I presume to be Mr Dundridge and his stupid pedantry.

I fold my arms across my chest and glare back.

"Obviously not. But what am I – ten feet off the path?"

His florid face becomes, if anything, even redder and he jabs a finger at me.

"You lot, you're all the same. Absolutely no

59

respect for private property, with your so-called Rights of Way. Trampling my crops, dropping litter. I'm damned if I'm having you wandering around the rest of my land as well. Bloody nuisance, the lot of you!"

I get to my feet and move to face him. He is shorter than me and as I look down into his angry, bloodshot eyes I observe a small nervous tic I had not noticed before.

"The only nuisance around here is standing in front of me."

I see his jaw tighten with rage. "Are you going to get off my land or am I going to have to call my gamekeeper?"

I itch to smash my fist into his face. I find myself wondering if the tic would stop if I hit him hard enough. But there are too many people here to make it worth getting into a fight.

Suddenly I am weary with the confrontation. All I want to do is get away and carry on with my cycle ride.

I start to gather my things into the rucksack.

"Don't worry, I'm going," I say.

And I set off back down the path.

My day had been ruined. The fragile sense of wellbeing that the endorphins had induced in me had been shattered, blown away beyond all hope of repair. And all because of the totally unnecessary unpleasantness of one over-privileged yob.

It is hard to imagine a more benign, unthreatening bunch of people than those who chose to don walking boots or a cycling helmet and set off for some fresh air in the Buckinghamshire countryside. Yet this uncouth throwback, brain probably atrophied by

60

generations of inbreeding, makes it his mission to inflict his petty misanthropy on anyone who dares do so.

It was then, as I reflected that Mr Dundridge was no more deserving of life than either Martin Kevin Elliott or Derek Harkness, that I had my Revelation.

Just because I enjoyed the act of killing did not make it wrong. What mattered was the nature of the person being killed. Killing a normal, decent citizen would be wrong however I felt about it. But by the same token, the execution (for that is what it would be) of a nasty little jerk like Mr Dundridge would be justified, equally irrespective of my feelings. It would be a Public Service, pure and simple.

This was a revelation so powerful that it literally took my breath away. I must have stood by the path for several minutes simply thinking about it. (I imagine I looked very strange. I recalled later that I had received some very odd glances from passersby).

Of course, this did not mean that I was about to chase off down the path and exact my revenge on Mr Dundridge. The Rule was there for a purpose. I still never wanted to face a police investigation again.

But perhaps, I thought to myself, when people really, *really* deserved it...

...the Rule did need to become a little more flexible.

*

Monday morning. And I am stuck in a management meeting.

The meeting itself is no more pointless and irrelevant than usual. (Though some might find it strange that a proposal for the appointment of a Gypsy and Traveller Awareness Officer features on the same agenda as redundancy plans for most of the borough's library staff.) But today I find it difficult to control my impatience. I have more pressing matters to attend to.

As soon as I return to my desk I consult the council's employment records, specifically those for the Planning Department. There are two Janes listed – Gardner and Olukayode. I have a good idea which one of these is my Jane, but I check the photograph on file just in case – it would be most embarrassing to make a mistake. But I am right, and I can now think of Jane somebody by her proper name.

Jane Gardner.

I prepare an email.

'Hi Jane,

Hope all is well with you. Just wanted to say how much I enjoyed our conversation the other evening – as we said, it's good to be able to chill away from the office sometimes. Just as well we left when we did, though, I was nearly late for my whist evening!

Regarding meeting up again, just wondering how you're fixed this week? You may be busy, of course, but if not I'm pretty free most days except Friday. If not, no worries – there's always another time!

Ciao,

Ambrose'

I read it back carefully, checking it for tone and style. I want to sound upbeat and friendly, but relaxed. Not pushy. Mildly illiterate, with unnecessary and excessive use of exclamation marks, which is how I have noticed young poorly educated people write themselves. It is a manner with which she should feel comfortable. I am particularly pleased with the implicit assumption, which is almost certain to be wrong but which will be flattering to her, that Jane Gardner has a thriving and busy social life.

And of course, nothing incriminating, or that cannot be explained away, in the event it is ever read by unfriendly eyes.

I put in one more exclamation mark (after the 'sometimes') then press the Send button. Then I turn my attention to my own In box.

My expectation is that Jane Gardner will be surprised to receive this email, that she will read it through a number of times looking for hidden meanings, and generally take her time before deciding how to respond. (I am hoping that she does not ask the advice of a girlfriend. I am not too worried about this though as I have the impression from our last meeting that she does not have many, not in the office at least.)

She will be flattered and intrigued, and will eventually conclude that no harm can come from having a friendly drink with a happily married colleague who is probably just a bit lonely. But she will herself not want to appear too eager, so I expect a response, in the affirmative, sometime this afternoon.

So I am myself surprised to see pop into my In box no more than two minutes later a reply.

'Hi Ambrose, im good thx drink sounds fun. This eve? Shall we meet in car park, what time?

J'

I read the message through myself several times.

63

But the only hidden message here seems to be that Jane Gardner is either very busy or did not pay enough attention in her English lessons at school.

But I am pleased with her response. Her enthusiasm to see me is encouraging, and should make my task easier. I reply.

'Great! Six o'clock okay with you? In the car park.
See you then.
A.'

I return my attention to the rest of my In box.

7

I arrive at the car park a few minutes early. I was brought up to believe that it is bad manners to keep a lady waiting.

I am realistic about the prospects of gleaning anything useful from this evening's rendezvous with Jane Gardner. I was lucky last time. But if there are any more skeletons concealed in the Planning Department's dusty cupboards, and specifically any dirt to be dug on Alan Grant, she is the person to tell me about it. I have met her type before. Quiet, almost invisible, people forget she is there at all. Then they lower their guard, let things slip.

Things that the Jane Gardners of the world hoard away in their minds, even if they do not know why they do so.

So maybe I will be lucky again.

I need to be.

I see her approaching and wave a greeting. She waves back.

I notice that she looks different today. Her hair is dry, of course, and she seems to be wearing a little more make-up, but there is something else as well. Then it occurs to me – she is not wearing glasses. Perhaps she has acquired some contact lenses.

"You look nice," I say as I hold the passenger door open for her.

She blushes a little. "Thank you."

"Any ideas where you'd like to go?" I ask as we drive off. "I don't really know the pubs around here very well."

This is not true. But as before I am keen to avoid running into anyone that I know while drinking with Jane Gardner.

She shrugs. "Not especially. Where we went last time was nice enough."

Nice would not be the word I would use to describe The Halfway House. But it is adequate for my purpose.

"The Halfway House it is then," I say.

*

"How was your weekend?" I ask.

We are inching our way, painfully slowly, through the rush hour traffic. This always makes me want to rip everyone who is blocking me out of their vehicles and smash their stupid faces onto their windscreens until they get out of my way. It makes it hard to maintain an attitude of relaxed bonhomie.

"Oh, brilliant!" she replies. I am so surprised by the enthusiasm in her voice that I turn to stare. She is grinning. "I met up with some old school friends and we went clubbing in Croydon. It was absolutely mad."

"I wouldn't have put you down as a clubbing sort of girl."

"Maybe there's a lot about me that you don't know."

This now seems quite possible. I must be careful not to jump to conclusions about Jane Gardner.

"In which case I look forward to finding out," I say.

This produces a giggle.

"What about you?" she says. "Good weekend?"

"Quiet," I say. "Helen had two weddings on Saturday, then church all Sunday morning and again in the evening, so I hardly saw her. A lot of our weekends are like that."

I sense her watching me. "That's a shame," she says. "What do you do when you're on your own?"

I shrug. "This and that. I like cycling, so quite often I'll go off and do a long ride in the country."

A sideways look followed by another giggle. "That explains it then."

This puzzles me and I glance at her. "Explains what?" I ask.

"You looking so fit." She holds my gaze for a moment then turns her attention back to the rush hour traffic.

"Still. It must get a bit lonely for you, I expect."

"Oh, I'm fine. I'm used to it by now. I can usually find something to do to entertain myself."

*

We sit at the same table and again I have a pint of lager and Jane Gardner has a large glass of chardonnay. It occurs to me that already we are falling into routines, like a couple. I find this idea disturbing and put it from my mind.

"How's work?" I ask. "Busy?"

67

She shrugs. "So so."

"Only I got the impression this morning that you were in a bit of a rush."

"This morning," She frowns. "Oh yes, when you emailed. Alan was trying to talk to me. He wanted something done on one of his applications..."

Suddenly her eyes widen and she claps her hand to her mouth. "Oh my God!" she says. "It's not – I mean, you being married to a priest – it's not the same..."

"Sorry?" I say. I endeavour to conceal my excitement at her words, instead to look mildly baffled. "I think you've lost me."

"This application. It's to pull down an old Rectory and build a block of flats. I'm sure I've seen the name Hillier on one of the letters opposing it. Is that you?"

"Well, yes. I have to say, I'd rather not get too involved, but my wife feels very strongly about it."

"But we're getting loads of letters against it – it seems to be hugely controversial." She pauses and her brow furrows with uncertainty. "I wonder if I should be talking to you at all."

"Now hold on, hold on," I say. I swallow hard and choose my next words with care. "Let's get one thing clear – this is Helen's thing, not mine. I couldn't give a damn about it, really. It's far too big for one couple, costs a fortune to heat, and on top of everything else is practically falling down. As far as I'm concerned, they can pull the bloody thing down next week. I certainly don't want it coming between us."

I stop there to allow Jane Gardner to digest my

words. I am pleased with the sincerity I have managed to put into them. Together with her inherent respect for my seniority and experience I am confident that they will allay her fears.

"Okay," she says. "If you're sure. But we probably shouldn't talk about it."

I shrug and drain the rest of my beer. "Suits me," I say. "Same again?"

*

"So tell me about Croydon," I say when I have returned with our drinks. "Do you transform into some sort of Goth for the weekends, or what?"

She giggles. "Not really. We dress up a bit, obviously, but Goth's not really my style."

"What then? It's a while since I've been that way myself do I don't know what the current look is. Fishnets? Basque?"

She laughs again and gives me a sideways look, flirtatious yet also calculating. "Is that your thing, then?"

I meet her gaze. "Depends who's inside them, I guess."

She smiles and drops her eyes to her drink.

I am pleased that we are getting on so well. Though I do not really want to think of Jane Gardner in either fishnets or a basque.

"What's your boyfriend say?" I ask.

She shakes her head and takes a sip of her wine. "Haven't got one," she says.

"Ah," I say. "Playing the field."

Her mouth twists. "You could say that."

"I'd have thought a girl like you would have fleets

69

of blokes after her," I lie.

She gives what I believe is meant to be a shrug of false modesty. "Wouldn't exactly call it fleets," she says. Then she fixes my eyes meaningfully. "Course, I prefer older guys myself. Someone a bit more mature, you know what I mean?"

I swallow hard. "I do indeed."

I break the short silence that follows this exchange. "Of course, Helen has to dress pretty conservatively. Fine if you like all black and dog collars, but otherwise..."

"I dunno," she says. "Some guys get off on nuns and stuff." I raise my eyebrows and she grins. "So I'm told, anyway."

"Hmm," I say. "Not so sure that would work for me. I think if I'm out for a bit of fun I'd like something a bit less clerical, if you know what I mean."

She nods. "I can see that."

There is a pause.

"So go on then – what do you wear when you go clubbing?"

I receive the sideways look again. "Why are you so concerned about what I wear?"

I shrug. "I don't know. Just interested, I suppose."

She takes a slow drink from her wine, staring at me as she does so. Then she puts the glass down.

"What's Helen think? About you going out with me after work, I mean. Does she mind?"

I am taken by surprise by the change in subject but take the question at face value.

"We haven't really discussed it. I don't think she minds. It's not as if I do it all the time, after all."

"Will you tell her who you're with?"

"I suppose I'll just tell her I was out with a colleague."

She smiles. "Smart move."

The implication that I would deliberately mislead Helen about my relationship with Jane Gardner makes me feel mildly queasy, even though I know that I have absolutely nothing to feel ashamed of. Emotion is a strange thing.

She leans back in her chair, and the smile broadens. "Maybe I'll bring some photos next time. Of me in Croydon."

The assumption that there will be a next time goes unquestioned by either of us. This provides a convenient opportunity for my next task.

Earlier in the day it had occurred to me that if it does indeed become expedient to develop some sort of relationship with Jane Gardner it would be best if it was not conducted via the office email. Nor do I want a whole load of calls and texts clogging up my mobile. I am sure that it would never occur to Helen to check up on me this way, but accidents do happen. So during my lunch break I popped out and bought a cheap pay-as-you-go phone. It is this that I now withdraw from my pocket.

I return the smile. "That's something to look forward to. By the way, shall we swap mobile numbers? I'd just feel a bit more comfortable if we didn't have to use email all the time, you know what I mean?"

Still smiling, she raises her eyebrows, which I now

71

observe are heavily plucked. "Oh yes. I know exactly what you mean."

She opens her handbag and pulls out her phone. "You don't have to worry. I can be very discreet, you know."

I pat her hand. "I'm glad you're so understanding. I mean, this is all very harmless, but if people found out..."

"Of course."

"It's best if we neither of us talk about it to anyone. Not family, not friends. Our little secret. It's more fun that way, anyway, don't you think?"

She appears surprised at this and I wonder for a moment if I have overdone the caution thing. But then she leans across with a conspiratorial smile. "Maybe I should call you by a code name, just to be doubly safe?"

This is an absolutely absurd suggestion which I find most appealing.

"Why not?"

"What then?"

I have a sudden vision of my dead tramp.

"How about Martin?"

*

I decide to avoid the matter of the planning application for a while. Instead I flirt with her, which is tedious for me, but I believe expected. I wait until we are on our third drink before I return to the subject.

"I know we're not going to talk about the detail of the thing, but just for my own curiosity, is it Alan Grant who's taking the lead on this Rectory application?"

A frown crosses her face. The third large

chardonnay is clearly having its effect (I have, without telling her, switched to non-alcoholic beer, which is disgusting, but a necessary sacrifice) and she seems to be having trouble switching her focus from our previous conversation about her favourite reality TV shows.

"That's right," she says. "Why?"

I shrug. "No reason. It's just – I know I said I don't care either way about it, but Helen obviously does, and... This is going to sound ridiculous, but because I work at the council I sort of feel responsible for making sure everything is done properly. Like I sort of represent us all, you know? Though I know that sounds daft."

She leans across the table with a serious look on her face. "I don't think it sounds daft at all," she says. Then she puts her hand on my arm and gives it a squeeze. "In fact I think it's rather sweet."

I look down at her hand. It is white, apart from the red nails, smooth and unwrinkled. Some people might consider it a pleasant hand. But I just wish she would take it away.

After a few seconds she does, and I am able to relax again.

"Anyway, I'm glad we've got good people on the case. You do hear some horror stories about planning. Not here, of course, but there's a few tales I've come across from other authorities – people taking backhanders, buying off the politicians – you name it. I'm just thankful that we've nothing like that here, that we've got someone like Alan on the case."

I am just talking, scattering words around, looking

for a reaction, a pointer to some weakness, some vulnerability I can exploit. But Jane Gardner says nothing. She simply sits, staring into her glass.

I wonder if perhaps I have overdone the wine, and she is ill.

"Jane?" I say. "Are you all right?"

She looks up and flashes a quick smile, but when it is gone she still looks troubled. "Of course. Why wouldn't I be?"

"I don't know. You just look, I dunno – upset. Have I said something wrong? I know we agreed to not to talk about the Rectory, but all I meant was..."

"No!" She interrupts me, leans forward and pats the back of my hand. "Of course you haven't said anything wrong. It's just..." She breaks off, biting her lip.

"Just what?" I ask.

She shakes her head. "No. It's nothing." She glances at her watch. "Wow, is that the time? We'd better get you back, or you'll get a right bollocking."

*

The drive back to the house where Jane Gardner lives is conducted mainly in silence. This gives me a chance to think back over the strange ending to our conversation.

I am inclined to accept her word that I said nothing wrong. I cannot myself believe that I did, and she has subsequently shown no animosity towards me, just an unaccustomed thoughtfulness, anxiety even. Which leads to the intriguing question: why should a discussion of the integrity of our planning approval process (for that is when the change of mood happened), and specifically the mention of Alan Grant, prompt such a reaction? Is it too much to hope that there might be something there to help with my ongoing campaign?

This is a question which I shall be very interested in learning the answer to. But I sense that pressing her on this matter would be counterproductive. Which means, frustratingly, that I shall not be getting that answer this evening.

Which in turn means that I have no choice but to see Jane Gardner again.

*

We reach her street and I stop the car. I turn off the engine and look at her.

"Well," I say. "That was fun. Thanks a lot."

She smiles. "No need to thank me. I enjoyed it too."

I smile in return. "That's good. So – shall we do it again next week? Maybe we should try somewhere else. It doesn't have to be the same pub every time."

She slides closer to me and puts her arm around the back of my seat. I smell the wine on her breath, and her scent, which is something citrus.

"No," she says, blinking into my eyes. "It absolutely doesn't have to be the same pub every time."

She holds my gaze and I realise that something else is expected. I move forward myself, intending to brush my lips against her cheek.

But at the last moment she turns her head, and instead of her cheek my mouth makes contact with her lips.

75

I close my eyes and hold the position, as this is clearly what she wants. Her lips are soft and moist and slightly parted, although to my relief her tongue is not in evidence.

I count slowly to five then gently withdraw from the kiss, for this is what it is. I open my eyes to find her smiling at me.

"My my, Mr Hillier," she says. "You are full of surprises."

Then she turns and opens the door. "Until next week, then."

I wait until she is inside her house then I take my handkerchief from my pocket and wipe my mouth.

8

I lie awake along time, wondering about Jane Gardner's odd conduct. Something I said bothered her, enough to change her manner towards me entirely, and make her bring our drinking session to an abrupt end. This is, I would say, uncharacteristic behaviour for her, although I cannot be sure of this. I have only met her twice.

I have thought back over my own words carefully. They were in the main utterly vague and general, apart from my comment about Alan Grant. So there must be a good chance that whatever it was that disturbed her is in some way connected to him. But she would not (or could not) tell me what.

Of course, it may be nothing relevant to my situation. I may be wasting my time with Jane Gardner. But something tells me otherwise. The trouble is, on the evidence of the evening just past, it is likely to be hard to tease whatever she is concealing out of her.

Arranging another meeting will not be difficult. I believe that she likes me, and she also appears to find me attractive. But this also brings problems. Flirting with her, discussing her tedious home life and her maudlin hopes for the future are one thing, but the thought of anything more physical fills me with revulsion. Our Rectory and its garden are, after all, nice, but not that special. Also, I do not believe that Helen would be at all happy with such a development, although of course I should not tell her.

But then I remember her face, harrowed and drenched with tears at the idea that there might be no more Children's Parties. And my resolve is hardened. I have to stop these plans.

And for that I need more ammunition.

So I have a difficult balance to strike. I have to show enough enthusiasm for Jane Gardner that she will be happy with the pace of progress in our relationship, and will feel comfortable confiding in me. But I must also be careful not to rush things in a way that would put me in an awkward situation before I have found out what I want.

I decide that I should stick with my original plan, and arrange to see her again next week. It is most frustrating that I shall have to wait that long without even knowing if there will be anything worthwhile at the end of it. But it cannot be helped.

*

In the morning I am tired. I have been in the office about an hour, being tetchy with the junior staff and drinking too much coffee, when I hear my new mobile ping.

I have a message from Jane Gardner.

I open it.

'Call me when u can. x'

78

I reply. 'Sure. Give me one minute.'

Curious to know what can be so important, I go to one of the small interview rooms nearby. (The walls of my own office are flimsy and it is far too easy to be overheard.)

I select a random file from a cabinet. Then, ostentatiously studying the file (although I do not believe that there is anyone watching me), I seat myself down and press the call button.

She picks up after one ring.

"Morning, you." There is the sound of traffic in the background, and I guess she has left the building to receive the call. "So how's my Martin today?"

"He's well, thank you. And his Jane?"

"She's fine. Just fine."

I sense she is smiling as she speaks. I wait for more but there is none, and I realise that she does not actually have anything to say. The call is simply part of the ritual that follows what she will be thinking of as a date.

I also realise that I will have to play along with this ritual.

"Actually, I'm a bit tired. I didn't sleep too well. You know – thinking about 'things'."

I put a heavy emphasis on the last word. It probably does no harm for Jane Gardner to know that I lie awake in bed thinking about her. Though not, I imagine, in quite the way she would expect.

A giggle. "Yeah, likewise." She pauses and I have the strange sensation of hearing a motorcycle accelerating noisily both over the phone, then, a second later, through the office window.

79

Then she continues. "Anyway, I just wanted to say how much I enjoyed myself last night."

"Me too."

"You didn't mind, then?"

This puzzles me. "Mind what?"

"You know." She pauses. "Me lunging at you like that. And you being a married man and all."

"Well, I didn't exactly fight you off, did I?"

Another giggle. "Not exactly. But that's good. I wouldn't want you thinking I was too forward."

"Hardly. In fact, I'm grateful you took the initiative. I'm so out of practice at these things, if it was left to me we'd probably still be sitting in the car now!"

A laugh, this time a proper one. "Cool. Look, I'd better get back. I'll see you next week, will I?"

"Definitely."

The background noise diminishes – I sense she has moved the phone closer to her mouth. "So why don't we do something different this time? Maybe you could buy me dinner or something?"

Her voice is breathy, almost a whisper. I swallow once, twice before I am able to speak.

"Why not? Shall I sort something out?"

Yet another giggle. She is in a giggly mood today. "You do that."

"Until next week then."

I ring off, and lean back in the chair.

What, I ask myself, the hell am I getting myself into?

*

When I return to my desk there is a voicemail. It is from Doug, my boss.

"Can you pop round and see me, Ambrose. There's something I want to bounce off you."

I pop to see Doug, wondering as I do so what he wishes to 'bounce' in my direction this time. Friendly, informal language like this from him normally means trouble for me. Some task that is too irksome, perhaps or has too much potential embarrassment with his political paymasters, for him to undertake himself.

He is on the phone when I tap on his door. He gestures me in and I take the seat in front of the desk while he finishes his call.

Doug is a big man, with close-cropped blonde hair and a red face. He always wears a suit and tie to the office, today with a yellow shirt that is a little bright for my taste.

"Carol, I've already told you, it's my top priority. Yes. It'll be done today, I promise. No, no problem at all. I'll see you at the committee meeting on Monday then."

He slams the phone down. "Bloody miserable old cow," he says. "Thinks I've nothing better to do with my time than organise her damned survey."

"Councillor Raymond?" I ask, though I already know the answer. Most people who come into contact with her would agree that 'miserable old cow' is a fair description of the representative for Easton ward. I reflect, as I often do, that there is much about Doug's job that I would not enjoy. Though I should not object to the extra money. Or the car. Or the conferences to discuss important matters with other local authorities that always seem to happen at country house hotels with golf courses attached.

"The same," he says. "Now, what did I... oh yes."

He leans back in his chair and fixes me with his solemn look. It is the one that tells me he is about to come out with a stream of politically expedient drivel that he does not believe a word of. "I have a little task for you, Ambrose. It's a while since we've had a proper review of our policy towards Diversity, and I'd like you to undertake one. See how it's doing, what improvements can be made."

I stare at him. This is even worse than I had imagined.

"You want me to review our policy towards Diversity?" I repeat.

"That's right," he says.

I continue to stare at him. Like many people, Doug is uncomfortable with silence. It prompts him to produce additional, unscripted points of justification, which are generally more informative than his original comments.

He fidgets and waits for me say more but I do not. My nerve is stronger than Doug's and I shall win this particular contest.

Eventually he shakes his head. "I've had Councillor Lambert on. She says she hasn't heard much about it recently, and is suspicious that we're back-pedalling on it. With the election coming up she's liable to make an issue of it unless we give her something."

This explains a lot. I have not met Councillor Lambert but like everyone else I am aware of her

82

reputation. Ambitious, ruthless, and utterly unscrupulous in using anyone or anything to further her career. She is expected to go far in politics.

I do not wish to get involved with Councillor Lambert.

"The reason she hasn't heard much about it recently is because it's working," I say.

I am using the word 'working' loosely in this context. Our Diversity policy is a stifling straitjacket on the work of our organisation, forcing individuals to leave their common sense at the door and work instead to a series of breathtakingly idiotic dogmas. The best that can be said for it is that it often provides a great deal of (unintentional) hilarity.

This is just a personal view.

I continue.

"All the data is fine. We've had no complaints. If she was hearing a lot it would be because it wasn't working and we'd had complaints. Then it would need reviewing. But not now. Now it doesn't need reviewing."

"You know that, and I know that, but unfortunately that is not how the politicians' minds work. They need something to play to the gallery with."

This is, I am aware, true. But that is the politicians' problem, not mine.

"Anyway, why me? I've got nothing to do with Diversity. Why not Ivy Boakye? She's already got a whole army of people fussing over it. She's in a far better position than me to do any sort of review."

Ivy Boakye is our Chief Diversity Officer. A black,

lesbian single mother with a criminal record (for grievous bodily harm), she is the living embodiment of her role. To such an extent, unkind observers quip, that she rarely seems to feel the need to do any actual work.

Doug nods as if this is a question he is expecting. "Absolutely – the current policy is very much her baby. That's why it's important that it's reviewed by an independent third party. But of course, you'll be working closely with Ivy."

"With respect, if it's this important, shouldn't you be doing it yourself?"

Though I already know the answer to this question. Councillor Lambert is well-known for destroying the careers of officials who displease her. Doug would want to keep the maximum distance (and at least one human shield, in this case me) between himself and her.

He shrugs. "You know how touchy Ivy can be. I feel like I'm treading on eggshells all the time with her."

This comment is somewhat disingenuous. Ivy Boakye has, it is true, what some would call 'an attitude problem'. Many people would say they feel they are treading on eggshells with her. But Doug behaves more as if he is dancing on the eggshells. Deliberately.

Then he puts on one of his cheesiest grins. "But if anyone can charm the lovely Ivy it's you, Ambrose. You're perfect for such a sensitive role, so highly regarded by everyone. St Ambrose – that's what they call you."

This is not the case. Though it is an appealing notion. (The saint bit. Not the bit about charming Ivy Boakye).

"And anyway," he continues. "It's probably no bad thing for you to keep yourself busy right now, you know what I mean?"

I stare at him, wondering if this is some sort of a threat.

"I'm quite busy enough as it is, thanks very much," I say.

This is true. I really do not need any extra work right now. All my efforts, all my energies must be directed towards stopping the planning application. In other circumstances, the opportunity to drive Ivy Boakye into a foaming rage by sweeping a scythe through the nonsensities of her Diversity policy would be irresistible. But not now. I do not have the time.

I look at Doug, and observe the smile on his face. It strikes me as sly and I realise that he has this all figured out.

"Listen, Doug," I begin. "I'd love to help, but..."

He raises a hand to cut me off. "Ambrose, this is not a request. It is an instruction. Do I make myself clear?"

I note that the smile has disappeared. He is not going to let me wriggle out of this.

A surge of resentment flows through me that I shall have to waste time, precious time that should be spent saving Helen's Rectory, on this charade, just to protect this worm's oversized backside.

But I also accept that there is nothing I can do about it.

For now, that is. I shall make sure that Doug pays for this, one way or another.

"Okay," I say. "You win."

*

"So what do you want me to actually do?" I ask. "If the policy works as it is there's no point in changing things just for the sake of it."

Doug purses his lips. It makes him look as if he is puckering up for a kiss. This is a most unappealing notion.

"I think you should come up with some initiatives."

"Some initiatives?"

"That's right."

"What sort of initiatives?"

He spreads his hands. "Hey, that's what the review's for, to find out."

I do not smile. "What's the timescale on this?"

He suddenly looks uncomfortable. "That's the other thing. With this election coming up we can't afford to hang about. I've told her we'll come back to her with some preliminary findings within a month."

"Within a month! You're joking, right? We're in local government, for Christ's sake, not Ground Force. Most policy reviews take longer than that to think of a name for themselves!"

"I know, I know. Listen, Ambrose, I am totally aware you don't want to do this, but you know what these politicians are like. Councillor Lambert wants to be able to bang on about diversity in the election, and if we don't give her something to bang on about, she'll bang on about us instead. And I for one do not want to

86

be banged by Councillor Lambert." Then he pauses. "Though actually, now I come to think of it..."

I raise an eyebrow and stare at him until he goes red. If I am to be stuck with this ridiculous project I shall at least get some entertainment value out of it.

"All right," I say. "But you owe me one, Doug."

As I am leaving the room he calls me back.

"Ambrose?"

I turn. He is frowning at his screen.

"What's this note you've sent me about Graham Forbes? He's in Accounts, isn't he?"

"At the team meeting the other day we were talking about cost savings and Accounts was mentioned as a target area. So I had a look through the files, and Forbes stood out as a sub-standard performer. I think he's a good candidate for the redundancy programme."

His face brightens. "Good. That'll save us a few quid. Well done."

*

I am still seething when I return to my office. On top of everything else I now have another problem to deal with.

Councillor Lambert is pure poison. If this review does not satisfy her, life will become very difficult for whoever she deems responsible for the failure. This would in the natural course of things be Doug. But he has, equally naturally, arranged for someone else to be in the firing line instead.

Me.

I wonder briefly if this is all some Machiavellian plot of Doug's to get rid of me, but I dismiss the idea.

He would not need to use Councillor Lambert for the purpose. Indeed it would pose too many risks to himself. No, this is self-defence, pure and simple.

It is not that I am myself incapable of dodging this particular bullet. I did not get to my present position without learning how these things work. It is the time that is involved that is the problem, time that I cannot afford.

However, my first priority must be to provide myself with my own human shield, in case things turn nasty.

Ivy Boakye should suffice for that purpose.

9

It is Friday evening. Helen and I are on are on a tube train, on our way to have supper with our friends Naomi and Ben in Crouch End.

Naomi is an old university friend of Helen's. She is now a social worker. Ben is a history teacher. Also present will be Phil, who also was at university with Helen, Naomi and me, and his wife Ali. Phil is a freelance journalist, Ali used to be a nurse but is now a full-time mother. They live in Shepherds Bush.

Ben and Naomi and Phil and Ali are, like us, enlightened, progressive types, with impeccable liberal (with a small 'l') credentials. They are all clever, and individually entertaining (except Ali). But for some reason, when we all get together the conversation has a tendency to become stiflingly, soul-sappingly politically correct. Sometimes I find this amusing. But more often it is simply dull.

I have therefore developed a game which I play with myself. I call it Right-On Bingo. (I got the idea from a cartoon strip some years ago, Alex, I believe). I make (mentally, of course) a list of those topics most likely to provoke a liberal foaming of the mouth, and cross them off (again, mentally) as the evening progresses. Iraq, tick, police brutality, tick, bankers, tick, American intransigence on global warming, tick, and so on. Sometimes I have to raise a subject myself if it looks like it has slipped everyone else's mind, but I always get my card completed, as it were, by the end of the night. My personal record was achieving 'House' by nine twenty, but that was in the summer when we had started early.

I do not think I shall do that well tonight.

But they are our friends and so I like them. Helen in particular enjoys these evenings. Up here in Crouch End she is not the Reverend Helen Hillier, she can let her hair down and be just Helen. It is good for her.

I like that.

*

We sit on stripped pine chairs around the stripped pine table in Naomi and Ben's kitchen. Helen, Ali and Naomi are discussing organic pasta, Ben is pouring red wine.

He hands me a glass. "Come on then, Ambrose. Tell me what you think of this one."

Ben loves his wine, and is indeed quite knowledgeable on the subject. He knows his Rhones from his Riojas, and is able to tell you many surprising things, such as that the '98 has too much quince and the '02 not enough banana, which is impressive given his limited budget. But he very much dislikes being called a champagne socialist.

I also enjoy wine, but have little time for the

90

preciousness of it all. I myself classify wines into three groups. Not Very Pleasant, Pleasant, and Too Expensive. This works well for me in most situations.

I swirl the wine around the glass in the approved manner, and take first a sniff, then a sip.

"Very pleasant," I say. I drink some more.

Ben nods. "It is, isn't it? It's an Australian cabernet. On special offer at Tesco – amazingly good value."

Ali's head snaps round at his words.

"Did you say Tesco?" she says.

All conversation stops at the mention of the great Satan of the angst-ridden middle-class.

A faint flush suffuses Ben's face.

"Well, it is our nearest big store. There's nothing else convenient."

Ali's nostrils flare, like a vampire scenting blood. Which is, now I come to think of it, a very good analogy for Ali.

"There's your local High Street. I thought we'd all agreed, we don't believe in supporting Tesco."

"Yes, well it's not so easy on a teacher's salary. We use the local shops when we can but..." He glances at Naomi for support.

"No, it's not so easy," she repeats. She starts handing round plates of lasagne. "But I do at least bake my own bread."

The dig at Ali's limited culinary skills, though not strictly relevant, is enough to force a retreat. I mentally congratulate Naomi.

"I wish I had the time for that sort of stuff," says Helen. "If it's not one thing it's another. I've got two weddings tomorrow. Poor old Ambrose, left on his own again." She sniffs. "Mmm, that lasagne smells delicious. Well done, Naomi."

I wait as my own plate is placed in front of me.

"Thanks," I say. "So you guys got anything exciting on this weekend?"

Ben shakes his head. "Nothing planned," he says. He leans across the table to top up my wine glass. "Just chores. What about you?"

"I'm hoping to take the bike out to the country. That's if the weather stays fine."

Naomi gives an approving nod. "Good idea. I always sort of worry that you'll just be sitting around on your own."

"I wish you'd take Phil with you," says Ali. "Don't give him any more lasagne, Naomi. I'm trying to get him to lose weight. Look at him! He looks like a stranded walrus."

Despite ourselves, our eyes turn to Phil, who glances resentfully at his wife but says nothing. It is indeed hard to believe that twenty years ago he was a county standard hockey player.

But that does not excuse her speaking of him in that way. I am glad I am not married to Ali.

"You can come with me if you like," I say.

He peers at me over his wine glass, his expression doubtful. "Where are you going?" he asks.

"The Chilterns. It won't be a long one, I probably won't be starting until after lunch, and it's pretty hilly. Maybe forty or fifty miles?"

He mutters something about perhaps another time, and Ali barks a laugh.

For a few minutes we concentrate on the lasagne, which is very good.

"Talking of supermarkets, I tell you who I bumped into the other day," says Phil. "Rosie, do you remember? Was reading psychology, I think, and had a weekend job at the Co-op."

"God, yes, Rosie," says Ben. "Nice girl." He turns to his wife. "You remember? She shared a house for a while with Tim Redfern and Mandy whatshername."

Naomi looks up from her food and frowns. "Not sure I do, actually. What did she look like?"

"Oh you know, slightly chubby – dark, curly hair?"

Naomi shakes her head.

"Used to wear those really bright shirts all the time, with long dangly earrings. You must remember."

Naomi continues to shake her head. "Sorry – can't picture her."

Phil breaks in. "Naomi, what your husband has failed to mention is that Rosie was in fact black."

Naomi waves her fork at him. "Ah, that Rosie. Of course." She glances at Ben. "Why on earth didn't you say so?"

The corners of Ben's mouth turn down in disapproval. "Personally, I don't believe that it's appropriate to define someone by their race. I didn't think you did, either."

"It's not defining anyone by anything to describe what they look like when you're asked," says Phil. "She was pretty near the only black girl in our group, for goodness sake. By refusing to mention it it's you who's being racist, as if there's something shameful about it."

There is another shocked silence. An accusation of racism at this table is serious indeed. Even more serious than when Ben suggested that Phil should be working for the Daily Mail.

Helen shoots me an enquiring glance. "What do you think, Ambrose? You're the expert on these things now."

I draw myself up into my chair and adopt a solemn look.

"Yes, well, speaking as the person who has been asked to conduct a review of the council's policy on Diversity, I feel I may have something to contribute in this matter."

All eyes turn to me. Helen, having used me to defuse the situation, sits back with a mischievous smile, but I do not mind. We are accustomed to playing the diplomat in these gatherings.

The others wear expressions of guarded respect, tinged with envy. However irritating it is to me be dragged into Doug's review, in this company at least there is major kudos in being regarded as an authority on Diversity.

"Wow," says Ben. "How did you land that one?"

I shrug. "My boss wanted a review, and someone independent of the existing policy unit to run it. So he came up with my name. I'm not really sure why."

"How come there needs to be a review?" asks Ali. "Do you have a problem with Diversity?"

"Not in the way that you mean," I say. "Or at least not a very big one. No more than five foot two."

Their faces remain blank. I sometimes find this,

that others do not quite appreciate my sense of humour.

"It's called Councillor Lambert. One of these young, going-places politicians. Rumour is she wants to go national, stand for Parliament. God knows she's unpleasant enough. Anyway, she's planning to use Diversity in her election campaign, so either we give her something positive to use or she'll simply have a go at us."

"What, so you mean it's not really a proper review at all?" says Naomi. She sounds disappointed.

"The system is fine as it is," I explain. (This is neither the time nor the place to expound my real opinions on the subject). "Obviously if I find a few things to tweak I'll do so, but I'm not expecting anything major."

"I don't think you should be going into it with a negative attitude, though," says Ben. "You've got a terrific opportunity here, to make a real difference."

I gaze at his earnest face without rancour. Ben's heart is in the right place, even if it is unfortunately disengaged from his brain. He has been trying to make a 'real difference' in a sink school for over a decade. I know he is wasting his time, just as I know that I will be wasting my own (albeit much less of it) with this Diversity nonsense.

But he is unaware of these truths, and it is not for me to disillusion him.

*

"More lasagne, anyone?"

I am already quite full, and I wish to leave room for the cheesecake that is sitting in the fridge. But Phil

95

pushes his plate towards Naomi.

Ali glares at him. But he ignores her and pointedly turns to the end of the table where Helen and I are sitting.

"So what's this problem you've got with the Rectory? The church wants to pull it down, did I hear?"

A barely audible mutter from Helen. "Bloody vandals."

"That's what they're planning," I say. "And they intend build a bloody awful block of modern flats. It's a total disgrace. It's a very historic building, and the garden's the only proper green space in the area. It really is just vandalism."

"Who would be in the flats?" asks Ben. "Would they be sold, or rented, or what?"

"Some sold, some kept as affordable rental," I say.

He turns to me. "Surely that's a good thing then?" he says. "There's a massive shortage of affordable stuff in your area."

"Obviously, but that doesn't mean you have to destroy the soul of the place to provide it."

"Not in your backyard, anyway," murmurs Ali, topping up her wine glass.

I stare at her in dislike. "How is your search for a decent primary school for little Oliver going, by the way? Still thinking of going private?"

She returns my gaze, challenging me. She thinks she can overawe me with the force of her personality, just like she does with her poor husband. But I am not so easily intimidated. I hold in my mind an image of her pinned against the wall, my hands around her throat, her eyes wide with pain and terror.

And I smile.

"And of course there's the crime to think of, as well," says Phil. "They still haven't found the bloke

who did those two murders near your place, have they?"

I wonder what relevance, if any, this has to anything we have been talking about. But before I can think of a suitable reply Naomi speaks.

"Don't you have any influence'?" she asks. "You know all the people involved, I imagine."

I shake my head. "It doesn't work like that, sadly. It's a completely separate department."

"But you're in HR, after all. I bet you could dig up some dirt if you tried."

Helen laughs. "I've asked him the same thing already," she says. "But he's way too honest to try anything not completely above board. But I'm sure there must be something he can do."

Our eyes meet, and we both smile, a smile of mutual understanding.

I sometimes wonder if anyone's life turns out as they expected. The idealism of youth gives way to pragmatism. Compromise is the stuff of our middle years.

Once I swore that I would never lie to Helen, never mislead her. In those far-off days I associated deceit with hurt. I never imagined that I would be faced with a choice between inaction that would bring her pain and deeds of which she would disapprove.

But here I am. There is so much about me that would break her heart if she knew.

Yet there is no real choice for me.

Still smiling, I turn back to Naomi and shake my head. "I'm sure you're right. But you know me. It's not really my style."

10

It is surprisingly easy to get to the Chilterns from central London. The A40 starts at Paddington, and you then just follow it all the way out until it turns into the M40. That assumes the traffic is not too bad, of course.

I park in the same car park as last time. It is pay and display, which I find mildly offensive in the middle of the countryside, but it is not expensive, just annoying if you do not happen to have the right change on you. Today I have made sure that I do though.

I pull the bike out of the back of the car and set off. The first part of the cycle lane is wide and smooth, and I am able to keep up a good pace, despite there being plenty of other cyclists and walkers using it. I wonder vaguely if I shall meet Mr Dundridge again today. I hope not, the experience last time completely soured my day. And I might not be able to resist the temptation to rid the world of his noisome presence on a second occasion.

Hard cycling is an all-consuming activity. The

exertion, tend to crowd out everything else. It is difficult to worry about work, or the Rectory, or even Helen when my legs are pounding and my muscles are burning and the wind is singing in my ears. It is good. It is when I am happiest, apart from being with Helen, of course .

After an hour and a half or so I am tired and hungry, and ready for a break. I find a suitable tree to lean against, and take out the sandwiches that I have packed for my lunch. My bike is a few feet away, lying in the grass in front of a holly bush.

There is no sunshine today, just grey skies occasionally visible through the breaks in the leaf canopy above. It is not warm, but I am sweating from my exertions and take frequent gulps from my water bottle.

We are not far from a village, and the path is busy. In the space of ten minutes I see a group of six pensioners, all with those ski pole things that walkers carry these days, even on the road; a middle-aged couple, a very tall woman with an Alsatian; and a young male jogger.

Two women on horseback pass by. One young, one older, perhaps mother and daughter. It reminds me of the time that Helen and I went riding, in the New Forest. After an hour of increasingly painful bouncing up and down I decided that it was not for me. But Helen took to it, moving easily in the saddle, laughing at my efforts. The look suited her, as well. Tight trousers, high boots, hair pulled back in a pony tail. I always meant to buy her some boots like that.

But I never have.

I adjust my position. My back is stiff from the cycling and the hard trunk of the tree is not comfortable. Also, I am beginning to get cold. I shall not stay here much longer.

I hear a rustling. Someone is approaching, they are out of sight around the corner for now, but the sounds are getting closer.

It is a woman. On her own, no dog, just another ski pole walking stick. Middle aged, stout.

She smiles, and nods. I do the same. It is what country walkers (and cyclists) do.

"Lovely morning," she says.

It is not a lovely morning. But I observe the pleasantries.

"Yes," I say.

Her smile falters. I believe that she is disappointed in my response. Perhaps she is lonely and wishes to make conversation. But I am not in the mood for conversation today. If she is lonely she should buy a dog.

She continues on her way.

I finish my sandwich and start packing my things into my rucksack when I hear voices. A man's voice, raised, and a child's.

They come into sight. The man is unlike most of the walkers here. He is I guess in his mid-twenties, with a shaved head, dressed in jeans and a grey hooded jacket. Tattoos covering most of his neck. A Pikey Thug, in fact. The child is a sort of mini-me, a boy dressed almost identically and with close-cropped hair. But no tattoos.

The Pikey Thug is dragging the boy along too fast.

101

Several times I see him stumble, only to be roughly pulled to his feet again. The Pikey Thug is shouting at him.

"I don't care what your fricking mother says, I'm not taking you to the bloody cinema. You'll stay the afternoon at your nan's, same as usual. Come on!"

With the final word he yanks the boy so hard that he falls completely to the ground. The child starts to grizzle. As the Pikey Thug pulls him upright again he sees me watching. His mouth twists into a scowl.

"What the fuck are you staring at?"

The correct answer to this question is that I am staring at an unspeakable monster that is torturing a defenceless child. But I am too angry, too utterly consumed with outrage at what I am witnessing, to speak.

I rise to my feet and walk towards the pair. I stop three feet in front of the Pikey Thug and search for my voice.

"I think you should go a bit easier on the kid," I say.

I am proud at how moderate this response is. My instinct is to launch myself at the Pikey Thug and squeeze the life out of him. But the child (probably his son) is there, and it would not be good for him to witness such a thing. Instead, I try to imagine how my Helen would react in this situation.

The scowl turns to a sneer.

"Yeah? You going to make me?"

"Maybe," I say, still calm. I take a step towards him. "You know, you really..."

I get no further with my sentence. The Pikey

102

Thug's knee has come up and connected, hard, with my groin.

I sink to the ground in agony. The Pikey Thug gives a short laugh then continues along the path, dragging the boy behind him. I hear his snarling voice as they go.

"Right, you. I hope you saw that. Let that be a lesson to you, okay?"

The boy starts grizzling again. He receives a sharp slap on the side of his head as a reward.

The Pikey Thug's blow has been vicious and expertly aimed. I remain slumped, burning with pain and anger and humiliation, for a minute or so before I am able to stand properly again. By this time he and the child are out of sight.

My instinct is to chase after them and teach him an even more unforgettable lesson. A painful, protracted, permanent one. But even in the midst of my rage and fury, I know I cannot do this. For one thing, there is the child. For another, I will not get away with such an execution, however justified, in broad daylight on a busy cycle path.

But oh, how I ache to feel his thick neck, with its stupid tattoos, in my hands. To hear the crack of bone, and see his face contort with his final agony. It would not be vengeance, it would be justice. For me, but even more so for the child.

The child that would have made Helen weep.

*

I try to burn off my anger, and the adrenaline that courses through my body, with another long, strenuous cycle ride. Not quite as far as I told poor

Phil, I don't have time. But long enough.

After a while I realise that I am thirsty. I see an ice cream van and stop to buy a lemonade.

I am right on the escarpment. I sit, admiring the view across the Aylesbury Vale, which is truly spectacular. But my mind keeps returning to my encounter with the Pikey Thug.

It seems that I cannot leave my home at the moment without running into some lowlife or other. The Pikey Thug, Mr Dundridge. Two very different characters, but with much in common. Neither of them deserving to walk the streets of this green and pleasant land. And both very, very lucky that they met me when I had no choice but to exercise the most massive self-restraint.

Next time, I promise myself as I take the final gulp of my deliciously cold lemonade, they, or their equivalents, will not be so lucky. I shall be prepared.

Then I realise what I have just said.

Words, so idle and so glib. But that does not mean that they cannot be made fact. I really can be prepared.

More than that. I will be prepared. The next time I return to these hills I shall be ready for the likes of the Pikey Thug and Mr Dundridge, the scum of the world. And if I do happen to run into them, I shall exact justice on them.

To hell with the Rule.

It is like my previous Revelation, only more so. Revelation Mark Two is not just an acceptance of a state of mind. It is a practical proposition, a template for action.

104

I stare across the plain stretching out in front of me. It seems a metaphor for the decision I have just made. The world is at my feet, waiting for me. I see no justice in it. No justice for me, no justice for anyone.

But the world is about to meet a new Ambrose Hillier. Just as Mr Dundridge and his like make it their mission to bring misery to it, I shall make it safer and more pleasant. And, of course, I shall have some fun while I am at it. (Fun, that, may I say, I feel I am very much overdue.)

The realisation of my new identity, my new purpose, is almost overwhelming. It is so momentous that I feel it must be manifested in some way physically as well. Surely I cannot have changed so much inside and still be the same outside?

I have no mirror but I look carefully at both my hands and my legs. Even pull up my jumper to inspect my stomach (just on the round side of flat).

Nothing. No difference at all.

I realise this must make me sound like some deluded teenager who thinks he is a superhero. This is not me. When I talk about being prepared, this does not mean I shall be acquiring a cape. I shall simply be making sure that when circumstances require a certain course of action, I have both the tools and the willingness to carry it out. It is as rational and simple as that.

Simple, but not easy. I have much to think about, much to plan.

I buy myself another lemonade.

*

I arrive home to find Helen stretched out on the sofa, her eyes closed.

She looks up as I enter the room and smiles.

"Good ride?" she asks.

I nod. "Hard going out there. Pretty hilly. How was your day?"

She too nods. "Yeah, Busy, but in a good way, you know?" She yawns. "I like weddings."

She looks tired. She has not been sleeping well this last few nights, partly I believe because of anxiety over the Rectory. It is beginning to worry me.

"Cup of tea?" I ask.

Her brow furrows in thought. Helen takes her tea seriously. "Tell you what, I'd like one of those new peppermint ones my sister gave us."

"Coming right up," I say.

*

I have a shower while the kettle boils. I had wondered if she would notice the change in me. But she has shown no sign of doing so. Perhaps she is too consumed with her own concerns.

My poor Helen.

When the tea is made I join her on the sofa. We sit, mugs steaming on the table in front of us, her head resting on my shoulder.

After a while she stirs.

"They looked so young."

I crane my neck to look at her. "Sorry?"

"The couples. The second one, anyway. Barely out of their teens. And so happy, and hopeful."

"Well, of course. If you don't look happy on your wedding day, when do you?"

106

"I know. And I'm happy for them. But sometimes it makes me sad to think of all that optimism, what's going to happen to it. To them."

"Hang on, just now you said you liked weddings. Now you say they make you sad."

She wriggles against me. "I'm a woman. I'm allowed to be inconsistent. Especially when I'm tired."

I run my fingers through her hair, probing her scalp. "What you need," I say. "Is a good long soak, and then a nice, relaxing back rub from your adoring husband."

She twists around so that she is facing me.

"What, now?"

"Why not?"

"It's a bit decadent, isn't? I mean, there's dinner to get ready, and..."

I touch my finger to her lips. "All that can wait. I think you deserve a bit of me time."

She leans forward and plants a kiss on the end of my nose. "Okay. Since you're offering..."

I get to my feet, and she does likewise.

"Do you think they'll be as happy as us?" she asks." My couples, I mean."

I shake my head.

"No," I say. "No one can ever be as happy as us."

*

She comes out of the bathroom, a towel clutched round her. She lays the towel out on the bed and studies herself in the wardrobe mirror.

"I'm getting so fat," she says. She turns sideways on and slides her hands down towards her hips. "Look at all this! I need to go on a diet."

I go to stand behind her. "I am looking," I say. "And I see no need for dieting at all."

I slide a hand around her waist then up towards her breast, feeling the weight of it in my palm. "And we certainly don't want any less of this, do we?"

She raises her eyebrows. "I thought I was getting a massage?" she says.

I drop my hand, giving her bare buttock a squeeze on the way. "Indeed you are," I say. "Get yourself on the bed and I'll get ready."

While she was in the bath I lit candles, and now I put a CD on the player by the bed. The soundtrack to The Virgin Suicides, by Air. Not a very romantic title, but very chilled, atmospheric music. Perfect background for a massage, apart from the annoying bits where there is talking.

As she arranges herself on the towel I strip off my own clothes. Then I position myself over her, my knees on either side of her hips.

She glances round. "I see. It's that sort of massage, is it?"

"Just making sure my trousers don't get creased."

"I see," she repeats.

She sighs as I make my first contact.

I feel my fingers curl around her neck. For a second I am reminded of other flesh I have touched, or wanted to touch, not with love, as here, but with anger and a burning desire to destroy. I put the thought from my mind. Such ideas have no place in this room. At this moment there is nothing and no one else in the world but Helen.

I knead her shoulders. Gently at first, then

108

gradually increasing the pressure, working the thumbs around the top of her spine. She is tense, the muscles tight and resistant. She grunts and gasps as I find the hard, knotted places but does not speak. Nor do I. Words add nothing to what is passing between us.

Slowly I work my way down and across her back, around the shoulder blades, my hands running the length of her spine, never breaking contact with her skin. I sense the tension through my fingers, and try to draw it from my wife's precious, tired body.

I shift my position so that I can reach the lower back and buttocks. I allow my hands to glide upwards, then out and down, caressing for a moment the sides of her breasts, before returning to repeat the process in slow, sweeping circles.

I lower myself onto her. I support my weight on my arms (I do not wish to crush her) and start to move.

My chest slides over her buttocks and up until my face is next to hers. Down, and then up again. Down, and then up again. I feel myself grow hard. Helen feels it too, and moves her legs apart to accommodate me.

I lie motionless, poised. My head is resting on her head, and for a moment I need nothing except to listen to her breathing, take in her just-bathed smell. I whisper in her ear.

"I love you, Helen. I love you so very, very much."

11

I have two important tasks on Monday morning. First, I must text Jane Gardner to organise our dinner date this week. This is not something I am looking forward to. Having to feign interest in her and her humdrum existence for an entire evening will be testing in the extreme. But it has to be done, and it has to be done soon. The official consultation period for the planning application will be over in less than a fortnight's time. While my own methods are not bound by the same timetable, I cannot afford to leave things too late.

My second task is to arrange a meeting with Ivy Boakye to discuss the Diversity review. This is also not a prospect which fills me with joy. Doug has told me that she has been informed that the review is taking place, so my call will not come as a surprise to her. But I am not expecting a very warm welcome from our Chief Diversity Officer.

I reflect again that the timing of all this is most annoying. On any other occasion I would be more than pleased at the opportunity to yank Ivy Boakye's chain. But now, with all this planning business to worry about, it is just a distraction that I cannot afford. I need to devote all my efforts to this. Helen is relying on me.

I cannot let Helen down. Not now. Not ever.

*

I send my text to Jane Gardner, cheerful and chatty, suggesting either Tuesday or Wednesday evening for our 'date'. As is now our melodramatic custom I sign myself 'Martin'. Then I pick up the phone and dial the extension of Ivy Boakye.

A female voice answers. Young, pleasant manner. Definitely not Ivy Boakye.

"Office of the Chief Diversity Officer, Joanne speaking. How may I help you?"

"It's Ambrose Hillier here. I need to speak to Ivy. Is she there?"

"I'll see if she's available." A short silence, then Ivy's voice on the line, flat, guarded.

"Hello Ambrose. I was expecting to hear from you."

"Ah, Doug's spoken to you then. I was wondering if we could get together this afternoon for a quick chat, work out how we take this thing forward?"

"Out of the question. Possibly next week..."

I recognise this for what it is. In local government (probably all offices, for all I know), 'I am busier than you' translates into 'I am more important than you.'

Nice try, Ivy.

"No, sorry. Doug wants us to get this going. How about two o'clock?"

There is a pause while she calculates. Ivy Boakye,

111

mighty in the implacable name of Diversity, is used to calling the shots. But Doug is her boss. Even she will not ignore a direct instruction from him. (Or so I believe. I could be wrong about this).

"Fine," she says. I imagine her teeth gritted, her knuckles white as they grip the phone. "But it'll have to be done in half an hour."

"No problem," I say. "I'll see you then."

I check my mobile. I am expecting an instant response from Jane Gardner, but there is none.

Perhaps she has some work to do.

*

I spend the next hour and a half in a meeting. Afterwards I check my mobile again. Still no reply.

This now strikes me as very odd. It is quite out of character for Jane Gardner to play hard to get. I wonder if she has disobeyed instructions and talked to friends or relatives who have advised her that this is what she should do. If so, it is very irritating. I do not have time for such games.

I take my mobile into a nearby meeting room and dial the council switchboard number, then ask for her by name. I am put through, and after a few rings a male voice answers.

"Jane's phone."

I do not recognise the voice, but disguise my own (I choose a nasal estuary accent) just in case.

"Hi, is she there?"

"No, sorry, she's off sick today. Can anyone else help?"

"Oh, sorry to hear that. D' you know when she'll be back?"

112

"Not a clue, sorry. Who is this, anyway? Are you calling about a particular application? If so..."

"No, just a friend," I interrupt. "Don't worry, I'll call her at home."

So Jane Gardner is off sick.

I call her mobile. But to my irritation I get a number unobtainable message.

I cannot call Jane Gardner at home, because I do not have a landline number for her. Short of turning up at her house I have no means of communicating with her at all, and no way of knowing whether her illness is serious or just some pathetic sniffle which will see her back in the office in a day or two's time.

This is very annoying.

I am now in a very awkward position. Now that Tom Bates seems unlikely to be of any use to me I urgently need to be able to pick her brains (what there is of them) for something else that may give me some traction. If she is available again within the week, all will be well. But any longer, and there will be a risk that Alan Grant will have already started shaping his formal recommendation. I will then find it more difficult to get him to change tack. (Of course, there is always a chance that he has already made up his mind on the matter. These people never take any notice of the public consultations. I have not told Helen this, though. It would distress her.)

I decide that I shall give it until Thursday. In the meantime, all I can do is hope that whatever is afflicting Jane Gardner is not serious.

It is most frustrating.

*

113

It is some while since I have visited Ivy Boakye's Diversity headquarters, and I am impressed at how much it has expanded. I have to squeeze past the desks to get to her office, nearly tripping over a wheelchair ("Sorry, Gavin,") on the way.

I find our Chief Diversity Officer seated at her desk, wearing a Free Nelson Mandela tee shirt (which must be very old). She gestures me to a chair in front of her without word or smile of welcome.

I glance around me. Ivy Boakye's office is bigger than mine. It also has a window, albeit only overlooking the car park. One of the other walls is decorated with posters and slogans. 'Women Who Seek Equality With Men Lack Ambition', 'Being Straight Isn't Normal, It's Common', and other pithy inspirational messages. I think I recognise a drawing of a Black Power clenched fist salute.

"Nice office," I say.

She gives me a hard stare.

Ivy Boekye uses her reputation to do a lot of her talking for her. Many people are unnerved by being in the same room as someone with a tendency to violent crime, which is useful to her. I am not so easily intimidated, for obvious reasons.

I try to recall exactly what it was that she did. If I remember rightly, she went for her ex-husband's lover with a frying pan when she came home early and caught them on the job. Extenuating circumstances were pleaded, but the court decided the ferocity of the attack, something like thirty separate blows to the head, put it beyond the realms of a simple crime of passion. Rumour has it that was when she decided she

114

had had enough of men, and switched sides, as it were.

"This better be quick," she says. "I've a meeting with our Atheists and Agnostics Group at half past. They're feeling excluded because of this new multi-faith prayer room that's been set up."

I resist the temptation to make a number of suggestions for where the Atheists and Agnostics Group could stick their sense of exclusion.

"Fine," I say.

She nods. She has made her point.

"So how did you get stuck with this?" she says. "It's not exactly your style, is it? I always had you down as one of the less odious of the reactionary tools we have around this place."

This (which passes as a compliment from Ivy Boakye) pleases me. "I'd like to think so. I guess that's why Doug picked me. He reckoned we could work together on this, constructively."

Her eyes narrow. "You've got to be kidding, right? You expect me to help you here?"

I am taken aback by the extent of the hostility in her voice. This is local government, things are reviewed all the time. It does not mean anything changes. Though now I come to think of it, she was very aggressive all through this morning's management meeting as well. Perhaps she is just having a bad day.

"Actually, yes I do. Look, I can find better things to do with my time as well, but Doug wants it done, so it's going to get done. All right?"

Her lips twist in a sneer. "Just following orders,

eh? Where have we heard that before?"

Her manner is now beginning to irritate me. "Ivy, what is your problem? I mean, what the hell do you think is going to happen here?"

She leans forward over her desk. "What do I think is going to happen? I'll tell you what I think. I think you're going spend a few hours here, being all smiley, doing your good old Ambrose routine, and all the time you're going to be making little notes about my people, checking up on them, picking them up on every tiny thing. Then you're going to go back to your fascist paymaster, and you're going to tell him that we're overstaffed and inefficient and he can happily get rid of three, or four, or however many pops into your nasty little head, of my brilliant, hardworking staff, who all do amazingly important work and achieve more in a day than you do in a month."

She finishes her by slamming her fist down on the desk so hard that the mug emblazoned with the motto 'So Many Men, So Little Space Under The Patio' emblazoned on it is shaken off its coaster.

Panting slightly, she wipes a fleck of spittle from the corner of the mouth with her sleeve. Then she sits back and glares at me.

"That's what I think is going to fucking happen."

We are all used to a degree of paranoia from Ivy Boakye. But this is extreme even by her own standards. I suspect there may have been some misunderstanding.

"Ivy, what exactly did Doug say to you?"

"Say to me? Bastard didn't even have the decency to talk to me himself. Just sent some poxy little email, telling me that you would be conducting a 'review' of my department. And we all know what that means."

"I'm not sure..." I begin but she carries on as if I had not spoken.

"Cuts, that's what it means. He sends his hatchet man in, and next thing you know, half the team have got their redundancy papers."

I wait to see if she really has finished this time. When it seems that she has, I speak myself.

"Ivy, I think you've got the wrong end of the stick."

She opens her mouth and I raise my hand. "No, let me finish. This is nothing to do with cuts. Doug has had Councillor Lambert on his case. She's worried that we're not doing *enough* about Diversity."

Ivy starts to interrupt again and again I stall her with my hand. "I know, I know, it's rubbish. But if we don't give her something she's going to make an election issue out of it. So Doug's promised her a review, and you and I are to work together to come up with some new initiatives to tell her about."

I pause to let her process this new information. Eventually she speaks.

"So no cuts?"

"No cuts," I agree.

She shrugs. "Why didn't you say so before? What's the plan then?"

This is better. Her tone could still not be described as warm, but I no longer feel that I need to be prepared to duck a missile (the mug, say, or her computer keyboard) at any moment.

"Right," I say. "First, I need to update myself on

the sort of work you've been doing recently. Have you issued any reports in the last few months I could look at?"

This is of course a rhetorical question. The closest the regiment of misfits seated outside ever come to any real work is to write reports.

"Naturally," she says.

"Good. So I'll go through them, and then we'll both have a think and we'll get together to come up with a few recommendations for the future."

She nods gravely. "Okay. I've got a few ideas myself, for things we ought to be doing. You've heard about my plans for the improvement of provision for the Travelling community?"

"I have. I must admit, I wasn't aware that we had a Travelling Community."

"We don't. But if we improve provision, we might. They do Travel, you know."

There are so many things I could say to this. But although Ivy Boakye is clearly a lunatic, for the next few weeks she has to my lunatic. I need her, and shall therefore have to humour her.

After all, if this goes pear-shaped (as seems on the evidence of today increasingly likely) I shall be relying on her to save my bacon.

"Of course," I say. "Silly of me."

She stares at me. Even to me her unblinking gaze is somehow unsettling. There is something about Ivy Boakye that is not quite right.

"By the way," I continue. "I should point out that it's important all these initiatives should be seen to be coming from you. The idea is that we're simply giving

118

Councillor Lambert a sort of sneak preview of stuff that you were planning to do anyway."

I let this register for a few moments before continuing.

"It's your show, Ivy. And we all want to keep it that way."

She continues to stare at me, drumming her fingers on the desk. "I don't trust Doug," she says after a while.

I give an understanding nod. This is a rare instance where Ivy Boakye is being completely rational. On the other hand, while I have no interest in sticking up for Doug, I do not want her being any more disruptive and provocative than is necessary.

"Normally I'd agree with you, but on this occasion I really don't think you have to worry," I say. "As I said, he's got just as much interest in this going well as you do. After all, Diversity's in his patch, any problems and it's a black mark against his name as well."

Too late I realise my mistake. Ivy Boakye's eyes shoot open, and she leans forward across the desk, breathing heavily. For a moment I think she is going to bite me.

"We don't use that phrase," she says.

Her tone is a mixture of appalled disbelief and repressive rebuke. Much as if I had just suggested a cheeky threesome with her and her mother.

Given the seriousness of my crime I recognise that contrition is the only option here.

"Sorry," I say. "I've got a lot on my mind at the moment."

She leans back but continues to glare at me. Forgiveness is not so easily granted.

As I get up to leave she has one parting thrust.

"I still don't trust him," she says.

12

When I return to my desk there is good news waiting for me. A small yellow Post-it note with a message scrawled on it.

'Pls call Jane.'

I go into the meeting room and try her number again. This time it is answered immediately.

"Hello?"

Croaky-sounding, but recognisably Jane Gardner.

"Jane? It's Ambrose. I got your message. Are you okay?"

"I think I've got the flu. It came on over the weekend."

"Oh no – poor you. Have you got it badly?"

"Not too bad. I could probably have come in today but Mum thought it would be better to rest it a couple of days. I'll probably be in later in the week though."

This is good news, very good news indeed. But it is important that I show an appropriate level of concern for her wellbeing.

"That's not so bad then. But you shouldn't come in unless you really are better. You don't want to take any chances with that sort of thing."

"No."

"Actually, I'd been wondering if you were okay. I called this morning and when I didn't get a reply, I thought that wasn't like you."

"Yeah, I thought you might have done. I'd have called myself, except I was out of credit, and I had to wait for Mum to go out and get me a top up."

I frown at the phone in disbelief. Top up? Surely only children were on pay-as-you-go these days? Apart from me. And I have very good reasons for doing so.

But this is not important.

"Of course. Anyway, the reason I called was to sort out a date for dinner some time. I was suggesting either tomorrow or Wednesday, but if you're not well..."

"No! Like I said, I should be okay soon. We could go for Wednesday, if you don't mind me still being a bit snuffly maybe?"

"Of course not, it would just be great to see you. But only so long as you're well enough – I don't want you making yourself worse. Promise you'll tell me if you're not up to it?"

She giggles. Though why this should be funny, I have no idea. "Oh, I don't think that's likely to be a problem."

"Okay, I'll sort something out. Until Wednesday, then."

Another giggle, then the sound of what may have been a kiss blown down the phone.

"'Til Wednesday."

In the evening Helen has a church meeting so I am on my own. Although I enjoy my wife's company this is convenient for me. I need to organise the restaurant for Wednesday evening. There is also a documentary on serial killers on BBC2 that I want to watch.

I prepare myself a gin and tonic and sit down in the study with a London restaurant guide.

I have a good idea of what I am looking for. My overriding priority remains that I should not be seen in Jane Gardner's company by anyone that I know. This is a risk that cannot be entirely eliminated, but it can be minimised. The handful of local places that Helen and I visit on a regular basis are completely out of the question, for example. But whether I will be better off going to some obscure suburb on the other side of town, Ealing, say, or somewhere busy and crowded with tourists, is a moot point.

In the end I plump for the West End. Jane Gardner is sympathetic to the notion that, as a married man, I have to take care with our trysts. But she will still be expecting something a little special. It is important that I do not disappoint her.

I need somewhere with an intimate atmosphere, that will inspire conversation and shared confidences, but not so obviously romantic that matters get out of hand. And the food should not be too complicated. I believe Jane Gardner to be a simple girl with plain tastes.

I decide on an Italian near Covent Garden. The pictures on the website show a small, cosy room, busy

123

with theatre-goers who will have no interest in us whatsoever. Perfect for my needs.

One phone call later, and it is all arranged.

*

I warm up some left over chilli con carni, pour myself a large glass of red wine, and settle down in front of the television. I enjoy programmes such as these, but it can be awkward to watch them with Helen. I am too likely to be afflicted with a desire to laugh out loud at how wrong they can be. Laugh, or else scream at the TV screen like a grumpy old man.

The first mistake I often find the pompous, self-aggrandizing so-called experts make is to spend so much time worrying about 'why? 'How', or even 'how often' is much more interesting. This man's parents split up when he was six, that one was bullied at school for being gay, she was raped by her uncles, and so on. Many people have bad childhoods, and still grow up to have dull, blameless lives. Equally, there are those (such as myself) who are perfectly well-adjusted and happy as kids but still develop into slightly more adventurous adults. It is such nonsense.

Then there are the 'trigger' merchants. The ones who are obsessed about what finally pushed so and so over the edge. Accident, my dear boy, accident! At least it was in my case. I never meant to kill anyone. Sometimes these things just happen.

The one thing that the killers featured on these shows do have in common is how stupid they all were. Stupid not to plan things properly, stupid to do things the same way each time, stupid to make it easy for the police to catch them. But this is never properly

124

analysed.

For example, how unbelievably idiotic are these people to keep souvenirs! Surely it is the act itself that is important, not some pathetic trophy, like a lock of hair or a pair of old knickers. Owning that cannot recreate the feeling of the moment, any more than you can relive a good meal by looking at the dirty plate. It is pointless, stupid and dangerous.

But of course there is a reason why the studies always focus just on the stupid ones. Because the clever ones, the ones like me, do not get caught.

*

The programme ends and I go to the kitchen to refill my glass. I wonder now, as I always do afterwards, why I bother watching these things. It seems a good idea at the time. This is, after all a subject in which I have a strong personal interest. But more often than not I just end up getting irritated. I have little patience with stupidity.

In general I find I am a much calmer person these days. Partly that is to do with greater age, and maturity. But I am sure that much of it is because of my self-awareness, which gives me an outlet, a sort of safety valve. When someone is really getting on my nerves, whether at work, or on the bus, or like Ali was the other evening, instead of getting myself worked up, I simply imagine what I would like to do to them. And because, unlike most people, I really *could* do those things if I wished, it has a naturally soothing effect on me. There is nothing like visualising someone's face turning blue and their eyes popping out of their sockets for keeping the blood pressure

125

down.

But stupidity is something else. It really annoys me.

*

It is now gone nine o'clock and still no Helen. Her work often keeps her late but I can never avoid the frisson of fear that strikes me at such times. Sudden and sharp and cold as an ice axe, the terror that something may have happened to her, that she may never come home again.

A thought that is too much to bear.

I pick up the telephone and dial her mobile. I know it will be turned off, but I cannot help myself. It is just me.

It is turned off.

I mount the stairs to our bedroom. I open her wardrobe and lean forward to put my head inside. I position myself between two of her dresses (the grey silk and the serious navy one) and I shut my eyes.

Even in her absence the wardrobe is pervaded with her scent. Her makeup, her perfume and even a hint of her hair shampoo all mingle in the darkness into that unique fragrance that I call, to myself, the Essence of Helen.

I drink it in.

Helen does not know that I do this. I would be most embarrassed if she were ever to find out.

But it does no harm. It is one of my more harmless pleasures.

*

I return downstairs just in time to hear the

126

telephone ring. I rush to it, wondering if it could be Helen.

"Can I speak to Barry Frith, please?"

The name is vaguely familiar. Then I remember.

"Are you the same idiot who was phoning last week?"

A pause. "I didn't phone last week. Is that Mr Frith?"

He is right. The voice is Scottish, but less adenoidal.

Though this is not the point.

"No, it is not Mr Frith. As I told your colleague last week, no one of that name lives here, or has ever lived here. You have the wrong number. Is that clear?"

Another pause. "Okay. But if you do see him, can you tell him to contact Southern and General Finance Corporation as a matter of urgency?"

I am about to scream into the telephone that I cannot tell Barry Frith this as I will not be seeing him as I have never heard of him. But my caller (perhaps fortunately for him) has hung up.

As I stare, still fuming, at the mute receiver, I reflect that I am possibly a less calm person than I had imagined.

*

I am still musing on these matters when I hear the front door slam. Helen is home.

She throws herself into an armchair with a sigh.

"How was the PCC?" I ask.

"Complete nightmare. We spent half the meeting discussing the crèche and the Sunday school and how much noise they make."

127

"What about it? A bit of noise pretty much goes with the territory, I'd have thought. It's only in the family services anyway, isn't it?"

I get up to fetch her some wine and her voice follows me into the kitchen.

"Exactly! Yet apparently some of the older members of the congregation find it, and I quote, 'disruptive and inappropriate'. They want the children shut away in the church hall, not just for the communion part as they are at the moment, but for the whole service. It's ridiculous."

I put her glass down in front of her and top up my own. "Totally ridiculous," I agree.

I do not really care where other people's children sit. When I was a child I detested church, and would happily have sat anywhere but on the hard, cold pews, listening to the vicar's interminable sermons. But Helen does, and I shall loyally share her outrage. "So who's that a quote from?"

"I'm sure you can guess. Joyce bloody Burnside. She presented a letter, signed by no fewer than twenty five of St Nicholas's finest. God knows how long she'd been going behind my back organising that."

I watch as she takes a gulp of wine.

"I don't know," she continues. "Some people are so uncharitable, so self-centred. You'd think they'd be pleased to have some young families in the congregation. Lord knows, there are plenty of churches out there crying out for them!"

"True," I say.

I wonder whether I should not rethink my self-imposed ban on the removal of Joyce Burnside. She

128

upsets Helen way too much.

"I'm afraid, my darling, that there are a lot of not very nice people out there. And, yes, some of them go to church. Human nature is what it is, sadly."

She grimaces. "That's for sure. We both see enough of that."

She takes another deep gulp of the wine. "Anyway, enough of that. How was your day?"

It is not lost on me that I see Helen drinking a lot more these days. It is to help her relax, of course, and distract her from all the things that weigh on her mind, but it is still worrying.

"Oh, nothing exceptional," I say. "I had a first meeting with Ivy Boakye about this Diversity thing. And of course everyone's getting revved up about these cuts. Lots of meetings, offsites, that sort of thing to talk about them. In fact I've got one over dinner on Wednesday evening."

"That's all right," she says. "I'm out, anyway. Where's it happening?"

I had not thought that Helen would ask me this and I have not prepared an answer. "You know, I'm not sure," I say. "I'm sure the email said, but I've completely forgotten."

She smiles. Helen knows me well and recognises my discomfiture. It is fortunate she has no idea as to the reason.

"Old age catching up with you," she says. "Either that, or you're having an affair."

Almost no idea.

It is a joke but I feel so uncomfortable lying to Helen, even in a good cause, that I am unable to laugh it off. I get up from my chair and go over to her. Then I take both her hands in mine.

"That's one thing I can promise you, unequivocally. I am not having an affair, and never will do. I will never be unfaithful to you, Helen."

She gives a puzzled smile. That line about the lady who protesteth too much pops into my mind.

"That's good," she says.

13

Jane Gardner and I have arranged to meet at the restaurant. This suits us both. There will not be the awkwardness (for me) of having to share the time between the end of the working day and our reservation, or the quasi intimacy of being crushed together on a crowded tube train. And she gets to go home and tart herself up for her 'date'.

I arrive early (as I have said, I was taught never to keep a lady waiting) and order myself a gin and tonic. A large one. I am not looking forward to this evening.

Though I am optimistic that the food at least will be good. It is a while since I have had a nice traditional escalope Milanese.

She is late.

This annoys me. I personally set great store on punctuality, and try never to be late for anything. Sometimes it cannot be helped. For example, if you are stuck in traffic because of a motorcycle accident. But more often it is sheer laziness.

Unforgiveable.

was expecting her. By this time I have finished my gin and tonic and am in a bad mood.

She is flushed and out of breath.

"Really sorry I'm late," she says. "I couldn't decide which dress to wear."

I stare at her dress. It is unlike the clothes she has worn previously. It is made of a green, satin-like material that is very low-cut and shows a great deal of cleavage. I have not seen the alternatives but I suspect they would have been a better choice.

I lean across and kiss her on the cheek. "No worries. I wasn't sure what socks to wear either."

She smiles at this, recognising it as a joke.

"But wow," I say. "You look fantastic."

She goes a little pinker and thrusts out her chest. Jane Gardner is proud of her breasts.

"Thanks," she says.

A waiter comes to our table and hovers. "Anyway," I say. "What do you want to drink? Shall I just get us a bottle of white?"

She shrugs. "Sure."

I turn to the waiter. "A bottle of the Pinot Grigio, please."

He leaves and I lean across the table. "So how are you? You seem to have got over the flu okay – you look really well."

In fact the light is dim and she is wearing far more make-up than usual, including lots of black eyeliner and some very red lipstick, so it is difficult to tell what she looks like underneath. But she does not sound ill so I am hoping she is not still contagious.

"Yeah, I'm fine. Just one of those twenty four

hour things, I reckon. But my Mum insisted I stayed at home for a couple of days. You know what Mums are like."

"Indeed. Though I had been wondering if you'd just been overdoing the clubbing again."

The corner of her mouth flickers. "What, me? Overdoing things? The very idea!"

*

We fall silent in order that Jane Gardner may study the menu. I pretend to do the same, despite the fact that I have already spent twenty minutes doing so and know exactly what I want. Then we order. Her the spaghetti Bolognese, me the Milanese.

The wine arrives, is tasted, approved and poured.

I raise my glass. "Well, Miss Jane Gardner, very nice to see you."

She giggles. "And you, Mr Ambrose Hillier."

We both drink.

"I've been meaning to ask you, actually," she says. "Ambrose. I've never heard it before. Where's it come from?"

"He was a saint," I say. "Saint Ambrose. He was the Bishop of Milan in, if I remember correctly, the fourth century."

"Is that why you like the escalope Milanese?"

This has never occurred to me. "Very probably," I say.

She grins. I grin back.

Empathy. That is what this evening has to be about. Establishing such a strong bond of empathy between us that she will be unable to resist telling me whatever I want to know.

"But actually," I say. "It means something else, as well. Immortal. It's ancient Greek for immortal. Though some translations would say divine."

This is true, and has long been a source of satisfaction to me. There is something both reassuring and impressive about being named 'immortal'.

Jane Gardner does indeed look impressed. "Really? Gosh. I don't suppose my name means anything."

I sense an opportunity to earn some brownie points.

"Well, I think we can guess what the 'Gardner' bit might mean, but..."

I pull my phone – my proper phone, not the cheap pay-as-you-go - out of my pocket, and open up the browser.

The signal is poor and everything takes longer than it should. I begin to grow irritated and wish that I had never started the stupid exercise, but Jane Gardner watches me patiently, polite interest etched all over her broad features.

Eventually I have what I want.

"Here we are – Jane. 'God is gracious'. That's what it means – God is gracious."

She frowns. "God is gracious? What sort of numpty calls their kid that?"

I shrug. "It says here it's a Hebrew name. They did things like that in those days."

"Oh well." Then she smiles. Perhaps she is aware that she is not sounding at all gracious herself. "Thank you anyway. I now know something I didn't before."

I give a little bow. "You're welcome."

We both take a sip of wine. Then she puts her head to one side and looks straight into my eyes. "Actually, there was one other thing I wanted to talk to you about."

I catch my breath. Is she about to open up at last, and reveal whatever it was she felt unable to tell me last time?

"Go for it," I say.

She holds my gaze, toying with the stem of her wine glass.

"That first time we met, you know, outside the car park in the rain. Were you waiting for me specifically, or was it just, like, chance?"

I quell my disappointment and take a drink while I think about this question. From her manner it is important to her, but I do not know which answer she wishes to hear. If I say it was chance, will she feel less special? Or if I tell her that I had indeed planned the whole thing, would that make me sound like some sort of stalker?

I decide on a modified version of the truth.

I lean across the table and fix her with a solemn look.

"Do you believe in Destiny?" I ask. "You know, Fate? Do you believe that sometimes things happen for a Purpose?"

She blinks at me. "What, you mean like in the horoscopes?"

"That sort of thing."

She considers for a moment.

"Don't really know," she says after a while. "Maybe. Mine did say the other day that I was to

135

meet someone who would be very important in my life for a long time to come. So that might have been you."

I give a slow nod, as if her answer was wisdom most sublime. I also try to put from my mind the emetic notion of being very important in Jane Gardner's life for a long time to come.

"There you are then. So I wasn't waiting to meet you. That meeting was waiting for us!"

Her eyes widen. "Blimey!"

*

"So how did your brother's doctor's appointment go?"

We have done work. Jane Gardner painfully avoiding saying anything 'compromising' about the Rectory planning application, me giving a light-hearted and suitable self-deprecating commentary on the Diversity review. Now we are on to the second bottle of Pinot Grigio it is time to get personal. Empathy must be maximised before I undertake my final assault.

She pulls a face. "Not so good. He said there was nothing wrong with Clive except being overweight."

I affect outrage. "But that's ridiculous! His knee's agony, you said. You can't expect him to work like that!"

"I know! I mean, he's big, obviously, but that's not his fault. We've got big genes."

I am puzzled at the relevance of this. "Big jeans?"

She laughs and leans forward to poke me on the nose. This is a habit that has become increasingly frequent as she has grown more relaxed in my company. I have been unable to think of a tactful way of stopping it.

"Big *genes,*" she says. "G – E –N – E – S. You know, the things that make you like you are. That's what Mum says, anyway. I'm just lucky I haven't got them myself."

I check for signs of irony. There are none.

"You are," I say. "So what happens now?"

"I don't know. He's refused to sign him off, so he won't get his benefits, not the full ones anyway. It's so unfair."

"I'll say. How much does he weigh, anyway?"

"Only a bit over twenty stone. Okay, it's a lot, but loads of people are that size these days. And it's not as if it was his fault. God! What I'd like to do to that doctor if I got my hands on him."

She is now worked into a fine state of indignation. Her face has gone red, though this may be partly from the wine.

I also contemplate what I would like to do to the anonymous doctor. Specifically, buy him a drink. Brother Clive, on the other hand, is another matter.

*

It is time to move on.

"Ah, well," I say. "No such excitements in our house. Except that of which we do not speak." I grin.

She gives me a quick glance. "Of course. How is she with all that?"

I shrug. "Oh, you know. A bit worried. She's very attached to the old place. But what will be will be. From my own point of view, so long as I can honestly look her in the eye and say we did all we could, and everything was as it should be, I'm fine with it. I'd hate her to lose it for the wrong reasons, if you know what

137

I mean."

I watch her closely. She nods at my words, but in a slightly distracted way, as if her thoughts are elsewhere.

But she does not speak.

I continue. "Of course, it's being in the dark, feeling helpless and out of control that's so stressful in these situations. You need to be able trust the people involved, but all you know is a name, you don't know the person."

I see her swallow. But still she does not speak.

I press on. "I mean, who do I know in Planning? I know you, of course, which is..." I pause as if seeking some suitable superlative. "Just amazing. And of course I trust you, I'd trust you with my..."

"Stop it!"

I gape at her.

My shock is genuine. I have never seen her like this before. Tears have appeared at the corners of her eyes and she is gnawing her knuckles. She looks utterly miserable.

At last I am getting somewhere.

"I'm sorry," I say. "I wasn't thinking. Listen, let's talk about something else. Did you see..?"

"No! Don't apologise. It's my fault. I should have said something before."

She twists her napkin in her hands and stares at the table. I pick up my wine glass and settle back in my seat to listen.

"Said what?"

"The other day – when you were saying about some councils being dodgy and how glad you were

138

that ours wasn't like that."

"Yes?"

A long pause.

"I'm not sure it isn't."

*

My heart hammers. "How do you mean?"

"I'm not sure, it may be nothing..." Her voice trails away.

I lean forward and speak in my most gentle tones.

"Listen, if there's something bothering you, why don't you just tell me? If it is nothing, well, it'll be off your mind. And if it isn't, at least I may be able to advise you on what to do."

She nods, then swallows hard. "Okay. Well, last year, I was doing some filing in the office next to Alan Grant's. I can't remember what, but I was sitting on the floor going through the bottom drawer, so no one would have seen me from outside. He wasn't there. Then his phone goes, and I'm thinking I ought to answer it, but then I hear footsteps coming down the corridor and going into his room and then his voice. 'Alan Grant', he says, quite loud."

"Yes?" I say. I want to shake her, force her to get to the point. But I know I must let her get there in her own time.

"And then his voice goes all quiet, he's whispering, and he doesn't think anyone can hear because he doesn't know I'm in the next room, but you know what those cubicles are like."

Of course I bloody know.

"Flimsy," I nod.

"Exactly. So then he says, 'I thought I told you

139

never to call me here. Like I said, in a whisper. You know?"

I dig my nails into my palms to prevent me from screaming. "Yes. A whisper."

"Yeah. So then the other person says something, and he says, 'well it's going to be more complicated than I thought, that's why the price has gone up'. And the other person says something again, then Alan says 'no, it's ten thousand. Take it or leave it'. Then he finishes up by saying, 'okay, I'll see you there then.'" She pauses and gazes at me, her expression anxious. "What do you think?"

What do I think? I think I may have just won the jackpot.

But I need more detail.

"What happened after that?"

She shrugs. "He hung up, and I stayed on the floor for a bit, 'cos I didn't want him thinking I heard him. But when I did, I caught his eye through the glass partition, and he looked like he'd seen a ghost. And then he was very nice to me for the next few weeks, which is pretty unusual for him, I can tell you."

"But you never said anything to him?" She shakes her head.

"Or to anyone else?" Another shake.

So Alan Grant thinks he has got away with it. Whatever 'it' is.

"But you don't have any more details? Any idea what this might be about?"

"No. Do you think it is something then?"

I heave a deep sigh, as if now bored of the subject. "Honestly? Probably not. But when exactly

140

was this?"

She considers for a moment. "It was the summer some time, I know that. Had I been on my holidays by then...?"

The seconds pass, slowly. I can hear my blood pounding through my veins.

Then she snaps her fingers. "I know, of course. I was trying to get the filing done so I could go to the shops and look at bikinis. I ended up with a nice leopard print one. A bit daring, but what the hell. We were going to Ibiza." She leans forward and raises her eyebrows. "Maybe you'll see it sometime."

I give a mechanical smile. I cannot believe that even now, in the midst of the most important conversation she and I have ever had (or probably will do), she is flirting with me.

"Right," I say. "So that would have been..?"

"Early July, at a guess."

She stares at me, her expression anxious.

I believe she has told me everything she knows. It is now down to me to make what I can of this new information. But I must still be mindful of her feelings. It is always possible that I may need her again.

I purse my lips. "Okay. Here's what I think. Whatever this was, it's obviously all done and dusted now. As you say, it could be anything. I think the best thing to do is just forget about it."

She looks relieved. "You really think so?"

"I do. And what's more, I think we should stop talking shop and enjoy ourselves. Now, where's that pudding menu?"

*

We take a taxi home.

I am euphoric with what I have learned this evening. At last, I have the leverage I need. The planning officer responsible for the Rectory application is guilty of about the most serious offence imaginable. He has taken bribes from an applicant.

I do not yet know the details, but it should not be hard to find out which cases Alan Grant was working on last July. I do not even have to find proof. Simply the threat of the allegation (which a full enquiry would doubtless corroborate) should be enough to make him fall in line with my wishes. After all, it is nothing he has not done before.

So I am relaxed and slightly tipsy and full of bonhomie when Jane Gardner leans against me, and I allow my arm to go around her shoulders. And when she moves her face to mine and starts kissing me, I do not resist.

And then it happens. The unthinkable, unforeseeable, incomprehensible.

I find myself enjoying the experience.

I smell her scent and feel her warmth against me, and my body betrays me. My mind, disengaged by excitement or perhaps the alcohol, does not resist.
Her hand takes mine and moves it to her leg. I allow my fingers to slide along her thigh. Her skin is softer and smoother than Helen's, the flesh less muscular, more yielding.

She pulls my head hard against hers. Our mouths are locked, our tongues moving against each other.

I am snogging Jane Gardner in the back of a taxi.

142

And I am enjoying it.

A distant part of my brain screams out, what about Helen?

But tomorrow this will be history, and Helen will never know.

And it is all in a good cause.

14

We are walking through the Rectory garden.

It is early evening. The sun slants through the trees, creating long stripes of gold across the grass. The lawn spreads out before us, an ocean bounded by distant mountains of wood and leaf.

We hold hands, Helen and, I walking towards the woods. Her face is raised to catch the last rays of the sun, it is darker now.

Suddenly she starts.

"What was that?" she says.

"What was what?" I ask.

"Over there." She is pointing into the shrubbery. "A movement. I saw it. Someone else, in our garden."

"You must be mistaken," I say, but she is already walking away from me, towards the woods.

I follow, but the sun is gone now, and I can no longer see her. I step between the trees, into the blackness, and there is nothing, nothing there but the trees and the shrubs.

I call out, "Helen!"

But there is no reply.

I wake. I have a headache, my mouth is dry, and I need to go to the bathroom.

But all I can feel is relief. Helen is beside me.

*

In the morning I am in contemplatative mood.

I know I should be thinking about my next steps. I may now have the means to bend Alan Grant to my will, but that will not happen of its own accord. There is still plenty to be done before the Rectory is finally safe.

But all I can think about is what happened in the back of the taxi.

I do not like to lose control. It has happened before, of course, but not often, and never in that way. So it is an interesting situation for me to find myself in.

Perhaps the most surprising thing is that I feel no guilt for my actions. I have never been unfaithful to Helen, and have always imagined that if I were I should be wracked with the most agonising pangs of remorse. But I am not. There is a vague feeling that it may have been inadvisable to encourage Jane Gardner's physical expectations, but that is a purely practical matter.

It is most strange.

Partly there is the sheer triviality of the act. A snog and a grope in the back of a taxi, no more than happens after every Christmas party in the land. But more importantly, I decide, there is no problem because, quite literally, my heart was not in it.

I had no intention to do anything with Jane Gardner. Nor did I even desire to, either, inasmuch as I felt no attraction to her as an individual. Put another way, would I have preferred that Helen had been

145

in the taxi with me, and that it had been her that I had kissed and caressed? Of course. Ergo, in my heart I remained completely faithful to Helen. It was just the body that slipped up.

And what is a body, anyway? Just a heap of flesh and bone and fluids. Does it really matter what one part of my body does, whether it enters the flesh of one particular person or another?

When you witness death, you see that flesh for what it really is. Meat. Nothing more, and no different to what we slice up as steaks or mince up for sausages. When the life has gone, and all is still, you realise. It is a shock at first, because we are taught to believe otherwise, but when it stares you in the face the truth is inescapable. Ultimately, all people are just...

Meat.

Except Helen. I have never thought of her in that way. Of course she is flesh, and she is beautiful, but she is also the most dazzling, noble soul. And that is what makes her special, what makes her different from all the others. What makes her Helen.

There is a photograph on my desk. It was taken the day she took up her ministry at St Nicholas. She is standing in front of the porch, an utterly radiant smile on her face.

I kiss the end of my finger then touch the finger to the photo. I whisper.

"Thank you God, if you exist, for my wife. She keeps me sane."

*

The telephone rings.
It is Ivy Boakye.

"Ambrose?" she says. "I've been thinking about what we were talking about the other day. And I've had an idea. It's really groundbreaking. Have you got a minute to talk about it?"

A Groundbreaking Idea from Ivy Boakye seems almost certain to be an a priori Awful Idea. But in my new role as her best friend and staunchest supporter I have to at least pretend to take these things seriously.

"Of course," I say. "Fire away."

"Drama workshops," she says.

I wait, but it becomes clear that she is not intending to elaborate further.

"Drama workshops?" I repeat. "In what context were you thinking?"

"Every context! Don't you see? That's the joy of them. Role playing can cover gender, sexuality, physical challenge. Just imagine – the most Neanderthal chauvinist old guard forced to role play the part of a gay wheelchair-bound black man, experiencing all the abuse and discrimination that individual faces every day."

I try to imagine Doug in this role. Ivy Boakye, presumably, would selflessly put herself forward to play the part of abuser/discriminator.

"It's an intriguing thought, Ivy," I say. "Who would be eligible to participate in these workshops?"

"Why, everyone!" She sounds surprised at the question. "It would be compulsory, obviously."

"And have you costed this out?"

"Cost? No, not yet." I imagine our Chief Diversity Officer at her desk, a hand airily dismissing such vulgar details. "But I can't see that it'll be a problem."

147

This is probably literally true. Ivy Boakye has turned the inability to see any problems with her pet schemes into an art form.

"Well, that's great," I say. "Let's see what Doug has to say, shall we?"

Her voice loses its enthusiasm and resumes its usual, astringent quality.

"Doug?" she says. "You think I'm letting that neo-fascist bigot tell me what I can and can't do?"

I hang up the phone with a sigh. This could be a lot harder work than I imagined.

*

I have arranged to attend the meeting of the council's Gay and Lesbian Group.

The GLG, as it is known, meets on alternate Thursdays in the staff canteen after lunch. I have emailed Julian Hatch, the organiser, stressing that this is part of my Diversity review. I do not wish Julian (who works in Recycling) to think he has a new member.

I myself am not homophobic. I have no interest in what consenting adults do with their own or someone else's bodies, in their own or someone else's bedroom. But equally, I care not a jot whether our resident dykes and shirtlifters think the 'council's Diversity policy is working for them' (as I put it in my email). As far as I am concerned, if they do their job well, fine; if not, they can bugger off. (Though clearly that particular phraseology would not be in line with the Diversity policy.)

But if my recommendations at the end of the review are to be taken seriously (and I am very keen that they should) the review itself needs to be seen to

148

be credible. While Ivy Boakye will doubtless insist on presenting her own initiatives (such as her drama workshop notion) I need some ideas that are, how can I put it, a little more practical.

I have read diligently the reports that Ivy's department has prepared. It is difficult to fault them for their thoroughness. On her own terms, she is doing a very good job, encouraging Diversity of age, race, colour, gender, religion, and sexual orientation (not to mention competence, experience and aptitude) in every aspect of council life. It is hard for me to identify areas where she is not already creating her own eviscerating agenda. But I believe there is an opportunity for me here.

There are about twenty people in the room when I arrive, mostly standing around talking, though a few are seated at a large table that has been created by pulling several smaller ones together. Most of them I do not know. But there are a few familiar faces.

Julian spots me as I enter the room and comes across to greet me.

"Ambrose, good to see you."

He is about ten years younger than me, tall and fit-looking (in the athletic sense). His hair is cut short but left spiky on top, and he is wearing chinos and a pink shirt.

He puts a hand on my arm and leads me towards the table. "I've warned the boys that you were coming to talk to them. I have to say that there was a bit of disappointment that you weren't actually joining the group." He leans towards me in a stage whisper. "I said to them, 'give it time, boys, give it time'."

I shoot him a glance. He was not this camp when I last saw him. But that was at a budget meeting. Perhaps that made a difference.

"Good to see you too. Tell me, does Ivy ever come along?"

He pulls a face. "Just the once. She didn't really – how can I put it? Fit in?"

This does not surprise me. It is hard to imagine many places where Ivy Boakye would fit in. Holloway prison, perhaps.

"In what way didn't she fit in?"

"I think she thought we should be more militant. You know, go on marches wearing pink knickers and so on. But we're much more relaxed than that. You know." He nudges me in the ribs. "Girls just want to have fun, and all that."

I cannot make out whether Julian is actually flirting with me, or whether this is his normal conversational style at these gatherings. I hope it is not the flirting.

"Indeed," I say.

I sit at the table and smile at the assembled group. Then I start my prepared speech.

"Thanks for agreeing to see me. I won't keep you long from your usual activities. As you know, the authority is very proud of its record regarding equal opportunities, and has put a great deal of effort into encouraging Diversity, and coming down hard on discrimination in any form. But we never like to rest on our laurels, so I've been charged with undertaking a review of how it's all going. And that's why I'm here today – to hear firsthand what you guys feel about things. So. Anyone want to kick off?"

I gaze around me. Most faces are blank, or show polite interest. A few appear bored. There does not seem any burning desire to speak out against injustice.

"Anyone suffered any discrimination recently?"

Heads are shaken, mouths stay firmly shut.

Julian looks embarrassed.

"What, no one?" he says. "Come on – Ambrose has gone to the trouble to come and talk to us all."

Still no one speaks.

Eventually a pale young man with a spindly ginger beard catches my eye.

"Yes?"

"My boss has been having a go about my sickness record recently."

I wonder what this has to do with discrimination. Perhaps the young man's illness is sexually transmitted?

"And is that because you're gay?" I ask.

The young man considers for a moment. "Don't think so. I think he's just a tosser."

There are a few titters around the table. Julian looks cross.

"I think you have your answer in that case, Ambrose," he says. "Everyone's pretty happy."

Another man, one of the few wearing a jacket and tie, clears his throat.

"I think calling it happy is a bit strong," he says. "Especially if you're working in Environmental Health. But that's nothing to do with discrimination. They treat us all like shit."

It is unclear whether this is a joke or not so I do

not respond directly.

"What about the positive side?" I ask. "Do any of you have any experience of the Diversity unit actually helping you with any problem you may have had?"

One of the few women present raises her hand.

"Actually, yeah," she says. "My line manager told me I couldn't dress how I wanted. So I complained to Diversity and they sorted it for me. Said it was discrimination against my lesbian rights."

I regard her more closely. She is wearing a denim waistcoat over a white tee shirt. Her arms are heavily tattooed, her hair cropped short.

"That's good," I say. "Which department do you work in?"

"Tourism. I person the front desk."

Our council's efforts to promote the borough as a tourist destination have had little success over the years. I have always assumed this was because we have nothing of interest to tourists. But I may have now discovered another factor.

"And these are the work clothes that your line manager tried to prevent you wearing?"

She nods. "That's right. And he even complained about my jewellery."

I take in her nose stud and her tongue stud, and count seven rings piercing her eyebrows. I have a sudden desire to place hooks through those rings, and use them to suspend her from the ceiling.

I tut in sympathy at her plight. "Extraordinary."

I have wasted enough time with these people. "Anyone got anything else? No? Okay then, I have one more question for you, if you'll bear with me. This is obviously a group for gays and lesbians such as yourselves, right?" A general nod. "So what I'm wondering is, what provision is made for our transgendered colleagues?"

I address my question to Julian, though of course this is not his responsibility. "Transgendered?" he repeats. There is surprise in his voice.

I nod. "That's right."

He frowns. "I'm not sure we've got any." He glances around the table for confirmation, receiving various shrugs and murmurs of agreement.

"But you can't be sure that you haven't, can you?" I ask.

No one speaks. My logic is irrefutable.

I continue. "So what I'm asking is, if we expanded this group so that it became the Gay, Lesbian and Transgendered Group, would there be any objections to that? I know that a number of organisations do operate that way."

I see a young woman at the far end of the table, one who has not spoken yet, whispering to the man sitting next to her. I fix her with my most inquisitorial glare.

"I should hate to think there was any discrimination within this group, of all places."

The young woman in question immediately looks guilty and nods her agreement to me. Other heads are nodding too.

I beam at them.

"Good," I say. "That's sorted then."

15

The next day is Friday. I call Tom Bates.

"Tom?" I say. "It's Ambrose Hillier again."

"Hillier? What do you want?" A note of panic enters his voice. "Listen, I told you..."

"It's nothing to do with that," I interrupt. "I've been asked to conduct a review into how well our policy on Diversity is running. I need to go through some Planning records, check a few things."

"Diversity? What's that got to do with us? I mean, we follow the code and everything. We've never had any complaints that I'm aware of."

"It's just routine. But I need to go through the minutes of all the Planning Committee meetings for the last three years."

There is a pause. When he does speak Tom Bates now sounds more confident.

"Well, they're all a matter of public record, so there's no problem with that. But I still don't see..."

"I've told you, it's just box-ticking," I interrupt. "But I need you to send those documents to me now."

I allow a little steel to enter my voice. "The

154

Diversity review requires them."

Another pause. "Fine," he says. "I'll get them right over to you."

I hang up and lean back in my chair.

I find I am enjoying the power conferred on me by my role as scrutineer of all matters Diversity. The very word acts like a talisman. Doors open, resistance crumbles. No argument. I imagine this is what it must have felt like to be a member of the Inquisition, or a secret policeman in some Soviet era state.

I wonder if there is any chance of making it a permanent part of my job description.

*

I am sitting at my desk some twenty minutes later when I have a surprise. None other than Jane Gardner appears in my doorway.

She is carrying a large number of files and seems out of breath.

"Hi," I say.

"Hi." She smiles and gestures with her chin to the files. "Where can I put these?"

I am being unchivalrous and I jump to my feet immediately.

"Sorry," I say. "I wasn't expecting to see you. Just down there will be fine."

She drops the files on the floor and straightens up.

"Tom said you needed these so I said I'd bring them over," she says. "He was in a bit of a state about it, to be honest, wanted to know what you wanted them for. Seems to think you were looking to make trouble. Of course, I couldn't say anything, but..."

155

Her expression is a mix of excitement and curiosity. I imagine that she too wonders why I want the files, though she knows me well enough (she believes) to be confident that I intend no ill to her department.

This is the first time I have seen her since our 'date'. I look at the mouth that I kissed that night, now framing a little, secret smile, and the eyes glowing with the pleasure of being centre stage, part of (as she sees it) a proper office intrigue. For a moment I feel a shudder of apprehension, a sense that I am getting myself involved in something that may one day be hard for me to control. But then I gather myself to the task in hand.

"I said to him, it's just a routine check. I told you I'd been asked to conduct this review of our Diversity policies, didn't I? This is simply to check for any bias in our Planning process."

"But I thought Diversity was just about how the staff are treated?"

I shake my head. "Absolutely not. It covers our external interface as well."

She appears doubtful. Or possibly confused. I continue.

"Take Housing, for instance. You wouldn't expect us to be favouring white families over black, would you?"

She looks shocked. "Of course not. But you're not saying we're like that, are you? Because..."

"No, I'm not saying that at all," I interrupt. "I'm just having a look, then I can say that everything is as it should be. And actually prove it as well. In any event,

156

what I'm looking at here are the committee's decisions. If there are any problems, it'll be the politicians in the frame, not you guys."

As I speak I pick the first file off the top of the pile and return to my desk.

I see her thinking about my words for a moment. Then she grins.

"That's all right then."

"Good."

I open the file and start reading. I assume even Jane Gardner will get the message.

But instead she eases herself into the chair in front of the desk.

I look up to find her gazing at me through widened eyes.

"So, Mr Hillier." Her voice drops to a whisper. "Or should I say Martin? How have you been since I last saw you? Behaving yourself, I hope."

I consider myself a resourceful sort of person. I am rarely rendered speechless. But at this moment I am quite literally lost for words.

It is ten o'clock in the morning, and I am in my own office. I have work needing my attention, work that is extremely important to our mutual employer (and even more important to me, though she does not know that). And she wishes to sit here, in full view of anyone who walks down the corridor, and make small talk.

She waits, smiling. I believe she expects me to be pleased that she is here.

This is very presumptuous of her.

But I am in an awkward position. I cannot simply tell her to go away. This would annoy her, and possibly cause problems in the future. It would also risk creating a scene, which would be embarrassing.

I therefore have no alternative. I must flirt with her.

I shall allow her sixty seconds.

I lean forward and smile myself. "Unfortunately, yes. It was fun though, wasn't it?"

She puts her elbows on my desk and rests her head in her hands.

"It most certainly was. Full of surprises, you are."

"Well, as someone once said, it's more fun that way."

She giggles.

I wish she would go away and leave me with the files.

"When can I see you again?" she asks.

I scratch my ear as if in thought. "The sooner the better, obviously. How are you fixed the beginning of next week?"

"Always got time for you Mr Hillier. How about Monday?"

I nod. "Perfect. What do you want to do?"

She holds my gaze. "I want to do anything you'd like, Ambrose. Anything at all. Do you understand what I'm saying?"

I swallow hard. There is little chance of not understanding what Jane Gardner is saying.

"That's certainly something to think about over the weekend," I say.

Her time is up. I pull a face as if forced to make a most unpalatable decision.

"Look, I'd love to carry on chatting to you, but..."

I gesture helplessly towards the file in front of me.

She gets to her feet. "Of course. I mustn't keep my important boy from his work."

She glances over her shoulder to make sure the corridor is empty then blows me a kiss.

"Until next week then."

I am left with my files and a feeling of nausea.

*

I take the files for last July, August, September and October and start going through them, case by case. One of these is the one that Jane Gardner overheard Alan Grant talking about. One of these will provide the ammunition I need to recruit him to my cause, that of saving my beloved Helen's Rectory. But I know that finding out which will not be easy.

Theoretically much of this information is available on the council intranet. Unfortunately, our intranet is not very good. From bitter experience I know that what should be a quick, easy way of accessing data normally degenerates into the technological equivalent of drowning in quicksand. So I stick with paper.

I have one interruption. Another call from Ivy Boakye, who wants to tell me her latest idea for an 'initiative'. She has had a complaint from a vegan in Environmental Health (how that works I cannot imagine) who is offended at the sale of meat products in the staff canteen. Ivy Boakye is inclined to agree with him that his vegan rights were being infringed. I perhaps express my views on this more aggressively than I might, and she hangs up in a huff. But I enjoy my meat and am not having my carnivore's rights infringed by anyone.

It also occurs to me that if this sort of garbage is the best we can come up for Councillor Lambert then someone around here is going to end up as dead meat as well. I just have to make sure it is not me.

I return to the files. I ignore those cases where the application was rejected. I am guessing that Alan Grant's corruption is more efficacious than that. That leaves me with a list of seventeen.

I believe I can eliminate nine of these as they do not appear to have aroused a great deal of controversy. This is on the assumption that no one would go to the expense (and risk) of bribing an official for an application that would be nodded through anyway. I could be wrong about this, of course. I know little of the realities of the planning process and it may be that the officers get a kickback on every case they process. In which case I am in the wrong job.

Of the remaining eight there are five where, as far as I can tell, Alan Grant had no involvement at all. That leaves me with three possibilities.

The first is for a change of use for the ground floor of a building from residential to retail use. The second is the demolition of an existing block of flats and the erection of a new one three stories higher. The applicant is a firm called Paramount Developments, a name that seems familiar, though I cannot immediately remember why. Perhaps it simply reminds me of the company that makes films. The

160

third concerns a proposed extension of floor space for a Turkish restaurant.

I am fairly certain that it must be one of these. But which?

I read through the documents again, looking for clues. But there are none.

This means there is only one way I am going to find out which of the three is Alan Grant's illicit paymaster. I shall have to ask them.

Annoyingly I have back-to-back meetings for the rest of the day. Stupid meetings, pointless meetings, meetings that exist solely to waste other people's time and money. But they are meetings I cannot avoid. I will not now be able to find out the truth about Alan Grant until Monday.

It is most frustrating. I shall be hard put to contain my impatience.

Patience. Patience is a virtue. But this much patience would be a struggle even if I were Saint Ambrose.

But I am getting closer to my prey. Closer to the moment when I am able to place my demands in front of Alan Grant in the certain knowledge that he will have no choice but to agree. Closer to my victory over the damned, bloody church authorities who are causing Helen so much misery.

16

This evening Helen and I are meeting James for dinner. And, I believe, his latest squeeze, though I do not know her name. We are going to a new restaurant called Octavius. James assures us it has very good reviews, though I suspect this matters more to him than to us.

He is insisting that this is his treat, as indeed it often is when we meet up. Helen is uncomfortable about this, but I recognise that it is simply because we could not afford to eat at many of the places that he enjoys, and he has no interest in slumming it in the type of faded bistro that we frequent. Think of it as compensation for the fact that he should pay more taxes so that people like me could have a decent salary, I say, but she is unconvinced. Nor are Ben and Naomi and the others, when I make the same argument to them. But they do not like James, and have no sense of humour where he is concerned.

I am hoping that getting out for the evening, away from all the pressures of the parish and the anxiety about the planning application, will be good for Helen. A bit of glamour to take her mind off things, a chance to relax rather than worrying about everyone else all the time.

Her God must know she needs it.

*

The restaurant is full, and the tables are too close together, which I do not like. Everything is dark brown wood or dark brown glass, though the tablecloths are light brown. It is very noisy.

James is already at the table. With him is a thin girl with very short dark hair. Gamine, I believe the fashion is called. They both stand as we arrive, and James performs the introductions. The girl, who is called Beccy, smiles, showing a row of very even white teeth.

"Good to meet you," she says.

This is a pleasant surprise. Her accent is Australian, or perhaps New Zealand. Most of James's girls speak poor English (he once explained to me that he was not primarily interested in them for their conversation), meaning that such evenings can become quite hard work.

James pours some white wine. "Beccy's a translator at the Greek embassy," he says.

"My parents came from Greece," she explains. "Emigrated to Australia when I was a baby."

"What do you translate into?" I ask. It is intended as a joke.

"Oh, English, French, German," she says. She tilts her nose and I understand that she enjoys scoring this particular point. "And I help out with the Japanese sometimes."

I bow an acknowledgement.

"I consider myself duly returned to my box," I reply.

I take a sip of wine. It is delicious.

"So how did you two meet?" I ask.

Beccy glances at James. "It was at a reception for a senior official from the Greek finance ministry. James got very drunk and I had to get him out of the room before he made an idiot of himself."

"I was under a lot of stress," protests James.

"Yeah, right. You and everyone else in the room." She turns back to us. "But he was very nice about it. Not like some."

"But hey, you've finally found someone who can stop you making an idiot of yourself?" I say. "You should hang on to her, James."

Helen also laughs. "Absolutely," she agrees. "She's worth her weight in gold."

Even if that is only about six stone, I think.

Beccy pats James on the arm. "There you are," she says."You hear that?"

He picks up his menu. "I did indeed."

"How's business, anyway?" I ask. "Last time we met it was a bit fraught, if I remember rightly."

He shrugs. "Oh, you know. Up and down. The markets don't seem to know if they're coming or going."

"But you're okay?"

He looks at me sharply. "Why wouldn't I be?" Then he turns back to the menu. "Now. I think we should order."

*

"I need the loo," I say.

I have just finished my main course. Lamb cutlets, very nice.

James glances up from his plate. "Hang on a minute," he says. "I'll come with you."

Beccy raises her eyebrows. "I thought it was just us girls did that," she says.

It is a relief to get away from the babble of the restaurant.

Our attitude towards other people is a curious thing. We require them as accessories for our pleasure. Nobody wants to eat in an empty restaurant, even though logically both food and service should be better that way. Instead we need some faces, preferably attractive, or at least interesting, and a murmur of background noise, for 'atmosphere'.

But only in moderation. Too many faces and too much noise is not good.

The background to our lives, that is what other people are. Nothing more, nothing less.

James and I stand side by side at the urinal, eyes fixed straight ahead in the approved manner.

"She seems very nice," I say.

"Mmm," says James. Noncommittal.

He has been quieter than usual all evening. I steal a glance at him. The lighting here is brighter than in the restaurant itself and I see that the signs of stress I noticed on his face last time I saw him are still there, possibly even deeper.

"You sure everything's all right at work?" I ask.

He sighs. "Let's not talk about that, okay?"

We go to wash our hands. "Actually, I thought I

saw you earlier in the week," he says. "Wednesday evening. Getting into a taxi near the Aldwych."

It is as if I have received an electric shock. But I can sense he is watching me and I do not react.

"Wednesday?" I repeat in a casual tone. "No, not me. I was stuck at work. We were supposed to have gone out but they decided the budget didn't run to it, so they had pizzas delivered instead. Can you imagine?"

"Nightmare," he agrees. "No, I assumed it couldn't be you really. This person was with a girl. Very loved up, they seemed."

I feel as if I am going to be physically sick.

"Girl? Really? Was she good-looking?" I ask.

He shakes his head. "Nah. Bit of a plumper, actually."

I dry my hands and toss the used towel into a basket.

"There you are then. Couldn't have been me. I've never fancied a plumper in my life."

This is in fact true.

James is still watching me. He still thinks it was me he saw, but he also knows that it does not make any sense.

"It's a big city," I say. "And we're all supposed to have a doppelganger."

He shrugs. "I guess so."

We return to the girls and the rest of our meal. I wonder as we thread our way through the tables how many other people have seen me with Jane Gardner and thought to themselves that we looked 'loved up'.

I find I have lost my appetite.

*

166

Helen and I travel home on the tube.

"That was fun," she says.

I am thinking about Jane Gardner. I am still in a state of shock at being spotted by James with her. This time I have got away with it, but I may not be so lucky in the future. I resolve to put an end to the whole thing as soon as is practical.

I put such matters from my mind and glance at my wife. She still looks tired, but it is a good, drowsy tired, rather than an exhausted, stressed tired. I am pleased about this.

"Yes," I say. "And Beccy's a nice girl. Much more suitable than his usual efforts."

She smiles. "You can say that again. I wonder how long she'll last though. Why do you think it is that he just can't seem to settle down with anyone?"

I shrug. "I think he just likes playing the field."

"Doesn't seem to make him happy though. He was very subdued all evening, didn't you think?"

"I think work is getting down a bit. He doesn't like to talk about it but things haven't been going that well for him."

She sighs. "I don't know. All that money. And for what?" She pauses for a moment before continuing.

"I do sometimes wonder whether he's not secretly gay."

I turn to her, wondering whether she is joking. But her expression is serious.

"James? Gay? Are you kidding? You've seen him around women – he can't keep his hands off them."

"Exactly. He does all the right things – well, right in that context. But he seems totally uninterested in

167

having a proper relationship with any of them."

"True. But that doesn't make him gay."

"And this one looks like a boy."

I glance at her again. This time she is smiling.

"Maybe. But the last three didn't. Do you remember the Estonian girl? She nearly took that waiter's eye out."

She laughs. "Oh well. It was just a thought." She leans her head on my shoulder. "Perhaps we'll get wedding bells down under after all."

17

The rest of the weekend is tense.

It is now only three weeks to the Children's Party. Helen is involved with its organisation for most of Saturday, and by the evening is exhausted and very down at the idea that it might be the last one. The smiling, carefree Helen I had briefly yesterday evening after dinner with James might never have existed.

I am becoming increasingly worried about her. After the loss of our daughter she suffered a period of depression. That too was accompanied by a hefty increase in her alcohol consumption. I am afraid that if this planning application goes the wrong way it will trigger something similar.

It is utterly vital that I prevent this.

I believe that I have things under control. However it is very frustrating having to wait until Monday before moving to the next phase. It is only when that is complete that I shall be able to dispense with Jane Gardner's services. After my conversation with James this is now a matter of considerable urgency for me.

I try to distract myself by returning to the subject of my next Expedition to the Chilterns. Ever since my last visit there, and Revelation Mark Two, I have felt my excitement mounting at what I am about to undertake.

It is possible that this will be nothing less than my first actual premeditated execution. The first time I have gone out with the fixed intent of administering retribution for someone's inexcusably foul behaviour.

I know that for some these very words will seem utterly repugnant. Whether from personal morality, or merely a sheep-like adherence to society's taboos, it would be unthinkable for them to act in this way. But I am not like them. I think the unthinkable, and do the undoable. I am Ambrose.

It will be a momentous occasion. But unless I plan things properly, it could also be a complete disaster. The Rule may have been abandoned in its literal state, but if I am to avoid the tedium of a police enquiry I must still take proper precautions. So I have devised two new replacement Rules. Never Someone I Know, and Never Too Close to Home.

Fortunately for me, the execution of either Mr Dundridge or the Pikey Thug in the Chilterns would be in accordance with both of these.

As far as the practicalities are concerned, be prepared, I have said, but what does that actually mean? Be prepared for the deed itself, of course, but that is a relatively straightforward matter. I would imagine that I could always find a suitable lump of wood lying around, for example. Or in the last resort

170

there are always my hands. They have served me well enough before, after all.

No, the really important thing to be prepared for is the getaway. Whatever I do must be unseen, unnoticed. And there must be no way on the planet for the police to link me either with the place or the person.

After considerable thought I have identified my requirements as follows:-

A dry, but not too sunny weekend day. (People, but not hordes).

A car and a bike and a rucksack, two different sets of cycling gear, and a dark tracksuit.

A car park with no CCTV, and the correct change. (This is very much the kind of detail it is important to get right. Being forced to wander around the car park asking people if they have change for a ten pound note, or even worse, receiving a parking ticket, is exactly the sort of carelessness that could get me into serious trouble.)

Dark coloured carrier bags to place over my shoes.

Whatever weapon I am to use. In this case I have decided on a knife.

A stretch of footpath that is not too busy (but not totally deserted), without any intersections. I do not want people popping out at me from unexpected directions

There needs to be some undergrowth (for cover to do the deed) but not so thick that I cannot cut across country to a nearby...

...cycle path, where I have left my bike hidden.

171

And which joins a tarmac road (to lose tyre treads).

Which after a good few miles leads back to the car park where I have left my car, though only after having pulled the bike off the road to change back into my original cycling gear.

This last point is very important. The man who parked the Skoda and set off is wearing one set of cycling kit. The cyclist who might possibly be seen on the cycle path is wearing another. And the man who pulls either Mr Dundridge or the Pikey Thug or whoever off the footpath and severs his jugular vein is wearing a dark tracksuit and carrier bags over the treads of his cycling shoes.

There must be nothing to link a murder scene to a dark green Skoda estate registered to Ambrose Hillier of the Rectory, High End.

I am conscious that all this may sound a touch obsessive. I have certainly been described that way in the past. But the devil is in the detail, as they say. All I am doing really is what one of my favourite writers, Agatha Christie, might describe as planning the perfect murder. Except that sounds a bit melodramatic for my taste.

Fifty years ago it would have been much simpler. The train down to the country station, the quiet country lane, and the wait for the target to take their normal route home. It would all have been so easy. Now, the train ticket would have to be bought by credit card, the station would have CCTV, and there would be no pedestrians on the country lanes, only Polish container lorries sent the wrong way by their satnavs.

That is what is called progress.

After a few hours on the internet I think I have found what I need. A large car park where a Skoda estate with a bike in the boot will draw barely a glance, and a good network of cycle and footpaths leading to the area where I had my unfortunate encounters with both Mr Dundridge and the Pikey Thug.

Of course I am well aware that all my efforts could be in vain. Neither of my two potential targets might be out walking in the Chiltern Hills that day. But I am happy to leave that in the lap of the Gods (if they exist). I believe that I have been called to my mission for a purpose. All I can do is fulfil that mission to the best of my ability, and be ready. Ready for one (or both) of them to fall into my hands.

Literally.

The weather forecast for next weekend is perfect. Cold and windy but dry, although of course that could change over the next few days. But with any luck, it should be all systems go for Ambrose.

So many things going on at once. It is all getting very exciting.

*

I clear my regular Monday morning work (fatuous management meeting, meaningless emails) as quickly as I can and retire to the small interview room with my notes. Then I settle down to make my phone calls.

I have given considerable thought to the manner in which I should approach my candidate applications. I do not wish to scare off the guilty, or prompt such outrage in the innocent that they report my call to the

173

authorities. I have decided therefore on Absurdity as a tactic.

In my experience this is often surprisingly effective. Here, I expect it to result in my approach being laughed off by any innocent parties, while hopefully catching the guilty off-guard.

That is the plan, anyway.

My first call is to the proprietor of the Turkish restaurant that wished to expand its floor space.

There is no answer.

I move on to the man who wished to convert the ground floor of a house to a shop.

This time the phone is picked up immediately.

"Can I speak to Mr Harry Gilpin, please?" I say.

"You're speaking to him." London accent, cheerful tone. "What can I do for you?"

"My name is John Gardner. I'm the tax accountant for Alan Grant, and I'm calling about a payment you made to him last summer."

A pause. "Alan Grant? Can't say I remember the name. What was it in connection with?"

"Mr Grant works at the council, in Planning. The payment was in respect of your planning application. You did put in a planning application last year, didn't you?"

"Well, yes. And I paid a fee with it, though I can't recall exactly how much. Is that what you're talking about?"

"This was a payment of ten thousand pounds."

"Ten grand! Are you having a laugh? I know they're a bunch of bloodsuckers up there but there's no way I'd have paid anything like that. It was a few hundred, tops."

Harry Gilpin's incredulity sounds genuine. But I give it one more try.

"My understanding is that this payment was in addition to the actual planning application fee. For special services. I just need a bit more detail on those services for the documentation, that's all."

"Well, I can tell you right now, I didn't pay for any extra services. I certainly wouldn't have coughed up ten grand. I don't stand to make much more than that on the whole deal, not in this market. I think you'd better go back to your client and check he's got his facts right."

I sigh. "I think I'd better do that. Thanks for your time, anyway."

I hang up.

My job often requires me to spot when someone is lying to me. Naturally it is easier face to face, but you can also pick up plenty from a phone conversation. Little hesitations, changes in tone. Right now there is no doubt in my mind.

Harry Gilpin is telling the truth.

I turn to the company that wished to demolish one block of flats and build a bigger one.

It is engaged. I try the restaurant again.

This time the phone is answered.

"Hello?" A woman's voice.

"Can I speak to Mr Ozal, please?"

"Hang on, I'll get him."

I hear her calling out. 'Berk', it sounds like.

The phone is picked up again. "Berk Ozal here." A thick accent, presumably Turkish. "Who is this please?"

I start to run through my spiel. Berk Ozal interrupts.

"I do not understand. Are you saying that I owe this Mr Grant money? Because I paid everything..."

I interrupt back. "No, we have the money, I just need some more information..."

"If you have the money, where is the problem?"

I bite my lip in frustration. Patience can be hard for me when I am dealing with idiots.

"I'm trying to tell you, I just need some more details about what the money was for."

"And you do not know this? Why do you not ask your Mr Grant about this?"

"He is not available. So Mr Ozal, if you could just confirm that you did pay my client ten thousand pounds last summer..."

"Ten thousand pounds? Ten thousand pounds?"

Berk Ozal is now screaming. I hold the receiver away from my ear.

"Are you mad? Where you think I get ten thousand pounds to pay this man? You crazy! You think I..."

I hang up. Berk Ozal is not my man.

Though as I look at the address of his restaurant I wonder if I should diversify my interests into firebombing.

I try the block of flats again. A woman's voice, efficient sounding.

"Good morning, Paramount Developments."

"Can I speak to Mr Donald Dennis, please?"

"Mr Dennis is out of the office at the moment.

Can anyone else help?"

"Not really. It's him I need. Do you know what time he'll be back?"

"We're expecting him later this afternoon. Can I get him to call you?"

"No, that's fine thanks – I'll call back then. Thank you."

I hang up and lean back in my chair with a sigh.

This is getting very tedious. Having eliminated the other two applicants I can now be almost certain that Alan Grant's mystery caller was Mr Donald Dennis of Paramount Developments (or one of his associates). There are simply no other plausible alternatives.

But I need evidence. Still the final, conclusive proof eludes me. Yet again I must wait.

It is enough to try the patience of a saint. A real one.

*

I have a meeting in the afternoon and it is not until four o'clock that I am able to call Paramount Developments again. This time I get through.

"Donald Dennis speaking."

"Hi, my name is John Gardner. I'm Mr Alan Grant's tax accountant."

There is a pause of several seconds. I envisage Donald Dennis, taken completely aback by my words, frowning at the phone, wondering what is going on.

When he speaks again his voice is non-committal.

"Alan Grant. I'm not sure..."

"He works at the council Planning Department. You made a payment to him last summer and I just need to clarify a few details about it."

"Why would I make a payment to him? I don't understand."

"Well, that's my problem. He just said for 'extra services', but I need something a bit more detailed than that."

"What extra services could I possibly want from a planning officer? I have my own agents, surveyors and so on."

I sense wariness in his tone, but also curiosity. He could hang up now but then he will never find out how much I know.

"Like I said, that's what I need clarified. It must have been something good, though. You paid him ten thousand pounds. You can't have forgotten, that, surely?"

I hold my breath. I am hoping that the precise amount will convince him that I am above board, not just someone on a fishing expedition.

Of course, if the number changed for whatever reason after the phone conversation overheard by Jane Gardner, then I am screwed.

"Of course I remember."

Yes! I have done it. I punch the air with my free hand.

"But what I don't get is why you need anything clarified. Who do you have to clarify it for?"

"Well, for his tax form, of course."

Having got what I want, I am now just having fun. At Mr Donald Dennis's expense.

He does not disappoint.

"You have got to be kidding me!" he explodes. "You're not telling me he's declaring this on his fucking

178

tax form! How fucking stupid can he be?"

I adopt a shocked tone. "What, you mean you won't be entering it on your return? Because as a legitimate business expense..."

"Oh, for Christ's sake!" he interrupts. "Listen, get the bloody fool to call me. Okay? Meanwhile do not put anything about this on any forms. This is important. You got me?"

"Okay, Mr Dennis," I say. "I got you."

In fact, I got you, and your friend Alan Grant, right where I want you.

18

I have arranged to meet Jane Gardner at six thirty in the car park. We are going to the Halfway House. Our usual time, our usual place. I feel almost affection for her at the knowledge that it is to be for the last time.

I have my leverage over Alan Grant. Tomorrow I shall speak to him, and that will be the end of my involvement with the Planning Department. It will no longer be necessary for me to socialise with Jane Gardner.

I am conscious that I was similarly confident about my ability to influence Tom Bates. I was wrong about that, and I keep asking myself whether I could be making the same mistake again. But this is different. For one thing, Alan Grant's offence is much more serious. And for another, he does not have the excuse that the Rectory is someone else's responsibility.

No. There is no reason to worry that Alan Grant will not accede to my request.

Jane Gardner sees my car and waves, then trots

over to meet me. She is smiling.

She gets in and leans across to peck me on the cheek.

"Hiya," she says. "Long time no see."

"All of three days," I say with a grin.

She pulls a pretend sad face. "It felt like longer. Anyway, where are we going?"

"I can't be too late," I say. "So I thought just the usual pub, if that's all right."

She shrugs. "Fine by me."

We set off. She chatters inanely about her weekend. I rehearse (yet again) what I am going to say to her.

It is a tricky balance that I have to maintain. If I am not firm enough she may assume that I am simply getting temporary cold feet. I might then find she hangs around, waiting for me to change my mind. Too harsh, on the other hand, and things could get nasty. Hell hath no fury etc. I would rather she did not start making trouble for me at work.

I get our drinks - the same as usual - and after we have settled ourselves at a table – also the same as usual - she leans across and takes my hand.

I look down, at our linked hands. Then I look up at her face. She is smiling, gazing into my eyes, and once again I am conscious of a shiver of trepidation. It is earlier in the evening than I had planned, much earlier, but I suddenly feel that I cannot leave this issue a moment longer. I have to deal with it now.

"Listen, Jane," I begin. "I've been thinking, and..."

"No, you listen," she interrupts me. "I've been thinking too. About this planning application of yours, or rather the one that your wife is objecting to. I want to help."

I stare at her.

"You want to help?" I repeat. "Help in what way?"

"Well, I'm obviously not senior enough to have any influence on what happens."

I nod. I do not need to be told this.

"But," she continues. "I was thinking. You said your wife was very anxious about the whole thing, and that you felt responsible to her for it. So it seemed to me that it couldn't do any harm to just let you know what was happening, how things were going and so on. Then you'd be able to prepare her for the worst if it came to that." She pauses. "What do you think?"

This is a very good question. After Jane Gardner's po-faced refusal to even discuss the specifics of the application on our second meeting I had given up any thoughts of using her in such a direct way. She had her other uses, after all. But now she says she is prepared to be my mole in the Planning Department.

Strictly speaking I should not need this. But since it is offered freely, the chance to hear what Alan Grant is doing and saying almost real time, as it were, seems much too good to pass up. It will be a form of insurance for me, a way of checking that he is doing what he has been told. After my experience with Tom Bates I should not be complacent.

The downside is equally clear. I shall not be able to bid Jane Gardner a sorrowful farewell tonight. Instead I shall have to socialise and flirt and canoodle and fondle her again on at least one, and probably more occasions.

Everything has its price.

*

I lean across the table and kiss her gently on the lips.

"I think it's very generous of you. And if you mean it, I certainly won't say no. It'll mean a lot to me, being able to keep Helen in the loop. She's so worried."

She puts her thumb to her mouth and chews the nail. "It still seems weird, though. Doing favours for her. While we're..." I watch as a blush spreads slowly up from her chest. "Perhaps I feel guilty."

I give her my most solemn look. "Jane, I promise you, you have done absolutely nothing to feel guilty about."

She giggles, then leans forward. Then she irritates me immensely by doing her nose jabbing thing again.

"Not yet, maybe. But I wouldn't bet on it staying that way much longer."

Her eyes are fixed on mine as she speaks. As I register her meaning it takes a superhuman effort of will not to recoil at her words.

I buy some time by finishing my beer in one, long gulp.

"Absolutely," I say.

"So when?" she breathes, still maintaining eye contact. "I'm up for it. So are you, I can tell. It's why we're both here, isn't it? We both know it's going to happen. It's like you said. It's our Destiny."

I am fairly sure that I have never told Jane Gardner that it was our destiny to sleep together. But it is probably not a suitable moment to point this out.

But I do need to say something.

I cast around frantically in my mind, conscious all the while of her gaze. It is growing puzzled. I suspect she was expecting a more enthusiastic response.

"Of course, if you don't want to..."

I realise that I am out of wriggle room. Anything less than full capitulation will, I estimate, be taken very badly indeed. It would probably also result in the withdrawal of her offer of help, which would be a shame.

And surely I will only need to string her along for another week or so. After that I will know whether my stratagems are working. After that I will definitely be able to cut loose.

"The weekend after next," I say. "Helen is away on a sort of retreat cum conference type thing. I'll have the house to myself."

I reach across and smooth a stray lock of hair back behind her ear.

"So maybe I could cook you dinner. What do you think?"

She drops her eyes, biting her lip.

I wonder if she is being deliberately coy. Or perhaps, now that her game is turning into reality, she really is struck with shyness. Either way, it is irritating.

But after a few seconds she looks up at me and smiles.

"Okay," she says.

"Great," I say. I pick my empty glass. "In which case, I think a celebration is in order. Same again?"

*

"So how's it going," I ask. "The Planning

application, I mean. Are they still getting in loads of objections?"

I have returned with the second round of drinks and Jane Gardner and I are sitting companionably, talking about inconsequentialities. Having fixed the date for The Big Event it appears that neither of us feels the need to discuss the matter further. Though I suspect for very different reasons. But having made my pact with the devil, I am determined to get my money's worth.

She shakes her head. "No, it's slowed right down. Just as well, if you ask me, otherwise we'd get way beyond schedule."

"And how's it looking?"

"Well..." She hesitates, glances at me sideways. "Nothing's actually being properly discussed yet..."

"Come on, Jane. You said you wanted to help. There's no point in holding back, you know. You won't be doing anyone any favours by making out things are better than they are."

She sighs. Then she gives a slow nod. "I know. Right. All I can say at the moment is that Alan is pretty dismissive of all the objectors. You know, when the subject comes up. Like he doesn't think they've got a strong case."

I smile at her encouragingly, as if she were a not very intelligent dog that had just managed a basic trick. "Okay. Thanks. At least we know where we are now."

Inside I am seething. So Alan Grant is dismissive of my darling Helen, is he? Thinks she hasn't got a strong

185

case?

We will see about that.

She continues. "He'll begin working on it properly soon, so I'll be able to tell you more then."

I nod. "The consultation ends tomorrow, doesn't it? I guess he'll start after that."

"He would do," she corrects me. "Except he's on holiday this week."

Her words are casual, but to me they are a bombshell. I struggle not to show my dismay.

Alan Grant is on holiday until next week. So I will not be able to talk to him until next week. Which means that I will not get any feedback from Jane Gardner until later that week...

...which takes me terrifyingly, gut-wrenchingly close to the weekend when I have just promised to sleep with this abomination of a female sitting in front of me.

As I stare at her, with these thoughts ricocheting around my mind, she leans across the table and puts her hand over mine.

"Anyway, can we stop talking about that now? I want to talk about us."

19

The next day I am summoned by Doug.

I have declared a truce with Doug. Not that he knows this, of course, any more than he knows that I have determined, once the Rectory is sorted out, to exact my revenge for landing me with this bloody Diversity farrago in the first place. But that is the point. Saving the Rectory must come first, while still protecting my own back from the putative wrath of Councillor Lambert. So with yet a further delay to my plans I must keep other distractions to a minimum.

It is all very tedious. But unavoidable.

"So how's this Diversity review going?" he asks as I enter the room.

I take my time settling into the chair in front of his desk before speaking. (Doug has better chairs in his office than I do). "Fine," I say. "I think we're on track."

"Good." He studies something on the screen in front of him for a moment. "And you're getting on with our Chief Diversity Officer all right?"

I give a shrug. "It's a bit like juggling hedgehogs

187

dealing with her, obviously. But she's been extraordinarily creative in her pursuit of Diversity across the whole gamut of what we do. I think her heart's in the right place."

Doug frowns at this. He is annoyed that I appear to be taking Ivy Boakye's side. This was, of course, my intention in saying what I said.

"If she's got one," he murmurs.

"She claims she's now the council's biggest profit centre."

He glances back at the screen. "Cost centre, I can see. Her headcount is up fifty per cent in two years. But profits?"

"She's in the process of estimating how much money we've saved on lawsuits through her programme of Diversity and Anti-Discrimination Training Days. She reckons it could be millions. I think she's going to ask for a bonus."

"Jesus wept."

"Indeed he did. No macho nonsense about the good Lord."

This earns me a sharp look. Doug can never be quite sure if I am joking when I say such things. But even he dare not mock the great God Diversity.

"I hope you've got something for me to give Councillor Lambert?"

"Oh yes. We'll have a couple of nice fresh initiatives for you."

"Good. I've arranged a meeting for the end of next week, to run through our preliminary findings."

This is new (and not very welcome) news. "Next week? That's a bit tight. What's the rush?"

"I'll be in Canada a couple of weeks later. About a dozen of us are going on a fact-finding tour."

I stare at him. "What facts do you need to find in Canada?"

"They did an awesome job a few years back in getting their public spending under control, cutting their deficits. We're going to see if we can pick up a few ideas."

I think about this for a moment. "So let's just check I'm understanding this right. A dozen senior managers are going on a transatlantic jolly for a week, in order to cut our costs. Is that about the gist of it?"

He gives me his blandest management smirk. "No pain, no gain, Ambrose. Anyway, so I thought we'd sit down with Ivy on Monday to go through what we're going to say."

Alarm bells ring in my head.

"Sorry, do you mean you're intending that we present the report without Ivy?"

He looks surprised. "Well I certainly wasn't planning on having her there. Do you have a problem with that?"

Yes, I have a problem with that. A very large problem. But I have no intention of explaining the precise nature of it to Doug.

I settle for putting on my most sceptical expression. "If you think that's wise..."

Surprise turns to a frown. "Too bloody right, it's wise. Are you saying you want to put Ivy Boakye in the same room as Councillor Lambert? You know what a loose cannon she is. She's entirely likely to start spouting complete twaddle, like we've got a problem

189

because most of the senior management are white middle-aged males or something."

"Well, they are." This earns me a glare. "But, anyway, that's exactly my point. If we don't bring her in with us, won't it look like we've got something to hide?"

Doug considers for a moment. "Not really, no."

I try again. "This review is intended to endorse what we're doing, highlight our successes. There's no mileage in appearing critical of Ivy, all that'll do is make us look bad. So here's what I suggest. You introduce me, I give a bit of a chat, give Ivy a pretty good write-up, then let her talk about her stuff for a bit. We conclude by giving the good Councillor a sneak preview of one or two new initiatives that are in the pipeline. Okay?"

"Fine. But I still don't understand why you need Ivy there."

I wonder if he is being deliberately obtuse. "Because if I present them as my initiatives, it will look as though she hasn't thought of them. If they come from her it underlines the fact that she is doing a good job. That's why she needs to be there, fronting it all up with us."

"And you don't mind her getting the credit for your work?"

This question, and the look of disbelief that accompanies it, explains Doug's problem understanding me. His bureaucratic mind, honed by long years in local government, balks at the idea of foregoing political credit.

"Absolutely not." I speak firmly. "The last thing I

need is to be Councillor Lambert's go-to-guy on Diversity."

Doug nods. This he understands.

"But still," he says. "I'm not happy about it. Ivy is borderline psychopathic."

I shrug. "That's why she's got her job. To show that our employment policies discriminate against no one, not even the criminally insane."

I get another sharp look.

"I'm serious," he says. "I mean, what did she attack that bloke with? A saucepan?"

"A frying pan," I say. "But don't worry. I can control Ivy."

His eyebrows shoot up at this. "You reckon? What are you planning on doing, hiring a straitjacket for the day? Frisking her for kitchen utensils?"

I lean forward and give him my most earnest expression.

"You've got to trust me on this, Doug."

For a long moment he regards me, his expression unreadable. It is of course not me he has a problem trusting, it is Ivy Boakye. In normal circumstances I would be entirely sympathetic to this (just as she is right not to trust him). But these are not normal circumstances, and I need Ivy Boakye at that meeting.

Then he nods.

"Okay. Have it your way. But I hope you're right about this."

So do I, Doug. So do I.

*

Helen has a meeting that evening so I prepare dinner for the two of us. Sausages (pork and leek),

191

mashed potatoes, and peas.

She is tired and once again very down. I wish there was something I could do to lift her spirits.

There is a corked-up bottle of Rioja on the counter and I pour us each a glass. There is just enough. Then I put on some soothing music, Scarlatti harpsichord sonatas.

"Good meeting?" I ask.

She shrugs. "Oh, just more stuff for the Children's Party. There's so much to do, and of course I'm away on this wretched retreat next week."

Mention of the retreat is an unwelcome reminder of Jane Gardner and my irksome duties to her. It is not something I wish to think about.

"So what've you got planned?"

"The usual. Various stalls, coconut shies, tombolas, that sort of thing. Cakes and fizzy drinks. Some school sports day type stuff, you know, races and tugs of war and so on, some for the parents. Some make-up artists. And this year there's one of the young lads from the church, he's in a band. Some of the PCC have checked them out, and apparently they're not too unsuitable for a kid's party. So we've got them playing." I watch as she pushes a sausage around the plate without enthusiasm.

"Sounds good."

She nods. "We reckon it'll be a record turnout this year. Better than ever. And possibly the last ever."

She takes a large swig of wine.

I gaze at her beautiful, exhausted face, and know I have to help her. Not in several weeks time, but now. I want to see her smile, now. And I want her to enjoy

192

her sausages, which are very good.

I know I should not but I cannot resist. Yes, it is a hostage to fortune, but it cannot do any harm. And it will mean so much to her.

"Actually, I've got a bit of news on that. But you have to promise not to say a word to anyone."

She frowns. "What are you talking about? The application? But they won't be making any decision on that for several weeks. How can you have any news?"

"Okay, not news as such. But something. But you really do have to promise not to mention it. It could get me into big trouble."

She shakes her head. "Of course I won't say anything. But how could you get into trouble? You haven't done anything stupid, have you Ambrose?"

This is typical Helen, all big-hearted innocence. She is now more worried about me than the planning application.

I laugh. "Of course not. No, I've just been asking around, seeing what I can find out. You know that girl in Planning I mentioned a couple of weeks ago? Well, I thought it couldn't do any harm to pump her a bit, nothing untoward of course, and see how the wind was blowing. It's all completely harmless, but it might look bad in the wrong hands. And I don't want to get her into trouble." I push a forkful of sausage and mash into my mouth.

She shrugs. "Okay, I can see that. So what have you heard?"

I finish my mouthful. "Nothing definite, of course. The consultation period's only just coming to an end. But it sounds like the planning officers involved are not at all happy with the proposals."

Her face lights up, and so does my heart.

"Really?" she says. "But that's amazing. I thought they really liked the idea of the affordable housing."

"They do. But they also respect that the garden is a rare resource for the community. And it's a lot harder to build new green spaces than it is flats."

"But that's fantastic!" Then her expression clouds. "But it's not their decision, really, is it? The politicians will have the final say."

"True. But you know how lily-livered they are. If the officials tell them that it will be bad for the community and therefore unpopular with the voters I imagine they'll fall into line soon enough."

"Fantastic," she repeats. Having looked on the point of tears only a few minutes ago, she now cannot stop grinning. I feel a warm glow at having wrought such a transformation. "But how sure is your source? What's her name by the way? I can't keep calling her 'she'."

"Jane. She's called Jane." It feels strange, talking about Jane to my wife thus. "You know how these things are. Until it's all down in black and white you can never take things completely for granted. But according to her, they already seem pretty clear in their thinking."

"Bless her. I shall have to buy her a drink when all this is over."

I nearly choke on the last slice of my sausage.
"Better not," I say. "It might embarrass her. I shouldn't really be saying anything to you about it at all."

"Fair enough," she says. "You'll just have to do it

194

for me." She gets to her feet and gestures to the empty bottle. "Talking of which, I think this calls for a celebration. Shall we be completely reckless and open another?"

"Absolutely," I say. I also get to my feet. "But I'll fetch it. You finish your sausages."

20

Saturday is overcast and blustery. Perfect weather for my Expedition.

I find I have been looking forward to this. After all the traumas of the last few weeks, the stress of having to deal with Alan Grant and Ivy Boakye at the same time as keeping our Chief Diversity Officer and Doug from each other's throats has definitely been getting to me. Not to mention trying to do a day job with every shyster in the council looking to stab you in the back (or at least that is how it feels).

At least I am making progress. On Monday I shall speak to Alan Grant, then on Tuesday or Wednesday I shall check with Jane Gardner to see how he is taking it. Then all being well, I shall be able to dispense with her services for good.

And Helen is happier. The prospect of losing the Rectory was sapping all the life out of her. With that threat lifted (or perhaps I should say lifting, I do not wish to tempt fate) I have my old Helen back again, bubbly, vital, a joy to all around her. Good news indeed.

But today, today is my time. My little self indulgence.

I spend the whole morning restless, unable to settle to anything for more than a few seconds. Helen notices, and says it is a good job I am going cycling this afternoon, to work off all that nervous energy.

Sheer, breathtaking excitement, and urgent, guilty anticipation. The danger, the knowledge that what I am about to do would be seen by most people as shockingly wrong, all are part of the thrill. I imagine it is the same feeling someone might have before meeting an illicit lover, or visiting a prostitute.

Not that I have ever done either.

*

The car park is much emptier today. As I expected, the weather has kept all but the most hardy at home. But there are a few cars. There will be some people about on the footpaths.

I start to follow my plan. I buy my parking ticket, then I take the bike from the boot of the Skoda, and my backpack. Inside is a second set of cycling clothes, and a dark tracksuit, plus a knife (I have decided that this time it would be interesting to watch someone bleed to death), several bin liners and two sets of rubber gloves. The knife and gloves were bought for cash from Sainsbury's as part of my regular shop (Helen does not have time).

I cycle away down the road. So far I have seen very few people. A few cars on the road, but no other cyclists, and as yet no walkers. After a few miles I reach a junction with a cycle path, where I pull the bike off the road out of sight and change into my second outfit. Then I emerge, miraculously, as another, different cyclist. Cyclist Number One was in royal blue shorts, a white top and a white helmet. Cyclist Number Two wears a black top, black tights, and a black helmet.

I set off again down the cycle path. I am following the route that it I took when I had my encounter with Mr Dundridge. If you want to catch a rat, you go to where the rats go.

But now that I am putting my plan into action it occurs to me how absurd my behaviour actually is. As I have previously observed, those who choose to ramble around the English countryside tend to be a benign bunch. I was most unlucky to meet two such objectionable individuals on my earlier trips. The chances of running into either of them or someone equally loathsome on a day like today must indeed be remote.

But that is all right. It is the cycling I am here for, after all.

Or so I tell myself.

I come to the spot where I took my break on that sunny day, only a few weeks ago but so much longer in my mind. Without really thinking about it, I get off my bike. I remove my helmet and put on the tracksuit over the rest of my cycling gear. I shove a pair of rubber gloves into the pockets for easy access.

Just in case.

Then I settle myself down against a tree, the same tree as last time. And I watch, and I wait.

*

It is not long before the first walkers pass by. An elderly couple, eyes firmly on the path ahead, oblivious to the man concealed a few yards away. Then a woman with a dog, too large for her, straining at its leash. Then two young mothers, comparing notes on breastfeeding, their babies slung in pouches across their fronts.

But none of them are Mr Dundridge.

After half an hour or so I am beginning to get cold and stiff. I realise that I have been foolish, and that I am wasting my time here. I could sit for weeks without Mr Dundridge coming down this particular path again. As I get to my feet and lean down to pick up my bike, I tell myself, life is not really like that.

But then suddenly, it is.

There is a voice, shouting. It is right in my ear.

I spin around. And there he is.

My acquaintance from my previous visit, Mr Dundridge. He is no more than five feet behind me.

"You! What the bloody hell are you doing here again? I thought I told you last time, the right of way covers the path, if you leave the path you're trespassing. Are you deaf, or stupid, or what?"

For a moment I cannot believe my eyes. In my heart I had not really expected that I would meet Mr Dundridge again today. It was a hope, a dream, a silly fantasy. I was resigning myself to the prospect that this afternoon would contain nothing more eventful than a bike ride. Yet here he is, standing in front of me.

I stare at him. His face is quivering red with rage, mean, angry eyes locked onto mine. Against all the odds, I have my wish.

I smile.

This enrages him even more.

"What the hell's so funny? I see nothing to laugh about. That's the trouble with your type, no respect for..."

I allow his words, meaningless waves of hatred, to flow over and by me. I reach my hands into my pockets to find the gloves...

And then disaster strikes.

*

From around the corner, not fifty yards away, on this half-forgotten path where on a day like today barely one person passes every five minutes, appears a group of four, no six, pensioners. All decked out in their brightly coloured hiking gear, their silly little ski sticks in their hands, they are striding along, chatting among themselves.

Until they see us.

Two grown men, one obviously, even at that distance, screaming abuse at the other. Suddenly we are the centre of attention.

And my plan becomes impossible.

I adapt the smile. It should now appear friendly rather than predatory.

"I'm so sorry," I said. "It's just that the countryside round here is so beautiful, I just lose myself in it. Me and signs, eh? I'm useless, I'm afraid."

I shrug and spread my hands and appeal for the sympathy of the approaching pensioners. "It was just that I saw a rabbit and was checking out where I thought its burrow was. So no harm done, eh? But I promise, it won't happen again."

I do not wait for an answer but wheel my bike along the path in the direction the pensioners have come from. I give them a friendly nod as I pass them. Most of them reciprocate.

Once I am around the corner and out of sight of the pensioners and Mr Dundridge I do not have to pretend to be genial and friendly and harmless and apologetic any more. I can be what I really am.

Utterly, completely, totally consumed with fury. I am seething, molten and volcanic, on the verge of eruption. I could not speak even if I wished to. I want to scream, to shake and maul and claw and slash the life out of anyone, everyone, but especially, more than I have ever wanted anything in my whole life, Mr Bloody Fucking Cunting Dundridge.

He has ruined everything. Hours of planning have gone into this Expedition, from the original idea, through the research and the reconnaissance, until every last detail was mapped out and foolproof.

And then he has to pick that precise moment to make his appearance.

How can I slash his, or anyone else's throat in these woods today after that? A loud argument, with six witnesses, would be the first thing the police would pick up on. And between them they would be bound to produce a recognisable description of me.

No. I have no option but to abort.

I stride along the path. I have to move, to do something. If I stop I know I shall be unable to control myself.

Images and imaginings flood my mind. I find Dundridge's home, and cut him slowly, see his

201

lifeblood seep away. The expression on his face as I explain why. Or I make him watch as I slice and dice his loved ones before his eyes, then do the same to him. I hear his desperate pleas for a mercy that he himself has long since destroyed.

Revenge. Thick and sweet and glorious.

I am walking quickly, eyes fixed on the ground ahead. I see no one, pass no one. It is just me, with my anger and the path and the woods.

And then suddenly it is no longer just me.

*

Something crashes into me. I am knocked from my feet, landing in bracken to the side of the path. I hurt both my hip and my elbow as I fall.

I look around. A cyclist is also lying on the ground, a few feet away. Next to him is his bike, a mud-spattered mountain job. I now see that a small track converges with my path at this point. This is where the cyclist must have come from.

The cyclist staggers to his feet. He is wearing a yellow short-sleeved top and black cycle shorts. There is a gash on his right arm which is bleeding, and a wound on left knee, which he seems to be struggling to put his weight on. He has a narrow, ratty face, and is glaring at me.

"What the fuck are you playing at? Why the fuck can't you look where you're going, you stupid old fart? Look what you've done. Moron!"

The shock of the collision had knocked the anger out of me. Now, faced with this totally unjustified abuse from Rat Face, it returns. In force.

I also get to my feet. "What have I done? You

fucking arsehole! You come careering out of there, without looking, and knock me over, and then have the fucking nerve to blame me! It's not even a cycle path!"

I do not believe he was expecting such an aggressive response. For a moment he looks taken aback. Then his mean little mouth tightens and he takes a step closer to me.

"Yeah? And what's that got to do with you?" he snarls. "Stupid old cunt! Why don't you just fuck off?"

This is the second time he has called me stupid and old. I am neither. Nor do I believe that I am a cunt.

"No," I say.

I also move closer so that we are only eighteen inches or so apart. "You fuck off."

His eyes widen in mock alarm. "Oh really? Well let's see about that. Cunt!"

With the final word he swings his left arm at me. But he is off balance from his knee injury, and I dodge the blow easily.

I kick him as hard as I can, on his injured knee.

He lets out a yelp of pain and clutches the joint. With my left hand I grab his cycle helmet and push it up and back, causing the strap to bite into his throat. I then take advantage of his exposed position to land a punch on his stomach, winding him.

"Cunt, am I?" I say.

*

I glance up the path from side to side to check whether we are still alone, then drag him as quickly as I can into the undergrowth. There is a clump of bushes about twenty yards in, well away from prying eyes, and I head for that.

Rat Face is shorter than me and wiry in build, so it is not too difficult for me. When we get behind the bushes I kick him again in the stomach and also in the balls to ensure that he does not run off. Then I return to the path for both of our bikes, pulling on the rubber gloves on the way.

I feel calm and in control. Perversely, now that I have a legitimate outlet for my rage, my anger has once again faded, and as I wheel the bikes over I am already thinking ahead.

Meeting Rat Face in this manner can only be described as serendipity. Fate has been teasing me, by first of all offering me Mr Dundridge, then snatching him from my grasp, only to present me with an even more perfect candidate in this odious, noxious youth. Removing Rat Face from the planet will be a true Public Service.

When I return he is on his hands and knees, grunting, and trying to get to his feet. He hears me and turns his head.

"I'll get you for this, you cunt," he says.

"Except that I've got you first," I reply.

I aim a kick at the side of his head to settle him down again and rip the helmet off. Then I open the backpack.

I take out two of the bin liners and the knife. Then I roll Rat Face onto his back and sit down on his chest, with my knees on his arms so that he can neither move nor defend himself.

"You have made two very serious mistakes today, young man," I say as I stuff one of the bin liners into his mouth. He flails his legs and thrashes his head from side to side but I have him held securely and there is no chance of his escape. "First, you were cycling, too fast, on a path where cycling is prohibited."

I take the second bin liner and spread it out across his upper body and throat. "And second, you were most rude and unpleasant to me. The combination of the two, I'm afraid, is very unfortunate for you."

I take the knife and hold it up where he can see it. "Quite terminally unfortunate, in fact."

He squirms even more. There is panic in his eyes and a desperate gurgling is coming from his throat, but the bin liner is an effective gag.

I steady the bin liner with my left hand and plunge the knife down into his throat with my right. A little blood seeps around the edges of the blade but the bin liner does its job, and no blood reaches my clothing.

I return my attention to Rat Face's eyes. At the moment the knife entered his body he arched in pain, but now he is simply lying back, staring up at me, helpless and hopeless. He knows the game is up, that it is only a matter of time.

I wonder what it must feel like in these final seconds. Knowing that life is quite literally draining away, that it is all over, and there is nothing that can be done about it. I am tempted to remove the gag and ask him, but of course I cannot afford to let him scream. But I make a mental note to arrange one of my Expeditions in such a way that my subject can speak, right up to the end.

I see blood spreading across the ground around Rat Face's head. The pool grows quickly. It cannot be long now.

It is not. Gradually the struggling fades and stops. The eyes cease to flicker and grow dim.

It is over.

I linger for a moment looking down. The eyes, windows of the soul. Why death should produce such an immediate, unmistakeable change in them I do not know. A hand looks much the same thirty seconds after death as thirty seconds before. But the eyes, they are different. Flat and glassy and lifeless as marbles, they could never be taken as part of a living thing.

I get to my feet and check my shoes and clothing for blood. All clear, just a few specks on the gloves. I was wearing them when I handled the knife and the bin liners, so I will not be leaving any fingerprints behind. Doubtless my DNA is around here somewhere, but as the police will have nothing to compare it with, I do not worry about that.

I strip off the gloves, wrap them in the remaining bin liner, and bundle that into the back pack.

And then with one last look at Rat Face, I set off on my way home.

21

I find it hard to concentrate as I drive back to London. I feel my mind is like the windsock I pass by the side of the motorway, pulled and buffeted every which way. Elation vies with anxiety, triumph with terror.

But interestingly, no guilt, no remorse.

And not a jot of regret.

I relive the scene over and over in my mind. I cannot believe that I have actually done it. Of course, I have killed before, but on both occasions it was on impulse, a primitive, visceral reaction to a shameful lack of respect to Helen. This was different. Although this morning I had never heard of Rat Face, never seen his vicious little face, it was by any measure a premeditated killing. I came out prepared to cut someone's throat, and cut someone's throat I did.

I did. I actually did.

Triumph, vindication, pride. A Public Service has been performed.

And yes. I enjoyed it.

But even in the midst of my euphoria, the fear is never far away. That gnawing anxiety that I have overlooked something, that tomorrow morning there will be a knock at the door (or in our case, a ring of the bell), and there will be the Plod, solemn and accusing.

That is my dread.

Of course, unlike last time I should never even come onto the police's radar. The perfect murder was planned, the perfect murder executed.

Apart from the little matter of six pensioners and Mr Dundridge seeing me moments before.

But what did they actually see? A man, in a black tracksuit, with a bike. Nothing to trace me to my home. Nothing even to connect me to the car.

I just have to stay calm, stay cool. If I do that, no one will ever be able to associate me with today's events.

Just stay calm.

*

This is easier said than done. Taking the life of another human being is not a trivial matter, and it is natural to be a little excitable after you have done so. When I arrive home I am still wired, and even after my shower I find it hard to stay in one place for more than a few moments.

Eventually Helen looks up from the newspaper she is reading.

"Are you all right?" she asks.

I affect a look of surprise and give a shrug, though of course I know exactly what she means.

"Why shouldn't I be?" I say.

"What, apart from looking like one of those polar

bears that have gone mad from being cooped up in too small a space?" (This is another of the things that Helen gets outraged about. Personally I have no interest in polar bears.) "You've been like this all day. I thought the bike ride would sort you out, but you seem worse than ever now."

I force myself to sit down and take a deep breath.

"Sorry," I say. "I guess I'm just still worried about this planning business. I can't get it out of my head."

Instantly she is all concern, moving to sit next to me and stroking my hair. (This makes me feel very guilty indeed. As I have said before, I hate lying to Helen.)

"But I thought you said it was all going to be okay?" she says.

"I know I did. But you know how it is. Many a slip between hand and whatever."

She plants a kiss on my cheek. "You're so sweet. You mustn't worry. You've done your best, and that's all anyone can do. It's in God's hands now. And anyway, at the end of the day it's just a building. So long as we've got each other, we'll be all right. Okay?"

"Okay," I reply.

It seems strange having Helen comforting and reassuring me. It is normally the other way around. But of course she is right (as usual). So long as we have each other, all will be well.

But on one point I do venture to disagree with her. I am absolutely not leaving this bloody planning situation in anyone else's hands.

Not even God's.

*

209

That evening I make a point of watching the news. There have been more street protests against the proposed cuts, and the local government minister has pledged to wage war on red tape and the 'fat cat culture within our town halls'. This reminds me of Doug and his freebie trip to Canada.

I wish the local government minister luck with his mission. I think he will need it.

But there is nothing about Rat Face. Presumably his body has not yet been discovered.

*

Overnight it rains.

This is an excellent development from my point of view. It means that what little in the way of trace evidence that I have left will be, if not washed away, diluted and mightily confused. I could not have planned things better.

Once again fortune smiles on the divine Ambrose. Perhaps he really is immortal. Or at least invincible.

However, I am curious to know the precise identity of Rat Face, and as Helen and I settle down in front of the late evening news on Sunday I find myself hoping that he has by now been found. Indeed, it would be more surprising if he had not. I did not leave him that far from the main path.

Sure enough, he has. A dog walker, predictably. The dog smelled something interesting and dragged its owner into the undergrowth.

And there he was. Darren Little, he is called. A small, common name, for a small, common person. It suits him. Though not as well as Rat Face.

He was twenty six years old, lived in Aylesbury

with his mother, and was unemployed.

That was it. There was nothing interesting about Darren Little's existence.

There is a telephone number for people to call if they have any relevant information and I make a mental note of it. I plan to use it tomorrow.

Helen is also paying close attention to this particular news item. But as so often she is viewing things from a different angle to me.

"How terrible," she says. "That poor boy. Just out for afternoon on his bike and that happens to him. No one's safe anywhere these days. Supposing it had been you?"

"They'll probably find out it was someone who knew him," I reply. "I mean, it hardly seems likely that there are hordes of psychopaths stalking the English hills, looking to pick off random cyclists, does it?"

"I suppose not."

"And anyway, it sounds like he was well off the beaten track. I'm a speed merchant, you know that – I stay on the main cycle paths. Nobody's going to attack me there, even if they could catch me."

She nods. "I know. But even so. I want you to be careful, okay?"

I lean across and put my arm around her shoulder. I give her a reassuring squeeze.

"You mustn't worry, darling," I say. "You know me. I'm always careful."

*

The next morning at nine o'clock precisely I telephone Alan Grant.

211

I am feeling very good today. I have a successful Expedition under my belt, and I am on the home straight of sorting this planning business once and for all. I feel strong and confident. There is surely little that can go wrong from here.

"Alan? It's Ambrose Hillier here, HR. I need to have a word with you, fairly urgently. Can you pop over?"

There is silence for a few moments before Alan Grant speaks.

"What, now? I'm sorry, it'll have to wait. I've just got back from holiday and I've got a shed load to do."

"No, I'm afraid it can't wait," I say. "It has to be now."

An impatient sigh. "Well I've already told you, it'll have to be later. What's it about, anyway?"

"I'll tell you that when I see you. But I'm afraid I have to insist you come over right away. Let's put it this way, you will very much regret it if you don't."

I fill the last sentence with as much quiet menace as I am able. My job gives me a lot of practice at this, and I feel I have become quite accomplished at it. I have every expectation that the tactic will be successful with Alan Grant.

It is.

"Okay," he says after a while. "But this better be bloody well important."

He hangs up, and I settle back to wait for my visitor.

Alan Grant looks as though he has been in the sun. But he does not look happy. His lips are tightly compressed, and his eyes, wary and distrustful, are

212

fixed on me balefully.

"Good holiday?" I ask as I usher him into the meeting room.

"Golf, in Spain," he replies. His tone is brusque, and there is the remnant of some northern accent that I hadn't noticed before.

He takes the seat opposite me. "Now what's this about? I told Tom I was coming over here and he gave me a very odd look. Are you having another go at the Planning Department? You know, more of your politically correct bollocks?"

I smile and shake my head. "Oh no, Alan. I can assure you that this conversation has nothing at all to do with political correctness."

The smile seems to annoy him. "Well what then? It may have escaped your attention, but there's some of us in this place have got a proper job of work to do. And it's bloody busy right now. So if I find you're wasting my time..."

"Yes?"

He leans across the table, wagging a finger in my face.

"Don't mess with me, Hillier. I know your sort. I've dealt them all my life. I'm not frightened of you."

He sits back and folds his arms.

He is challenging me. In his arrogance, he thinks he can take me down.

How wrong he is.

I do not like having fingers wagged at me. I shall very much enjoy wiping the smirk off Alan Grant's face.

I smile again, more broadly this time.

213

"Alan, Alan, let's not fight. All I want is for you to do me a little favour."

It takes a moment for this to sink in. Then he bursts out laughing.

"You want me to do you a favour?" he repeats. "By dragging me over here, with your nasty little threats? You've got a nerve. Either that or you're very stupid. Either way, the answer's no."

He stands.

"Aren't you interested in what I want?" I ask.

"Not really," he says. But he makes no further move to leave the room.

"I just need you to block a planning application. The one for the Rectory at St Nicholas, High End."

He nods. "Your wife's church." He must have seen my surprise for he continues. "Oh, yes, I know all about that. The answer's still no."

This time he does head for the door.

I call after him.

"After all, it's not as if it's something you haven't done before. Though of course, I can't afford to pay your normal fee."

Alan Grant stops dead. "And what's that supposed to mean?" he asks without turning round.

"Just that. That's why it would be a favour. Sort of barter, if you know what I mean. I could repay you with a favour."

Slowly he turns to face me. I am pleased to see that his air of smug triumph has disappeared.

"And what favour could I possibly need from you?" he asks.

"Why don't you sit down again and I'll tell you?"

He sits.

I pretend to think for a moment.

"How about... Yes, I know. How about, I don't tell anyone about the bribe you took from Mr Donald Dennis at Paramount Developments last year?"

I see him swallow, hard.

"I don't know what you're talking about."

I beam at him. "Of course you do. Ten thousand pounds, wasn't it? I certainly wouldn't forget a backhander like that."

He is silent, thinking about what I have said, what I know. From the amount of detail I have given him he must realise I am not bluffing.

"You don't really have any choice here, Alan. Either you're ruined, or you simply do what you do anyway. The only difference is, this time you don't get paid for it. Not in cash, anyway."

He shakes his head. "How the hell did you find out about all this stuff, anyway?"

"That's not your concern. What should concern you is that I do know, and am prepared to use that knowledge."

"It's not that simple."

"Seems pretty simple to me."

Again he shakes his head. He looks, I think, tired for a man who has just returned from holiday.

"It's not just me. There are a number of factors, some them quite – complicated. And don't forget the politicians. It's their decision at the end of the day, not mine."

"Crap. You know very well they'll take your recommendation."

215

He shoots me an irritated glance. "I can't just say, 'this one's a no'. I have to present an argument."

I wave a hand. "That's easy. The Rectory garden is a valuable and rare outside space, a green resource for the community. Saving it will be popular with the voters, too."

"Jesus. You've got this all figured out, haven't you?"

Then he sits back and gives me a hard stare. "But I'm afraid there's one other factor which you don't seem to have taken into account."

The sudden change in his expression is disquieting. "Which is?"

He gives a grim smile. "Did you ever look on the planning papers at who the applicant was?"

I shrug. "It's one of the church bodies, I can't remember which one. The Church Commissioners?"

He shakes his head. "No, they're the owners of the site. But they're letting someone else do the actual development."

"And that would be?" Although I suddenly have a nasty idea what the answer is going to be.

"Paramount Developments. So you see, there's no deal. I've already been bought."

*

I stare at the man sitting opposite me, with his silly overtanned face and his expression of self-satisfaction at having, as he sees it, caught me out. And I feel a surge of anger, white hot and pure. I am surprised that Alan Grant does not melt with the sheer force of it.

"Well, now you're being unbought," I say. Or

216

more accurately, snarl. "You'll just have to tell them they've been outbid."

He gives a little laugh. This adds to my rage. I hate being patronised.

"Like I said, things aren't quite that simple," he says. "These are just not the sort of people you say that to. I'm telling you for your own good, Hillier. You don't want to mess with them."

I have killed three people, one of them only two days ago. Alan Grant does not know this. But I am not used to being threatened in this way, and I do not like it.

My fingers itch to show him exactly how much I do not like it. A sharp blow from my desk lamp would soon sort him out. It is unfortunate that he is worth more to me alive than dead.

And his words do give me pause for a moment.

"All I want is to save the Rectory. Then that's the end of it. But I should warn *you*, just in case you, or your friends, were thinking about doing anything silly, that there is a letter with my solicitor. It is to be opened in the event of anything unfortunate happening to me, setting out everything that I know."

This is of course not true. But it might not be a bad idea. It is the sort of precaution one has to take when dealing with the criminal classes.

"Whatever. The answer is still no."

I lean across the table. "Listen to me very carefully, Alan. This development is not going to happen. And you are going to tell your friends that."

He too leans across the table. "You're out of your league, Hillier. Let it go."

217

To my amazement I realise that Alan Grant is mimicking me.

He needs to be taught a lesson.

I hold his gaze, forcing him to look into my eyes. And for a second, I do what I very, very rarely do.

I allow him to see beneath the mask.

I see him recoil.

I speak softly. "No Alan, you're out of your league. Now go away, speak to your friend, and do as you're told."

Interestingly, even with his suntan he seems to have gone pale. For a moment I wonder how that works.

"Okay," he says. "I'll do as you say. I'll tell him the deal's off. But don't say I didn't warn you."

He gets up to leave.

"Give Mr Dennis my regards," I say.

He does not reply.

22

During my lunch break I celebrate my victory by heading for the tube and travel four stops into town. For my next task I need the anonymity of central London. I do not know what ability the police have to track mobile conversations and identify the callers via aerial masts and CCTV and so on, or even whether they would want to for a call like mine. But I do not want to take any chances.

It has been a good morning's work, and I find myself humming as I leave the station. After my earlier disappointment with Tom Bates I was reluctant to count my chickens with Alan Grant but I now have what I need. He has agreed to recommend against the proposals.

So the stresses and strains of the last few weeks are finally nearly over. I have won. Helen's Rectory is safe.

And now it is time to have a little fun.

I position myself in a quiet street a few hundred yards from the station. Then I dial the number that I memorised from yesterday evening's news.

I put on a quavery, diffident voice.

"I'd like to speak to one of the officers investigating the murder of that poor young man in the Chilterns, please."

When I am put through I continue.

"Now listen carefully. I'm a pensioner and I don't want get involved, so I shan't be giving you my name or anything. My heart isn't good and my doctor doesn't want me having too much excitement. But my wife said I ought to say something, so here I am. We were walking near there on Saturday, and we saw a man, having a very loud argument, with a cyclist. Are you getting this?"

The young lady on the other end of the phone assures me that she is. "But we really would like to have your name and contact details as well," she says. "I promise we won't bother you unless we have to, but we may have some more questions later."

I allow my tone to rise a little, so that I sound suitably querulous. "I've already said no," I say. "I don't know any more than I'm telling you, so you won't need to talk to me again. Anyway, this man, he was shouting and threatening and saying the most awful things to this young cyclist."

"And can you remember what he looked like?"

"Of course I can remember, do you think I'm senile? He was quite young, certainly under sixty, and he had a red face and was wearing one of those green waxed coats."

"Do you know what the argument was about?"

"Well, it sounded like the man was telling the

220

cyclist to get off his land. And the cyclist was saying 'I'm very sorry, Mr Bumbrage, I won't do it again.'"

The young policewoman suddenly sounds very animated. "That's what he called him, was it? Mr Bumbrage?"

"That's what I just said, didn't I? Though I couldn't swear it was actually Bumbrage. It just sounded like it. Dumbrage, or Dundridge perhaps. Something like that. Anyway, you know what I know now, so I'll let you get on with chasing it up."

As I remove the phone from my ear I hear her final words, urgent, pleading. "No, please don't..."

But I already have.

Childish, I know. But after everything I have been through I feel entitled to indulge myself.

*

By the time I arrive back at the office my euphoria has vanished and I am in a sour mood. My favourite sandwich bar has closed down. Apparently the building it is in is scheduled for demolition.

Fucking property developers. Is there no part of my life they do not want to ruin?

This afternoon I am meeting with Doug and Ivy Boakye. It is a sort of dry run for the meeting with Councillor Lambert later in the week. I will outline the results of my Diversity review and she will talk about what I have instructed her to talk about. Meanwhile Doug will fidget and worry that I will say something to upset the politicians. It is called teamwork.

I go through my papers, rehearsing what I am going to say. I have been able to spend less time on it than I would have liked and I am not happy about this.

221

There is nothing of real substance, just empty jargon, a litany of petty meddling in the life of the council. This may of course be what Councillor Lambert wants to hear. But somehow I doubt it. For once I shall be pleased to have Ivy Boakye in the room with me.

However even now I find it hard to concentrate. My thoughts keep returning to this new development with Alan Grant, and Mr Donald Dennis, of whom I know very little, other than that he is a criminal and Alan Grant is afraid of him. It has thrown me off balance.

I have no doubts that the Planning Officer will do what he has been told. He has far too much to lose otherwise. But it is still disturbing.

*

Ivy Boakye is already in Doug's office when I arrive. It does not look like they have been engaging in small-talk.

"Ambrose, come in," says Doug. He gestures towards the chair next to our Chief Diversity Officer, who is today sporting a tee shirt on which the word 'Dyke' is prominently displayed, surrounded by a red star. "Sit down and let's get going."

I believe he is grateful to be rescued from Ivy Boakye's company. I have noticed on more than one occasion that he gets nervous when he is alone with her.

In my opinion his concerns are unnecessary. As far as I am aware she is only really violent (I do not count throwing staplers and things in this category) towards people with whom she has a close personal relationship. But I doubt there is any point in telling him that.

She nods a greeting to me. I have managed to maintain the semblance of a civilised working relationship with her through this process (so far at least) but it has not been easy. In particular she has taken great offence at my refusal to allow her to put forward her notion of compulsory re-education drama workshops. However on this I am adamant. This is my review and I will not have my name attached to anything so egregiously ridiculous as that.

But over the course of these last weeks I have developed an intense dislike for our Chief Diversity Officer and the appalling, debilitating drivel she peddles. When all this is over and I have more time I shall see if there is anything that can be done to contain Ivy Boakye.

This too is probably a lost cause. It is just the way the world is these days. But it will be fun trying.

*

I run through my review. Statistics, percentages, achievements, past initiatives. Ivy Boakye looks proud, Doug looks bored. When I get to the bit about the hypothetical money that Ivy Boakye has 'saved' the council by preventing hypothetical law suits and the massive cost to the taxpayer of their hypothetical settlement, he rolls his eyes.

Fortunately Ivy Boakye does not see this.

"Going forward," I say. "Ivy has a few new initiatives that she would like to share with Councillor Lambert."

I sit back and let Ivy Boakye do her bit, as scripted by me. The proposals for more inclusivity for our transgendered colleagues, guidelines to guard against sexism in the issue of free bus passes (I am particularly proud of that one), and plans for a review of racism in schools' PE curricula (she dreamt that one up for herself).

When she has finished I direct a confident smile towards Doug.

"So? What do you think? Personally I reckon we've got plenty there to keep Councillor Lambert happy."

For a moment he says nothing. Just drums his fingers and stares at me.

Eventually he shakes his head.

"Ambrose, you've surpassed yourself," he says. "That is the biggest load of crap I have ever heard."

I hear Ivy Boakye gives a small gasp of outrage. I cut in quickly.

"Not exactly the ringing endorsement I was hoping for, Doug. What else did you expect?"

He throws his hands in the air.

"I don't know! Something more than that tosh, that's for sure."

"Oh really? I thought you just wanted the minimum necessary to keep Councillor Lambert off our backs."

Another gasp from Ivy Boakye. Both Doug and I ignore her.

"Yes, but... Couldn't you think of something new?"

"There's loads there that's new! The bus pass stuff, the PE stuff..."

"Yeah yeah, you don't have to repeat the lot, I

heard it the first time. I was just hoping for something more – I don't know – groundbreaking?"

This is the wrong thing to say in front of Ivy Boakye. She leans forward and fixes her gaze on Doug.

"Well, now you come to mention it, there was one other thing," she says.

We both turn to her. I with irritation, Doug with suspicion.

"Ivy, I don't think we should..." I begin. But she talks over me as if I had not spoken.

"Ambrose said we should leave it for another time, but I think it's such a brilliant idea that we should definitely be showing it to Councillor Lambert."

Doug throws me a meaningful glance. "Really," he says. "Do go on."

"Ivy," I try again. "This isn't the appropriate..."

She spins around in her chair, eyes flashing.

"Ambrose, you heard what Doug said. And anyway, you may be in charge of this review, but it is I who am Chief Diversity Officer. I do not take orders from you."

I see Doug's mouth twitch in a smile. I slump back in my seat, awaiting the worst.

She turns back to Doug. "Drama workshops," she says. "A compulsory programme for all co-workers, to enable them to experience for themselves the abuse and discrimination inflicted on others."

From his expression anyone who did not know Doug might imagine he was impressed by this idea. I, however, do know him.

"I see," he says. "How's that going to work then?"

"The example I gave Ambrose was of a typical member of the oppressing majority, role-playing a wheelchair-bound gay black man."

"Really? And, just for interest, who are the typical members of the oppressing majority?"

"Typically, white males. But not exclusively, of course," she adds. This is what passes for magnanimity with Ivy Boakye.

Doug assumes an expression of surprise. "So, possibly me, then?"

She gives an enthusiastic nod. "Absolutely." She shoots me a spiteful glance. "And him."

Doug turns to me and smiles broadly. "Of course."

Then his expression turns serious again. "Tell me, Ivy, what would this cost?"

She gives a quick, impatient shake of the head. "That's what *he* asked. Why do you people always have to think of everything in terms of money? The importance of what we're doing here can't be expressed in purely financial terms!"

"Because that's what I'm paid to do, balance the books. As are you, as it happens. Not that anyone would ever believe it. Your budget has got more red ink on it than a whole tribe of Indians."

Ivy Boakye's jaw drops. For a moment she is shocked into silence. I shoot Doug a pained glance but I believe that he is too busy enjoying her discomfiture to notice.

"You can't say that," she splutters eventually.

Doug's chin juts out. "Why not? It's true."

"That phrase. It..."

"What, you're worried about me offending all the

Red Indians in the room?"

"And we don't... they're native Americans..."

"Ooh!" Doug's eyes widen. "Oh dear. Have I just jumped out of the frying pan into the fire?"

This reference to Ivy Boakye's weapon of choice is not lost on her. Her face sets and she shoots forward, bringing her face only a foot or so from his.

"Your attitude is utterly unacceptable," she says. "What century do you think you are living in, talking to me in that way?" she continues. "You think I am your slave or something? You think what I do, fighting for justice against the likes of you, is a joke?"

Doug's voice remains calm. "No, Ivy. I think you are my employee. And there is certainly nothing remotely amusing about either you or your job. But what is fucking HYSTERICAL," he slams his hand down on the desk so that both Ivy Boakye and I jump. "Is the way you think that you can lord it over the whole bloody world, spending money like water while the rest of us struggle to keep this show on the road in the worst crisis for local government in history."

Ivy Boakye does not reply immediately. Nor do I know what to say. Much of Doug's tirade is technically accurate (apart from the bit about the worst crisis in local government in history, I am sure that the Norman invasion, or the Civil War for example were worst crises. Nor do I see Doug himself 'struggle' much). But I do not understand what he is hoping to achieve by antagonising her in this way. It is just stupid. Stupid and unnecessary.

She gets to her feet. "I shall not stay here to be

227

insulted. But you haven't heard the last of this. I can assure you of that."

*

After Ivy Boakye has stormed out of the office Doug and I remain seated.

I believe he knows he has gone too far. He fidgets in his chair and will not meet my gaze.

"Bloody woman," he says.

I say nothing. I am too furious at his wilful sabotage of my efforts to speak.

My silence seems to annoy him.

"Come on, Ambrose, don't give me all that. You know as well as I do. She's a psychopath. A complete nutter."

Still I say nothing.

"Oh, for Christ's sake. Say what you really think for once."

Once again I do not understand his insistence on this point. We all know Ivy Boakye is a dangerously unhinged maniac. But we have never felt the need to talk about it before.

With difficulty I control myself. "Okay, Doug," I say. "What I really think is that we should be having this conversation in a few weeks time, once we've got Councillor Lambert off our backs."

He frowns but gives a resigned sigh. "You're right, of course. We need to get that sorted first. But someone's got to do something about her, you know."

I stand. "Agreed. But later."

As I am leaving the office he calls out behind me. "In any event, I'll tell you something for nothing. You

228

can forget all about bringing that psychotic bitch to the Lambert meeting."

*

I return to my desk, still fuming,

The phone goes. It is Ivy Boakye.

"Ambrose? We have got to do something about that man."

I am struck by two things about this statement. First, the uncanny resemblance to Doug's comments regarding her. Second, the use of the pronoun 'we'. It seems that in the face of Doug's outrageous behaviour, Ivy Boakye has put aside her displeasure with me (choosing the lesser evil, as it were).

"The man's a dinosaur. It's exactly his type that needs to be re-educated, and yet here he is, apparently in a position to block my ideas. It's appalling. He hasn't a clue about the importance of our work. You, you get it. But he's just not on the same wavelength as us. What are we going to do?"

I allow myself a second to take pride in the fact that I have fooled Ivy Boakye so comprehensively that she believes we are on the same wavelength. At the same time I hope that not too many other people feel the same way. I have a reputation to think of.

Then I return to the matter in hand.

"I agree he was well out of order back then, Ivy, and I've spoken to him about it. But I don't think we should be too harsh on him. After all, he set up this review in the first place. He's just got a lot on his plate at the moment."

I sense her scowling at the phone in her Diversity headquarters.

"Jesus, Ambrose, do you never stop trying to see the good in everyone? I'm telling you, the man's a complete chauvinist. Didn't you see the way he looked at me sometimes? Not to mention the way he spoke. Sneering, patronising..." Her voice fades away, as if unable to cope with the weight of her disgust. "I bet he's a rapist as well."

"I know, I know," I say in the most soothing tones of which I am capable. "But listen, let's worry about that once we've got this review out of the way, okay? We don't want to push Doug offside before that's sorted, do we? We can work out what to do about him then."

There is a pause while she considers my words. Waiting quietly is not in Ivy Boakye's DNA. She is more of a 'hit with a kitchen implement first, ask questions later' sort of person. But even she must see that on this occasion my advice is good.

"Okay, Ambrose." she says. "I hear you. For now. But I'm telling you. One way or another, I'm going to get that man. I'm going to utterly destroy him."

23

In the evening Helen is delayed at the hospital with one of her parishioners so I prepare dinner. I am doing cottage pie. Helen likes my cottage pie. I put extra cheese on the top to make it crispy. As I peel the potatoes I think back over the events of the last twenty four hours.

I am exhausted. What should have been a straightforward day progressing my plans has turned into a nightmare. I am surrounded by idiots, at every turn I meet nothing but obtuseness and corruption. It is very stressful.

But at least the situation with the Rectory and the Planning and Alan Grant is sorted. Even though in this Mr Donald Dennis I have a more active, malign and unscrupulous opponent pitted against me than I ever realised, I have won. The Rectory is safe.

With that out of the way I am free at last to deal with Doug and Ivy Boakye. They are like a pair of children, bickering in the playground, taunting each other and then complaining to teacher. Why the pair of them cannot act like grownups for once I do not know.

Of the two, I am naturally more sympathetic to Doug's views (though I wish he would keep them to himself, at least for the time being). Ivy Boakye is a menace. But I do not agree with his diagnosis that she is a psychopath. It is a term that is used very loosely and mostly incorrectly. I have read extensively on the subject and the key feature of the condition is that a psychopath has no empathy. He (or she) just does not care about others. So I, for example, could never be a psychopath, as I care about Helen.

In fact, I suspect there are actually very few dangerous psychopaths walking the streets. I imagine they are mainly running large corporations, where the ability to ruin numerous people's lives without compunction must be useful.

Ivy Boakye, in contrast, does care. She really believes that she is doing the right thing. She is just massively, horrendously deluded.

But I am not optimistic that Doug will be able to do anything about it. As Frankenstein discovered, it is sometimes easier to create your monster than destroy it.

Ivy Boakye's threat to turn her tanks onto Doug is more intriguing. And such is her firepower that she might even win. (Though not before I have properly safeguarded the Rectory. That is my clear imperative.)

Such an outcome would be outrageously unjust. Whatever his shortcomings, Doug is not remotely as poisonous and vicious as Ivy Boakye. He is at least sane. It is very clear where my loyalties should lie.

But on the other hand, I still owe him payback for getting me into this situation in the first place. And if she did succeed in getting rid of him, I might even be in line to get his job.

It is worth thinking about.

*

The telephone rings. As I dry my hands and make my way to the study I have a sudden fear that it might be Alan Grant calling to change his mind.

It is not Alan Grant.

"May I speak to Barry Frith, please?"

This time it is a woman. Again Scottish, with a lilting accent which in other circumstances might be considered pleasant.

Even so, I find myself forgetting my manners.

"No you may not speak to bloody Barry Frith, because he is not here, has never been here, and as far I'm aware is never going to be here. Why can't you fucking people get the message?"

There is a short, shocked silence. "There's no need to take that tone, sir. I'm only trying to do my job."

"As presumably were the two people who've called in the last few days. But I told them, both of them, that they'd got the wrong number. What is so difficult to understand about that?"

The unnamed Scottish woman laughs. It is an intensely annoying, patronising little laugh.

"The problem is, sir, you'd be surprised how many of our customers try that one on us once they get a bit

233

behind with their payments. 'What, him? No, never heard of him. No, he's never been here. You must have the wrong number'. Oldest trick in the book."

"Yes, well perhaps your Mr Frith played a blinder by actually giving you the wrong number in the first place. Had that occurred to you and your brain surgeon colleagues?"

The voice becomes less friendly. "Not likely, sir. We do operate a number of checks, you know. But I suppose it's possible that there may have been an administrative error. Let's just check a few details. What address are you speaking from, sir?"

A vision of some sort of Scottish cage fighter, with a single figure IQ, pit-bull straining at the leash, turning up on our doorstep and harassing Helen springs into my mind.

"I don't think so," I say. "I'm not enjoying the phone calls, I'm certainly not laying myself open to the threatening letters and personal visits as well. You'll just have to take my word for it you've got the wrong number."

"I see." The pleasant lilt has become positively stony. "You understand how suspicious that sounds, don't you?"

"I don't care. I don't want to hear from you again. If I do, I'm calling the police, okay?"

I hang up.

I have just returned to my potato peeling when the doorbell rings.

Once again I dry my hands, cursing to myself. As I make my way to the front door I reflect that if this is another tramp, Rules or no Rules, he may be lucky to make it back to the garden gate in one piece.

It is not another tramp. It is Joyce Burnside.

She contrives to look down her nose at me, even though she is standing at the bottom of the steps and I am over a foot above her.

"Yes?" I say.

"I need some papers," she says. "There's an electrical fault in the church hall and the man says he'll need the original plans. I think they're in the Rectory safe."

"I'll have a look tomorrow," I say. I start to close the door but she puts her hand against it, preventing me.

"Can't you do it now?" she says.

"No. I'm busy. I've said, I'll do it tomorrow."

She frowns, and looks as though there are more things she would like to say. But instead she settles for a strange snorting noise.

As I watch her back retreating down the path I am reminded of Ivy Boakye's mug. 'So Many Men, So Little Space Under The Patio'. The references to men and patios are of course too specific for me. But the general sentiment is one I can wholeheartedly agree with.

*

Once the cottage pie is safely in the oven I am able to put on some music (Mozart's concerto for flute and harp) and sit down with a gin and tonic. It is the first time I have had to myself all day, and as I sip the ice cold liquid my thoughts turn again to Darren Little. I try to think of it objectively, about what I have actually done, rather than fretting about the police and

235

whether I have forgotten some detail that might incriminate me. I have (naturally enough) gone over all that in my mind countless times in the last two days, and have always come to the same conclusion, that there is nothing, that I am safe. But the fact that despite all my earlier resolutions I have gone out and deliberately killed again, that deserves some consideration.

The execution of such a piece of worthless scum is an achievement which I believe I am justified in feeling some pride. Obviously in terms of the actual deed, which though I say so myself, was a near flawless piece of planning and execution. After all, there is artistry in perfection, even if the only person who will ever appreciate this is me. But more importantly, I have yet again performed a Public Service, of the type that few, if any, others are capable of.

For I, Ambrose Hillier, have rid the world of a parasite. I am proud of this. I feel no guilt about it whatsoever. In fact, I enjoyed doing it. And I am not ashamed of that, either.

I am aware that others might not fully share in these sentiments. But I have thought about this many times since that first life-changing encounter with Martin Kevin Elliott, and I have come to the conclusion that society has completely ambiguous attitudes towards death. Thousands die every year on the roads, in accidents, some caused by wilfully dangerous driving. Many, many thousands of innocent civilians die in the countless wars, large and small, that take place around the world. Likewise huge numbers die as a direct consequence of the greed of tobacco companies. And we read about these things in the newspapers and shrug our shoulders and do no more than wish it would all go away. Which is rational. We as individuals did not cause these events, and as individuals can do nothing to prevent them.

Yet consider the huge resources we throw into a single murder investigation. Especially if the victim is appealing, say a young, attractive, white woman. Hundreds of police working full time. Outrage and blanket coverage in the newspapers and on television. All that effort, for just one life cut short.

But even if the victim is themselves a murderer, or a rapist, or a paedophile we will devote millions to apprehending their killer. How stupid is that?

I have now killed three people. (That is less than a drop in the ocean of humanity, by the way. They were replaced within seconds.) But each of them had it coming to them. Certainly they were far more deserving of their fate than those whose bodies are shredded on our motorways on a daily basis.

What is wrong with that?

So maybe I will make this my mission. Maybe I will execute one or two scumbags like Martin Kevin Elliott or Darren Little a year.

It is just being public-spirited.

*

It is past eight before Helen arrives home. I can tell from her expression that her day has not been a good one either.

I pass her a glass of wine.

"How was the hospital?" I ask.

She shakes her head. "It's old Mrs Jenson. She's

237

had a stroke. The doctors say she probably won't last the night. The family are staying with her, of course, but..." She glances at her watch. "I told them to call me if there were any developments."

Developments. A bland, institutional euphemism for death.

I kiss her forehead and she flashes me a quick, tired smile.

"So cheer me up," she says. "Any news on the planning application?"

I think back over my day. The nasty, greedy, petty people I have to deal with, my frustrations with a corrupt and self-serving bureaucracy. I cannot help her with her priestly activities, but I am glad I can protect her from all that.

"No news," I say. "I'm seeing Jane tomorrow night, I'll have a better idea then. But everything's still on track as far as I'm aware. By the way, if you ever pick up the phone and it's somebody from an outfit called Southern and General Finance, don't tell them anything, all right?"

She looks puzzled. "Why? Who are they?"

"Debt collectors, I think. Got the wrong number for someone called Barry Frith."

She shakes her head. "Poor man."

That is Helen for you.

*

Later we watch the ten o'clock news. There is nothing very interesting. More banker-bashing, more trouble in the Middle East, and a super model has been photographed taking drugs with someone that may or may not have been a minor member of the royal family. But one item catches my attention.

"And there have been dramatic developments in the hunt for the killer of Darren Little, the cyclist found murdered in the Chiltern Hills at the weekend. A local landowner, Sir Hugh Dundridge, is being questioned by Thames Valley Police, it is believed following an anonymous tip-off. No statement has been made, but a police spokesman described the development as 'promising'."

So, more developments. This time good ones. And Mr Dundridge is actually Sir Dundridge.

I must remember that next time I meet him.

24

The next evening I meet Jane Gardner for drinks.

We go to our usual pub. For some reason it is busier today than on previous occasions, and noisier. As I stand at the bar I hear snatches of conversations.

"Bastard can stuff his sodding job..."

"I mean, it's a fucking joke! Twelve hundred a month for a shitheap like that?"

"If you don't stop staring at my sister's tits I'm gonna kick you so hard your balls'll get stuck in your throat."

Classy joint, the Halfway House.

Jane Gardner is excited tonight. Nervy. She cannot keep still in her seat. But it seems a good sort of excitement, she keeps breaking into smiles for no apparent reason.

I am hoping the reason is that she has good news about the planning application.

I lift my pint of lager. "Cheers."

She grins and clinks her large chardonnay against it. "Cheers."

"So," I say. "Long time no see. How've you been?"

She nods. "Actually, yes. Things are going pretty well."

Then she pulls herself upright and gives me a little smile. "Notice anything different?"

I believe from her expression that she is expecting an answer to this question so I examine her carefully. She is dressed in her normal way, that somehow manages to combine tarty with dowdy. I do not think I have seen that particular blouse before but that does not seem the sort of thing to qualify as 'different'.

Her hair also seems much as I remember it, as does her lipstick.

She continues to look at me expectantly.

In the end I decided to go for something that is obviously not right but will be the right sort of not right.

"You've lost weight!"

She beams at me. "I have! Three pounds!"

"Wow!" I say. I hope that this pathetic rounding error on her over-round form is not the only reason for her cheeriness.

But I do not have to worry.

"Anyway," she says. "I've got some news for you."

She leans forward and her voice sinks to a conspiratorial whisper. "I've been keeping my ear to the ground at work, like we said, and guess what?"

"What?"

She casts a worried glance at the tables on either side of us. The occupants are involved in their own conversations about, respectively, the relative merits of various football players, and their favourite clips on YouTube. I do not think they will be interested in planning applications.

"Go on," I say.

"Well it's amazing," she says. "I don't know why, but Alan seems to be coming round to thinking he should recommend blocking them knocking down your Rectory."

I feign surprised delight. Or rather, I feign the surprise. "No! Really? What's happened then? I thought you said he was all up for the flats?"

She shakes her head. "I really don't know. Perhaps he's been reading the letters of objection and likes the arguments? He didn't say why."

"What happened then?"

"Well, he was having a meeting with Tom in his office, and I was doing a bit of filing in the room next door, when I heard the word Rectory. So I kept my head down and stayed very quiet, and tried to listen. I had to be careful, I didn't want them thinking I was eavesdropping, especially not after that last time with Alan. As it was, I saw him looking at me a bit strangely later." She frowns at the recollection.

"And?" I say. Not for the first time, I feel I would like to pick her up and shake the words out of her.

"And I heard Alan say, quite loud, 'Well I must say I find the counter-argument about the open green space quite persuasive'. And then Tom says, 'Actually, I agree.' So I was really surprised to hear that, so I risked sticking my head up, and I saw them both staring at each other, like they were both surprised as well, at what they'd each said."

"And then?"

She shrugs. "As I said, they just stared at each

242

other, and Alan's frowning a bit, as if he's not sure Tom's serious. Then he says, 'In which case, I'll start drafting something up.' Then Tom gets up and says, 'Excellent. I'll be off then.' But then he doesn't go, he just stands there, looking at Alan a bit odd, but then after a bit he goes off to his own office and that's it."

She sits back, staring at me expectantly. "What do you think?"

I take a deep breath, and shake my head. "Amazing," I say. "It restores your faith in the structures of civil society."

She looks disappointed at this response. I realise she wants something a little more personal.

I pat the back of her hand and gaze into her eyes. "And thank you so much. You don't know how much this means to me."

The familiar pink flush spreads up from her chest. "That's okay," she says.

Then she leans forward and grins. "You can thank me properly on Saturday."

I feel the smile of appreciation that I am wearing freeze on my lips.

It is time.

I have thought much about this moment. In fact, this is the second time that I have gone out for a drink with Jane Gardner intending to end the whole nonsense. On the last occasion I came away instead having agreed to sleep with the wretched girl.

But in general my approach must be the same. Specifically, that I do not want her feeling so aggrieved that she makes trouble for me at work. Or even worse, at home.

243

So we shall part amicably.

I allow the smile to fade into a look of sadness. "Actually, I've been meaning to talk to you about that."

Her smile too fades, into an expression of concern.

"Why, what's up? Has your wife's trip been cancelled or something?"

I shake my head. "No, it's nothing like that."

I gaze into the middle distance. I am hoping that I look like a man both haunted and torn. "It's just that... I don't think I can go through with this. It was our wedding anniversary at the weekend." This is a lie, but Jane Gardner is not to know this. "And Helen wanted to look through the wedding photos, you know, as you do. And it all just made me think, you know? About the vows, and what we promised each other."

I swallow. For some reason I am having difficulty not laughing, but I am hopeful that Jane Gardner will think that I am in fact choking back tears.

"I'm sorry, Jane," I say. I take her hand and stare down at it. "I really like you, and I really wanted this, but – it's just not me. I'm just not the sort of guy that does those things. Can you understand that?"

I look up into her eyes. An unhappy man pleading for comprehension and forgiveness.

She is staring at me with what looks like disbelief. "You're kidding, right?" she asks.

I shake my head. "I'm afraid not."

"That's it? You're dumping me, just like that?" "I wouldn't put it like that..."

"Well, how would you put it?"

But before I can reply to this she sits back in her chair and folds her arms. "Anyway, whatever. If that's what you want, fine."

This matter of fact reaction to her rejection comes as a pleasant surprise. I had feared emotion, tears, possibly a scene.

"Really fine?" I say.

She shrugs. "You've just told me it's over, and that actually you're not interested in shagging me after all. What else is there to say?"

The tautness in her voice warns me that actually it might be less fine than she is saying.

"It's not that I don't want you, Jane. I do, you know that."

She makes a sudden snorting sound. "That's what I thought, anyway. You certainly seemed to in the back of that taxi. Or have you forgotten about that?"

"No," I say. "I haven't forgotten the taxi."

Though I have done my best to.

Abruptly she downs the rest of her drink and stands.

"Anyway, there's no point in hanging around this shithole any longer. Shall we go?"

25

On Wednesday we have supper with Phil and Ali in Shepherds Bush. Ben and Naomi are also there.

I am in a very good mood. Alan Grant is going to take care of the rectory for me, and I seem to have extricated myself from the Jane Gardner situation with no harm done. My major remaining concern is the Diversity Review. Specifically, Doug's refusal to allow me to bring Ivy Boakye along to Friday's meeting with Councillor Lambert, thereby putting me right in the line of fire when it all goes horribly wrong. But even there I cannot be too despondent. I have a meeting with Doug tomorrow, and am confident that I will be able to think of something (what, I have no idea), to bring him round.

Above all, Helen is happier and more relaxed than she has been for some while.

So all is well in the Hillier household.

This is noticed by the others as we sit around eating crisps.

"You seem on very good form," says Phil. He pours some white wine.

Helen glances at me. "Go on. Tell them. They are our friends, after all."

I gaze at my wife with mixed feelings. I do not regret relieving her anxiety, but I wish she could have respected my injunction not to speak of this. But she is such an open, guileless person, it is hard for her to conceal things.

"Well, I really shouldn't say anything, but we've had some good news regarding the Rectory. My spies in the Planning Department tell me the application is going to be blocked."

Ben looks puzzled. "How can you be so sure? Even if you know what the council officials are going to say, it's not their decision. Surely something like this will go to the Planning Committee?"

I nod. "You're right, we can't be absolutely sure. But it's the officials' job to interpret the council's development policy, and their recommendations are made in that context. And then it's the committee's job to implement that policy. So it's unusual to find the recommendation completely ignored, unless there's some overwhelming political issue at stake. Which there shouldn't be here."

"Still," says Ali. "It's a bit early, isn't it? If I remember rightly from what you were saying last time the consultation period only ended a few days ago. Didn't it?"

"Yes, but obviously they look at the objections and arguments as they come in, otherwise it's a very long, drawn-out process." This is a lie, but Ali is not to know that.

"Whatever." Helen is beaming. "Isn't it

wonderful?"

Ali wrinkles her nose. "It still all seems a bit reactionary to me. After all, there's such an appalling housing shortage in London. Are you sure you're not being a bit sentimental?"

Helen's face falls and I feel a surge of hatred for the smug woman sitting opposite me. All this effort, all this work to put the smile back on the face of my darling Helen and this spiteful little bitch has to bring her down again. For a moment I wonder whether something cannot be done about Ali.

It would not be quick and painless for Ali. I would find somewhere private where I could play with her properly for a while. Stick skewers through those big floppy tits and hang her by them, for example.

It is a cheering thought. And though against the Rules, it would be less risky than it first might seem. After all, Ali and I are friends. No one would ever suspect me.

Phil joins in. "That's why we're thinking of moving out of town. We've no hope of getting a bigger place round here."

I look around their modest sitting room innocently. "Why do you need anything bigger? This is fine, surely. You'd only be making the housing shortage worse for families that do need the space."

Ali glares at me and Phil shifts uncomfortably in his seat.

"It's not just that," he says. "It's the school situation, as well."

"I thought you were going private?" I ask.

Ali and Phil both start speaking at once.

248

"You know we don't really agree with private," says she.

"It's hard to get in there as well," says he. "And they're…" He glances at his wife. "So expensive, as well," he finishes lamely.

Now it is his turn to be glared at.

I laugh and turn to Ben. "Interesting. Which of those do you prefer, Ben? Middle-class parents sending their kids private, or middle-class parents moving out of the areas with poorer schools into their middle-class ghettoes?"

Ben's face sets, and Helen looks at me crossly.

For once I do not care. It is very tiring being Mr Nice Ambrose all the time. Occasionally, just occasionally, I need a break.

Still laughing, I get up to go to the loo.

*

When I return everyone has gone through to the kitchen. The room smells of pasta and cheese.

Things seem to have calmed down. Phil and Helen are laughing at something that Naomi has said, though Ali is stacking saucepans unnecessarily loudly, her mouth set in a hard line.

That is another thing I do not like about Ali. I cannot stand people who sulk.

"Well, I had the weirdest dream a few days ago," says Phil. "I dreamt that Ali was a professional footballer."

"Strange fantasies you have here in Shepherds Bush," I say.

Phil ignores me, but the next saucepan is slammed down especially hard.

"Which club?" asks Ben.

This is a typical Ben question. It was a dream. What does it matter which club?

Phil's brow furrows in thought. "Bournemouth, I think."

Ben shakes his head. "I don't think Bournemouth have a women's team."

Naomi rolls her eyes. But I am beginning to enjoy this game.

"Which position?" I ask.

Phil nods as if he was expecting this question. "Goalkeeper."

This at least makes sense. Something large and obstructive, deliberately getting in everyone else's way.

I sit down at the table and Naomi turns to me. "I was thinking of you the other day, when I saw about that cyclist being killed. That's where you go, isn't it? The Chilterns? I hope you're careful."

"That's just what I tell him," says Helen. "But you know Ambrose. He just laughs when you say something like that."

"The chances of something like that happening randomly are infinitesimal," I say. "It's almost always someone you know."

"But wasn't this some local landowner?" says Ben. "That's who they're questioning, anyway. Presumably the cyclist pissed him off or something. That wouldn't have been someone you knew."

Ali turns round. "No, they've let him go. They've issued a photo fit of someone else they want to interview, some man they reckon was hanging around looking suspicious."

My heart starts thumping so hard in my chest, it seems that everyone at the table must hear it.

"Photo fit, eh?" I say. "What sort of man?"

Ali shrugs and returns her attention to the saucepans. "I'm not sure they said much else. About fortyish, I think. Oh, and I think they said he was wearing a black tracksuit, or something similar."

I force myself to stay calm. Show nothing. Poker face, hands still.

As far as I am aware there was only one man hanging around and behaving suspiciously in a black tracksuit in the woods that day. I pray to Helen's God that the photo fit will be the usual image of a grotesque Neanderthal that gets shown on TV.

"Not another cyclist, then," says Phil. "A proper cyclist would never be seen dead in a black tracksuit. It's all brightly coloured lycra, way, way too tight."

"Normally with an extra sock or two shoved down the front for effect," agrees Ben. "God, they look gay."

Ali turns back to the table and gives me a frosty smile. "That true, Ambrose? That all cyclists are gay?"

I blow her a kiss. "Why, are you interested?"

She pulls a face. "Hardly."

I pretend to be sad at this. "That's a bit hurtful. I can always provide references if you're worried." I glance at Helen. "One, anyway."

Our eyes meet, and her lips twitch mischievously.

"Well, my memory isn't what it used to be. I might need a reminder before I can do that."

For some reason Ben, Naomi and Phil all look uncomfortable at this. But as I gaze into the eyes of my

251

darling wife, once again I do not care.

*

When we arrive home Helen is tired.

"I think I'll go straight to bed," she says, yawning.

"I'm just going to check a few emails," I say. "I'll be up in a minute."

I head for the study and wait to hear the landing creak with her footsteps. Then I turn on the computer.

I enter in the Search box: 'Chilterns murder photo fit'.

Up it comes.

I had not realised I was holding my breath. But I utter a long, relieved sigh.

The photo fit is visibly human. And if I was to show it to someone, and say 'this is me', they might spend a few moments frowning at it in a puzzled fashion, before giving a reluctant nod.

But it is not me.

It is strange, how something can be almost perfect in very detail, but totally wrong as a whole. My mouth is indeed that shape, but it does not have that sullen cast. The eyes also, a physically accurate representation, but mine are not so narrowly vicious. I, who look at myself every morning in the mirror, know this to be true.

Another stroke of luck is the hair. It may well have looked like that on the day in question. That crumpled, oddly-angled mess that occurs when a cycle helmet is first removed. But no one will look at it and say, 'ah, that is Ambrose Hillier's style'.

I have nothing to worry about.

But now that relief has replaced fear, and I am

252

able to think clearly, I seethe. I will not forget the way that Sir Dundridge has repaid my little joke on him.

I take one final look before closing down the computer and following Helen to bed.

26

I sleep poorly.

Images of the photo fit, images of me, drift in and out of my consciousness. I lie on my back, listening to the gentle rhythm of Helen's sleep, and wonder if I am not being appallingly cavalier in my dismissal of its power. These things are never perfect, but many criminals are apprehended with them each year. All it would take would be one person to call the police and suggest that the strange Neanderthal image on their TV screen reminds them, for reasons they cannot put their finger on, of one Ambrose Hillier.

Perhaps I should change my hairstyle? Or grow a moustache? (Though Helen would hate that). Or would that in itself be suspicious?

I sit up and have a drink of water from the glass by the table and force myself to relax. People do not think like that, I tell myself. Or at least not normal people, not people in High End, not people who have no involvement in a murder enquiry. There is no reason why I should not be safe.

Just so long as I never, ever go to the Chilterns again.

*

This nagging anxiety about the photo fit does not go away. It persists into the next morning, as I sit at my desk, pondering what I can say to Doug to make him change his mind about Ivy Boakye. When the phone rings it is a welcome diversion.

But not for long.

"Hillier? It's Grant."

His voice is curt, wary. There is the sound of traffic in the background. He has left the office to make this call.

But then Alan Grant has had plenty of practice at this sort of thing.

I contain the frisson of disquiet that I feel at the sound of his voice and force a cheery tone.

"Alan, what a nice surprise. What can I do for you?"

"I've spoken to our friend. I couldn't get through to him until yesterday evening, he's in Portugal for the week. But I have to tell you, he's not happy."

"Well, I don't want to sound hard-hearted Alan, but I'm not really interested in whether he's enjoying his holidays or not. I just need to know that he's going to behave."

He laughs. It is an odd, scratchy, humourless sound. "No, I mean he's *really* not happy. With you. And with me as well, for that matter, so thanks a bundle for that."

I am not very interested in this either. Because Helen is happy. And that is what counts.

"But he understands the situation?"

"Oh yes, he understands all right. I told him that if you blab, he goes down as well as me."

"So what's the problem?"

Again the laugh. "The problem, as you put it, is that this guy is used to getting his own way. And he very much doesn't like being told that it's not going to happen."

I am beginning to lose patience with this telephone call. I really do not understand why Alan Grant keeps on telling me whether Mr Donald Dennis is happy or not and what he does or does not like. My only concern is that the bloody planning application gets blocked.

But Alan Grant is continuing.

"I don't think I can go through with this, Hillier."

For a moment I wonder if I have heard this right.

Then he carries on. "You just don't know this guy. He's not someone to piss off."

Anger takes me. "And I'm not someone to piss off either. I thought we'd established that. You will fucking well do as we agreed. How you deal with your chum Dennis is your own concern, bit I am not going to allow this planning application to go through. Do you understand me?"

There is a pause before Alan Grant speaks again.

"Why don't you talk to him yourself? I'm just the bloody pig in the middle here. Why can't you two try to come to some sort of agreement?"

His voice has become weak, wheedling. It is even more annoying than his earlier patronising tone.

"Because there is no agreement to come to, other

than you agree to recommend against the application. Because I have no relationship with bloody Donald Dennis and no desire to have one. Because it is you who have got yourself into this mess with your greed and corruption, and I have not the faintest intention of doing your dirty work for you to get you out of it. Do I make myself clear?"

Another pause, longer this time.

"Yes, very clear." He sounds weary now. "But I'm afraid the answer's the same. You can threaten me as much as you want but the fact is I'm a lot more scared of him than I am of you. And he's got a message for you, as well. If you try anything with him, he'll take you down. That's what he said. And he means it, I promise you."

He pauses for a second.

"Drop it, Hillier. I'm warning you for your own good. Drop it."

He hangs up.

*

I look down at the phone. An insensate, inanimate object, but a purveyor of utter calamity. I notice that my hand is trembling, and I force myself to replace the receiver in its cradle.

But what I really want to do is smash it. I want to pulverise it against the desk, then punch my fist through the computer screen, then throw the whole fucking lot through the window. Above all, I want, more than I have ever wanted anything in my life, to have my hands around the throat of Alan Grant.

And then to do the same to Mr Donald Dennis.

This cannot be happening. It simply cannot be

true. Everything was sorted, everything was arranged. All that was required of Alan Grant was that he did the obvious, the right thing. And all Mr Donald Dennis had to do was accept that for once in his miserable, corrupt, destructive existence, he was not going to get his own way. But no.

Of course I can destroy them both. But while Mr Donald Dennis's threats hold no fear for me personally, the risk that he might find a way to get back at me by hurting Helen is too great. Even from prison, he could find a way. People like him always do.

I have always had a bad feeling about this man. Even while I had Alan Grant's words of capitulation still echoing pleasantly in my ears, and while Jane Grant was reassuring me that all was well, a part of me was worried that everything was too easy. That is where that sudden jab of anxiety came from a few minutes back (but how long ago that seems now) when I picked up the phone and heard Alan Grant's voice. Somehow, even then I knew something was wrong.

And now what?

I have run out of road. Tom Bates has let me down, and now Alan Grant has done the same. It was a miracle that I was able to find any leverage on the pair of them at all. The chances that a frantic scrabble through the files of their colleagues would do the same are remote (though perhaps not, it is always possible that the whole department is corrupt).

Even if I did find something I would run into the same problem as I did with Tom Bates. The only person who could actually direct Alan Grant to alter his recommendation is Andrew Vine, the boss of the whole department. But I do not hold out much hope of catching him with his trousers down. He belongs to some sort of evangelical Christian sect, and is known as a man of unremittingly grim probity.

It is hopeless.

I look at the photo of Helen, so happy and proud in front of her new church. At the edge of the picture a corner of the Rectory is visible, dull brown brick and faded cream paint, yet so much more than that. I put out my hand and allow my finger to trace the outline of her head, her shoulder.

"What are we going to do now, my love?" I ask it. "What the hell are we going to do?"

*

I have a meeting to attend. Meetings, meetings, meetings. That is all my life seems to consist of. All unutterably pointless, all mind-numbingly, slit-your-wrists- to get-out-of-there tedious beyond belief. By the time I return to my desk I have already forgotten (if I ever noticed) what this one was about and who was there.

There is a yellow Post-it note attached to my computer monitor.

'Pse call Jane asap. Urgent.'

I frown at the small scrap of paper. This is not in the plan. It was only yesterday evening that Jane Gardner and I bid our final, fond farewells. Well, not that fond, actually, which makes it all the more surprising that here she is, hounding me. And not even following our established protocols either.

I get out my pay-as-you-go mobile, which has been turned off for the duration of my meeting. Sure enough, there are three text messages, all in a similar vein.

I contemplate ignoring them. But logic dictates that if she has tried to contact me four times, there is likely to be a fifth, and a sixth, and so on. Or worse, she could actually show up in my office again.

No. It will have to be done.

She picks up immediately.

"Ambrose?" she whispers. "Wait a minute. Do not hang up!"

There is the sound of steps, and voices, then Jane Gardner's voice again, still whispering, but this time with a strange echo.

"That's better," she says. "Now - we need to talk."

Her tone is insistent, impudent. It irritates me.

"Well, I'm a bit busy at the moment," I say. "It'll have to wait. Where the hell are you, anyway?"

"In the ladies. I can hardly talk at my fucking desk, can I? Listen, Ambrose, I'm not asking you, I'm telling you. I need to talk to you right now. It's important."

This is of course what I had feared, but thought I had avoided. Jane Gardner refusing to take no for an answer, hanging around after me like a lovesick teenager.

I force my voice to sound caring and sympathetic.

"I'm sorry, but I don't think there's any point, Jane. I've thought a lot about this, and..."

"Jesus, will you just listen?" she interrupts me. "It's not about that. Not exactly, anyway."

I do not understand this. "What is it about then?" I ask.

"Here. What's going on here, in the department."

"What's that got to do with me?"

She gives an exasperated sigh. "That's what I need to talk to you about."

These words, with all their awful possibilities, hang in the air between us for a moment before she continues.

"So I need to see you now. To sort it out."

"I'm sorry, I'm busy." This is certainly true. I still have not properly prepared for my meeting with Doug this afternoon. "Can't it...?"

"No, it bloody can't!" she interrupts again. "It has to be now. For Christ's sake, it's lunchtime, you must be able to spare a few minutes. If not, I'm coming over to your office."

I do not like the sound of this. There is a new firmness to Jane Gardner's voice, a determination that I have not heard before. I am not going to escape this meeting.

But then, perhaps I ought not to even try. Whatever it is she has picked up on in the Planning Department, it may require some action from me.

"Okay, okay. I'll meet you in the car park. We can drive somewhere and get a sandwich while we talk."

I hang up and heave a deep sigh of my own.

Just when I thought things could not get any worse...

*

Jane Gardner pulls the car door shut behind her. I force myself to give her a smile.

It is not returned.

I pull out of the car park. "So what's all this about then?" I ask.

For a few moments she does not speak. When she does her voice is low and hard.

"You must think I'm really fucking stupid."

I am so startled by this that I almost swerve into a cyclist, earning a torrent of abuse, inaudible from within the car, but clear in its intent.

"What did you say?"

"You heard me."

"Yes, but it didn't make any sense."

There is a pause. Out of the corner of my eye I see her turn sideways, to look out of the window, before she speaks.

"What did you say to Alan Grant?" she asks.

"What?"

She turns back to me. "Jesus, are you frigging deaf or something? I asked you what you said to Alan Grant." When I do not speak she continues. "Did you tell him what I said to you? About overhearing him that time?"

"No!" I keep my eyes on the road, but shake my head vigorously. "Of course not. Whatever makes you think I'd do a thing like that?"

"Because he asked me. Outright. If I'd said anything to you. Now why would he do a thing like that?"

My head is now spinning. I need time to think. "Listen, I don't know what's going on here, but you're right, we need to get this sorted out. But let's leave it until we get to the pub and I can concentrate, okay?"

27

The fucking Halfway House again. I thought I had seen the back of the bloody place for good.

We do not speak again until I have returned to our (depressingly familiar) table with our drinks.

"Now," I say. "Tell me exactly what's happened."

She takes a sip of wine then purses her lips.

"Okay. You know I said the other day that he was looking at me strangely? That's happened a few times since. Then this morning, guess what? I was on my own in the office, and he comes up to me."

"And?"

"And he leans right over the desk, and he says to me, just like that, 'have you been talking to that cunt Hillier?' That's what he called you. Can you imagine?"

She sits back and watches me through narrowed eyes.

That was not very polite of him, I think. But nor is it important right now.

"So what did you say to him?" I ask.

"Well, I just stared at him for a minute, I suppose.

I didn't know what to say. Then I said I didn't know what he was talking about."

"And?"

"And so he says, 'you know exactly what I mean. Ambrose Hillier. That cunt who works in HR. Have you been talking to him? About me?"

"So you said...?"

"Of course, I said I hadn't. But I don't think he believed me. He didn't look as if he did."

I am well able to believe that Alan Grant did not believe Jane Gardner's denials. Caught off guard, the chances of her being able to lie convincingly seem non-existent.

She now looks me square in the eye. "But what I want to know," she continues. "Is how he got the idea in the first place."

I shrug. "Well, you did bring me those files the other day. Perhaps someone heard you had visited HR with some files, go the wrong end of the stick, and said something to him."

This makes her think for a moment. "That's possible, I suppose. Doesn't exactly seem likely, though, does it? What did you want those files for, anyway?"

"I told you. We were looking at the Planning Committee's decisions as part of the Diversity review. Checking for any bias."

"Really?"

Once again she is fixing me with that gaze. This is a new Jane Gardner, less gullible, less malleable.

I preferred the old one.

"Yes! I said so," I say.

Still she stares at me. Then she leans forward.

"How about this for an alternative theory? How about, you've never really been interested in me at all. How about you've just been playing me for a sucker, trying to find out stuff about the Planning Department that you can use to protect your manky old rectory, pretending to fancy me then dumping me as soon as you've got what you wanted? How about that, eh?"

I stare at her in genuine shock. I have seriously underestimated Jane Gardner.

"Jane, how could you even think such a thing?" I say in an outraged tone. "You know how much I care about you."

"Oh, cut the crap. I'm not that stupid. I just played the innocent little girl routine 'cos you seemed to like it." Her voice has risen and the only other occupant of the bar, an elderly man reading the Racing Post, looks across with interest.

"But do you know what really annoys me?" she continues. "That I fell for it. That I believed all that ridiculous bollocks about it being lonely in HR and wanting someone to gossip with. Or rather, I wasn't quite that much of a dumbass, I just thought it was your cackhanded way of getting into my knickers. And now I find not even that's true."

I do not know what to say to all this. Jane Gardner has transformed in front of my eyes from something harmless if irritating, like an overlarge and overfriendly dog, into a screaming harpy.

But I must try to calm her down.

"Look, I don't know if you've been watching too much Spooks or something, but that's not how things

265

happen in the real world. For goodness sake, do you think I was just lurking in the car park that day, waiting to bump into you?"

For the first time I see a flicker of doubt cross her face. But then she shrugs.

"Maybe. Maybe not. It's what's happened after that concerns me. Specifically the fact that one of my bosses is now majorly pissed off with me and thinking I can't be trusted." She gives a tight little smile. "So you know what I'm thinking? I'm thinking I should maybe go to Mr Vine, tell him all about it. He'll know what to do."

It is fortunate that at this moment I am not holding my glass. If I had been, I would almost certainly have dropped it. Suddenly my mild concern, which has principally been concerned with preventing Jane Gardner making a nuisance of herself, has morphed into full-blown panic.

If Jane Gardner speaks to Andrew Vine him about this, he will feel obliged to investigate, questioning both Alan Grant and myself. The whole story would then be bound to come out and I would lose any chance I might yet have to influence the Rectory planning application once and for all.

For these reasons this is very serious. Jane Gardner must be stopped from taking this course of action at any cost.

I make a pretence of thinking about her suggestion. Then I shake my head.

"I really don't think that's such a good idea. You'll be stirring up a hornet's nest, and Alan will then be absolutely sure you've been telling tales out of school about him. Surely it's best to let things just quieten down of their own accord?"

She gives a short laugh. "Funny, I kind of thought you might say that. But actually I think you're probably right. Best to let sleeping dogs lie and all that, eh?" As I breathe a silent sigh of relief she pauses and stares into her wine glass, as if there were something important written in its cool, pale depths. "But that still leaves us."

I shrug. "What about us?"

"You tell me it was all real. But I need to be sure about that."

I lean across the table and take one of her hands between mine. "Jane, of course it was real. How can you doubt it? Like you said yourself the other day, remember that taxi ride? Of course I want you. It's just, you know. Like I said."

"I know what you said." Her voice is tight and low again, and I feel a tremor of unease. "Words are easy. What about actions?"

"What do you mean?"

Her eyes suddenly fix me. "You say you want me. Well, prove it. Let's do Saturday night."

It is hard for me not to recoil at the intensity in her expression. "What, you mean like we planned?"

She nods. "That's right, like we planned. Before you chickened out. You cook me dinner and then we fuck."

She giggles, and for a second she is the old Jane Gardner, the one I felt comfortable with. "Or the other way round. I don't really mind."

Then the new one is back.

I stare at her. I realise that I have now finally run out of excuses, that there is nowhere else to turn.

I desperately cast around in my mind for some alternative that will satisfy her.

"How about we go out to dinner instead? I'll take you somewhere really smart up in the West End. How's that sound?"

A quick smile flicks across her face before disappearing again. "Nice try. And maybe I'll take you up on it."

I experience a brief moment of relief but then she leans forward.

"But, another time. Saturday, I fancy myself a shag."

*

I arrive back at the office still reeling from this further disaster. Only a few hours ago I was congratulating myself on the successful completion of almost every stage in my programme. Now I find that, like demented zombies in a cheap movie that refuse to die, both Jane Gardner and Alan Grant have heaved themselves off the floor and are charging after me, intent on my destruction. I am losing control.

And I am not happy.

When I reach my desk there is a message waiting for me. Doug is now busy this afternoon, and has cancelled our meeting. But he absolutely promises to see me first thing in the morning.

I hold the message, staring at it. For some reason it sits heavy in my hand, a dull weight, as if it is engraved on lead instead of scribbled on a scrap of paper.

I sit and hold my head in my hands. It also feels as if it is made of lead.

Tomorrow morning. Only hours before the actual meeting with Councillor Lambert. Not that it matters much anymore. Either Ivy Boakye comes with us or she does not, either it is a disaster or it is not, either Doug makes me the scapegoat or he does not. None of this will matter if I cannot save the Rectory for Helen. That is all I can think about. That, and the awful prospect awaiting me on Saturday evening.

And that I refuse to think about.

*

But when I arrive home I find that Helen is happy. She has been at a meeting regarding the forthcoming children's party, and is humming to herself as she potters about the kitchen, doing things to vegetables.

"You're late," she says.

I shake my head. "Something came up at work."

She glances at me more closely. "Problem?"

"Nothing that can't be sorted." I give her a peck on the cheek. "How're you?"

"Yeah, good, thanks. Only nine days to go now! Everything seems on track, though. It's just a nuisance that I have to be away this weekend at this wretched conference."

"That it is," I agree.

I pour myself a glass of wine and sit down at the table.

"But at least we don't have to worry about this planning thing anymore," she continues.

I must have been paying her insufficient attention because she comes over to me and puts a hand on my head. I look up. She is staring at me with concern.

"Are you sure everything is all right?" she asks.

I give a smile. "Of course. I'm just tired."

"Are you sure?"

I shrug. "Why shouldn't everything be all right?"

She gives a quick shake of the head. "I don't know – you just sound as if there's something."

Suddenly her eyes widen. "Oh my God! It's not the planning application, is it? They haven't changed their minds. Only..."

"Shhh!" I get to my feet and go and take her head in my hands. She looks up at me, her expression fearful. "It's all right," I say. "Everything's going to be all right."

Reassured, she returns to her vegetables. I sit down again, and return to my thoughts.

Words are easy, Jane Gardner said. How right she was. The words to calm my treasured wife, they are simple to say. Making them real is another matter.

But it must happen. I do not know how, but it must. Somehow I have to find a way.

For Helen's sake.

28

We are walking through the Rectory garden.

It is early evening. The sun slants through the trees, creating long stripes of gold across the grass. The lawn spreads out before us, an ocean bounded by distant mountains of wood and leaf.

We hold hands, Helen and, I walking towards the woods. Her face is raised to catch the last rays of the sun, it is darker now.

Suddenly she starts.

"What was that?" she says.

"What was what?" I ask.

"Over there." She is pointing into the shrubbery. "A movement. I saw it. Someone else, in our garden."

"You must be mistaken," I say.

"No, there. Look."

I follow her gaze. There is a figure cloaked in the shadows, unrecognisable in the gloom.

I call out. "Who are you?"

The answer comes back. "My name is Donald Dennis."

"What do you want?"

The figure gives a rasping laugh.

"Everything," it says.

Suddenly there is a great crash and the ground opens up beneath our feet. I hear Helen shriek, and between us there is no longer soft grass. Just a mighty, gaping chasm.

I reach out to her. "Helen!" I call.

But I am too late. She is gone.

I wake. I am drenched in sweat, my heart racing.

It was just a dream. But Mr Donald Dennis is real. And he has to be stopped.

*

It is Friday morning. I am sitting opposite Doug.

I slept badly again last night. Hours of restlessness, desperately trying to come up with something, anything, to use as a weapon against Mr Donald Dennis. Then brief, intermittent bouts of sleep, themselves rendered unrestful by dark, elusive dreams. Hardly the best preparation for a day as momentous as this.

"So, Doug," I say. "I need to talk to you about Ivy and this meet..."

"No."

"Now, hear me out, Doug. I have thought about this, you know."

"And so have I. It's too risky."

"Don't you think it's risky not bringing her? Have you thought how that will look?"

"Not nearly as bad as she sounds. Come on, Ambrose! You've heard her. She's a complete head case. Think what damage she could do to our careers if she gets going on one of her hobby horses. I'm sorry, the answer's no."

Our careers? It is Doug's career that he is worried about. We both know that he will throw me or anyone else to the wolves to protect that.

But I can see that further argument is pointless. Doug's mind is made up. I have lost this battle as well.

I am about to get to my feet to leave when he continues.

"Anyway, I'd have thought you'd have been glad of the chance to have Councillor Lambert to yourself, given your own problems."

I stare at him. What's that supposed to mean?"

He looks surprised at my reaction. "What? Well, just that she's on the Planning committee. And you know, all this stuff with your place..."

My life has become so surreal of late that I wonder if I have slipped into another dream.

"Councillor Lambert on the Planning Committee?" I repeat. "Since when?"

He shrugs. "I don't know. A couple of years at least. Quite a big cheese there as well, by all accounts. Not the chair, that's old Billy Randall, but he's a bit doolally these days so she calls the shots." He gives a puzzled shake of the head. "I thought you'd have known that."

No, I did not know that. I try to have as little to do with the politicians as possible.

I think back over all the minutes of the Planning committee I have read only a few days ago. How on earth could I have missed that Councillor Lambert sat

273

on it? I can only presume that I was in such a rush I only had time to look at the cases, and never even glanced at the attendance lists. But still. It is not like me to be so unobservant.

Then I remember something that I *did* see when I was looking through those files. Something that at the time I dismissed as being of no relevance to me but now...

But now..?

Now could possibly be the answer to everything.

*

"Ambrose?"

I become conscious that Doug is staring at me. There is an odd expression on his face, one that I have never seen before.

"Are you all right?" he asks. "You've gone quite pale."

That is the unfamiliar expression, then. Concern.

"Yes, I'm fine," I say. "More than fine. I just need a moment to think."

I feel much as I imagine Mary felt when the angel Gabriel appeared to her. Utterly overwhelmed, but in a joyous way. In receipt of a gift so transformational that words are simply inadequate to describe it.

But while God may have proposed, I still have to dispose (to completely mangle the metaphor). I have much to do, many details to sort out.

And very, very little time in which to do it.

"Doug," I say. "How would you feel if I gave you something that was absolutely guaranteed to keep Councillor Lambert off your back?"

*

I watch as the implications of what I have just said sink in. The bureaucrat's dream. Something to hold over an awkward politician.

But his expression quickly turns to one of wariness.

"Such as?" he asks.

"I can't tell you exactly how yet, I've still got to work out the details. You're going to have to trust me."

"Fine. Let me know when you've worked them out."

"There's just one thing though. I'm going to need Ivy at this meeting."

The wariness switches to full-blown suspicion.

"Right," he says. "How convenient."

I ignore the sarcasm. "I'm serious, Doug. I think I've got something that will have her behaving herself for months. At least."

He rotates his chair gently from side to side while he regards me.

"How do I know that it's not one of your tricks?" he says after a while.

"Because I don't play tricks. You know that."

This is true. Not that sort of trick, anyway.

Still he watches, still he moves from side to side. Then his jaw sets.

"But why do you need Ivy?" he says. "I don't get it."

I cannot tell Doug exactly what I am intending at this stage. It would cause his political antennae (as he refers to it/them, whatever they are) to go into meltdown. But it is clear that I will not get his

275

agreement without giving him something.

And I need to get to work.

"Okay. You know the 'good cop, bad cop' routine?"

He gives me a look. "Obviously."

"Right. Now the way this is going to go, someone's going to have to be the bad cop. Yes?"

He nods and I continue.

"So tell me this. If Ivy isn't there, who's going to be the bad cop?"

He shrugs. "Well, it's your idea, so..."

"No." Now it is my turn to be intransigent. "I'm doing all this crap for you, I don't see why I should get the grief so that you can get the glory."

Many people would be uncomfortable talking to their boss in these terms. But there is no point in being subtle with Doug.

This time there is a longer pause.

"So she's basically just the fall guy?" he says after a while.

At long bloody last! Give the man a coconut.

"Absolutely not," I say. "That is a totally outrageous suggestion. Ivy is there to represent her heartfelt views and beliefs."

Doug chuckles. "Of course."

Then he leans forward and jabs a finger at me.

"Okay, Ambrose. You win. But you make damn sure you keep her under control. If this goes tits up you'll find yourself in so much shit you'll need a mask and snorkel. You get me?"

*

I almost run back to my office. Tiredness and

276

depression forgotten, I itch to get to work to see if my theory (for despite what I said to Doug, that is really all it still is) will work.

A few hours. That is all that I have.

The files of past Planning Committee minutes are still lying where I left them in the corner. I haul them on to the desk and commence my task.

I find my first example, the one I remember from previously, easily enough. I photocopy the relevant pages and put them aside. Then I begin going through the remaining files, one by one.

To be absolutely sure about my facts I need to go check every single case since Councillor Lambert started on the committee. It is tedious work, and after searching for half an hour and finding nothing, I start to get dispirited. I begin to wonder if perhaps I was mistaken, and that what I need does not even exist.

Then I find another.

Excited, I check it again, more thoroughly this time.

It is perfect.

It takes me nearly two hours to plough through them all. By the time I have finished, I have found just one more example.

But it is enough.

I pick up the phone and dial the number of our Chief Diversity Officer.

"Ivy?" I say. "We have a slight change of plan."

29

It is Friday afternoon. Doug, Ivy Boakye and I are due to have our long-awaited meeting with the famous Councillor Lambert. Our report will go to the full council in due course, but she, as instigator of the review, gets an advance preview of the findings. And of course, first dibs at any political kudos going.

In recognition of the importance of the occasion it will take place in one of the grand council meeting rooms in the old part of the building. Dark panelled wood walls, stern portraits of local Victorian worthies who served their community, doubtless lining their pockets at the same time. Not much changes.

The meeting is scheduled for three o'clock. We are early, as befits our lowly status. Councillor Lambert is late, as befits hers. To my relief Ivy Boakye is dressed a little less provocatively than usual. Today she is wearing what appears to be the full regalia of an African chieftain.

Doug is jittery, pacing up and down. I am seated at the massive old table – mahogany, I believe – that occupies the centre of the room. I flick through the presentation I have prepared with Ivy Boakye, checking that we have not omitted anything important. It is hard to concentrate with Doug's constant muttering, but I decide not to speak to him about it. I do not need him even more on edge than he is.

The two of them appear not to be on speaking terms. This does not bother me. So long as they refrain from hurling abuse at the other in front of Councillor Lambert I shall not care if they throttle each other afterwards. In fact, I should be quite pleased if they did (especially if I were able to watch).

At twenty past two Councillor Lambert sweeps in and takes a seat opposite me. She does not apologise for being late, which is very rude. But I have been in local government long enough to recognise power games when I see them, and remain unperturbed.

Doug takes his seat and Councillor Lambert, still without speaking, looks at him expectantly.

He begins his prepared speech. Now that he is actually on parade, his performance anxiety disappears, and he is back to his normal form, just the right mix of confidence and toadying.

"Councillor Lambert, it's good of you to take the time to see us today. I don't believe you have met my colleague, Ambrose Hillier, who as one of my senior managers has been conducting this review of the council's Diversity policies."

Impenetrable dark eyes are turned on me, appraising me. I appraise back.

I knew that Councillor Lambert was young, but

even so I am surprised at her appearance. She cannot be much over thirty. And she is tiny. A sharp-featured face, prominent cheekbones set above a thin-lipped mouth, all topped with short, very black hair. Probably quite attractive, if you like boys.

Yet from that small frame exudes something intangible but impossible to ignore. Confidence, or power maybe. Certainly intelligence.

I must take care not to underestimate Councillor Lambert.

"Ambrose Hillier," she repeats. "I've heard about you."

I offer my friendliest smile. The one that Helen once said could charm the birds from the trees. "Nothing too awful, I hope. If it was, it isn't true."

Still those eyes hold mine, unsmiling.

"We'll see."

Not so charmed, then.

Doug is continuing. "And this is Ivy Boakye. She is head of our Diversity unit, and has been assisting Ambrose with his review."

A small frown creases Councillor Lambert's brow. "Is is usual to have the review of an area conducted by a team that includes the head of that area? Isn't it supposed to be independent?"

Ivy Boakye bridles at this but Doug answers smoothly. "If the review were prompted by problems, or perceived problems, so that in effect it was a disciplinary review, then yes. But that isn't the case here. We're simply having a look at where we've come from, what we've achieved, and what's still to be done. In those circumstances it is totally normal to include Ivy in the team."

Doug is good at that sort of thing.

Councillor Lambert gives a barely perceptible nod, then glances at her watch.

"Let's get started."

*

I hand out the presentation documents and start my own spiel.

"First of all, I'd like to say how pleased I am to have been asked to undertake this review. We are all aware of how seriously the council takes the issue of Diversity, and I regard it as a privilege to have been able to further its progress in this way..."

All through my patter, designed to ingratiate myself with the politician within Councillor Lambert, I am watching her. Waiting for her to preen herself, or give one of those self-satisfied little smiles that politicians specialise in.

Nothing. I could have been reciting the weather forecast. Nothing but that unblinking gaze.

This continues throughout my presentation. Once she asks a question, and scribbles several lines of notes on the presentation document. But she gives me no idea what she is thinking, whether she is impressed or disappointed with what she is hearing.

It is most unsettling.

I hand over to Ivy Boakye. I can now observe Councillor Lambert openly. And then I realise what is actually going on here.

She is bored. She has not the faintest interest in Diversity, only in the opportunities it may present for political point-scoring. And so far we have not given her any.

She has no idea of the bombshell waiting for her in only a few minutes time. I doubt very much that she will be bored then. But meanwhile I have to go through the motions.

Ivy Boakye finishes by outlining our new 'initiatives'. Councillor Lambert is by now drumming her fingers on the presentation document.

"And how much of this would be happening anyway, without the review?" she asks.

I answer. "As I hope is clear from our presentation, the proactive approach to Diversity has been working well already, so I think it's fair to say that most of what we've talked about would be going ahead in any event." I turn to Ivy. "But the policy towards bus pass allocation, perhaps? That's something new, wouldn't you say? And the increase in provision for transgendered colleagues?"

Ivy nods her agreement.

Councillor Lambert narrows her eyes. "And that's it? That's all you've got to show for all this expenditure of taxpayers' money?"

I ignore this blatant attempt to throw me off balance. "The most important thing, in my opinion, is the injection of energy a review like this puts into any programme. Even for a department as vibrant and enthusiastic as Diversity, I am prepared to go on record as saying that this process has been most helpful in taking things to the next level."

Even Doug looks impressed at this piece of bullshit. Ivy merely looks mystified.

But Councillor Lambert does not look impressed.

She shakes her head.

"I can't believe that's all you can come up with. This self-serving, meaningless crap."

Even I am now taken aback by the Councillor's directness. Not to mention her perspicacity.

Ivy Boakye has gone rigid. "Now see here..." she begins.

"No, you see here. We have real problems in this borough, real issues of discrimination. And as far as I can tell you're doing nothing about them – nothing at all! These two," she waves a dismissive arm at me and Doug. "That doesn't surprise me. But you!" She jabs a finger at Ivy Boakye. "I am disappointed."

I wait for Ivy Boakye to respond (perhaps defending Doug and myself against this flagrant piece of sexism) but she appears struck dumb.

Councillor Lambert gets to her feet and starts to gather her belongings.

"You can expect to hear more about this," she says. "As far as I can see this is nothing but a whitewash."

At this Ivy Boakye does find her voice. "That phrase is no longer acceptable," she croaks.

Councillor Lambert gazes at her for a moment.

"You're pathetic," she says. "I'm done here."

*

I, however, am not done.

"There is just one more thing that Ivy would like to raise," I say. "We didn't put it into the presentation document because there were concerns that it might be politically sensitive."

Councillor Lambert stops in her tracks. For the

283

first time she looks animated. She sticks her chin out, her dark eyes sparkling as she resumes her seat.

"Are you being serious? As you yourself have said, this is a subject of the utmost importance. How on earth can political sensitivity, as you refer to it, get in the way of any matter relating to Diversity?"

Ivy Boakye gives a fervent nod. "My sentiments exactly." She shoots a dismissive glance at Doug, who frowns at her. "I was confident you would take that view."

I have only had a few hours to script Ivy Boakye for this moment. It is very important that she gets her lines right. A lot depends on it. But if she does, it will be fun to watch.

I sit back to watch the fireworks.

"As you know," she begins. "Our terms of reference are not just to promote Diversity within all aspects of the council's activities, but also to protect against adverse perceptions. In other words, we must not only do the right thing, and be seen to be doing the right thing, but we must also guard against any allegation that we might not be doing the right thing."

I observe her with interest. She is taut with evangelical fervour, her voice exuding passion for her subject. It is as if the spat of only seconds previously had never happened.

Councillor Lambert just looks impatient. She knows all this. Arse-covering is as much a part of her world as it is ours.

"To which end," continues Ivy Boakye. "We have examined the external interfaces of the council to check for signs of problems. Not just evidence of actual problems, but instances where there may be a perception of..." Her voice tails off as she suddenly registers Councillor Lambert's expression. "Anyway, to cut to the point, we are worried about religious discrimination in the Planning Committee."

Whatever Councillor Lambert might have been hoping for it was not this. She jerks upright and her eyes shoot wide open.

"What did you say?"

A more sensitive soul than Ivy Boakye might have quailed at the way these words were spat out. Fortunately for me, Ivy Boakye is not a sensitive soul in any way.

"We're not saying there is religious discrimination of course, just that read the wrong way, some of the decisions taken in recent years could be interpreted in that manner."

Doug is starting to look worried. He was aware that I had something up my sleeve, but I doubt he was expecting such a direct attack on Councillor Lambert's own territory.

She glares across the table at Ivy Boakye. "What the hell are you talking about?"

Ivy Boakye frowns. I had not led her to expect such a violent reaction. (I did not want to put her off.)

"In recent years, there have been two applications from the Sikh community, and one from the Muslim community. All were turned down."

"So? They were bad applications. That's not evidence of religious discrimination."

"But no applications from the Christian organisations were turned down."

"That's because there weren't any!"

Ivy Boakye shrugs. "So I understand."

"So what the hell are you going on about? Like I said, there's no evidence of discrimination."

"But the problem is, there's no evidence that there isn't any, either," I say.

She looks at me. Both Ivy Boakye and Doug look at her. All of us (she, Doug and I anyway. I cannot speak for Ivy Boakye) know this is ludicrous. But the logic is irrefutable.

She is now looking very agitated. There is no doubt in my mind that if this had been almost any other conversation she would have got up and left the room by now. But she cannot afford to leave an allegation as serious as religious discrimination hanging over her. Not with a predominantly Muslim electoral ward like hers (I checked).

Doug is looking thoughtful. "It's like that bloke said about trees in quads," he says. "How do you prove that something isn't there when..?"

His voice fades away. Philosophy is not one of Doug's core competencies.

Councillor Lambert shoots him a look of disdain. "You mean Berkeley," she says.

I am impressed.

She leans across the desk towards Ivy Boakye. "Now listen, this is the most ridiculous thing I've heard in my whole life. Is it your idea of a joke? Because I'm warning you..."

Ivy Boakye bridles at this accusation. "No, Councillor. Diversity is not a joking matter, and I take my role extremely seriously. And where I see a potential problem it's my job to take precautions."

The Councillor's eyes narrow. "What do you mean, precautions?" she asks

"Nothing major. Nobody's being accused of anything, after all. Just a memorandum to all the council committees, warning them to be vigilant against discrimination of any kind, but especially religious."

A stunned silence falls around the table. I know, and Doug knows, and especially Councillor Lambert knows, that such a memorandum would be read as exactly what Ivy Boakye says it is not. An accusation. And it would not take long for the council grapevine to work out which committee's actions had prompted it.

Councillor Lambert has gone pale. "You can't do that," she says.

Ivy Boakye looks puzzled. I believe this is genuine. (This naivety is why she is so priceless to me.)

"Why not?" she asks. "After all, as I said, it's just a precaution. It's for your own protection, really."

Both Doug and Councillor Lambert appear to have been struck dumb. It is time for Reasonable Ambrose to intervene.

I lean forward. "Listen, I understand your concerns here, Councillor. I wonder if there's not something we can work out here."

Ivy Boakye looks surprised. This was not in the agreed script. I give her a reassuring smile.

"I mean, I don't think we need to rush into things. We could simply have this as something we have on the agenda to get round to in a few months time." Councillor Lambert stares at me, and once again I am struck by the intentness of her gaze.

"And how is that going to help?" she asks.

I shrug. "Well, the problem seems to be that over this particular time period, unfortunately, the way things have fallen out is that you've had several poor applications from religious minorities, which you've felt quite correctly you've had to turn down, but none from the Christian church. But if we give it a bit longer, say just the next meeting or two, it may be that you get a good application from the Muslims or the Sikhs, or perhaps a bad one from the C of E. And then the problem would simply go away."

I smile at her but her reaction to my words is unreadable.

"I hope you're not suggesting that we start making bad judgements just for the look of the thing," she says.

I raise my hands. "Absolutely not! Not in a million years. I'm just suggesting that if it did work out that way, it would be to everyone's advantage."

Doug is giving me a strange look. I am guessing that by now he has cottoned on to my plan.

I am not too worried at this. I do not believe he cares enough about it to make trouble for me. That would make him look bad as well. But if it did seem to be going that way, I would have to take pre-emptive action.

Perhaps I could set Ivy Boakye on him.

Councillor Lambert is frowning again. "Still seems pretty pointless to me," she says. "I have no idea what's coming up on the agenda in the next few months, but it would be a hell of a coincidence if there

288

was anything suitable."

I shrug. "Nor me. But it's surely worth a shot. And if it still looks like we have a problem in a few months time we can discuss it then." I look around at the three of them. "What do we think?"

Ivy Boakye looks disappointed. There will be one less memorandum circulating with her name on it than she had hoped.

Doug is still staring at me, wearing a calculating expression that I have not seen on him before.

I give him a faint smile and wait. After a few moments he nods.

"I agree," he says. "Let's give it a shot." He turns to Councillor Lambert. "I'm sure everything will work itself out."

For a moment she does not speak, but merely flicks that penetrating scrutiny from Doug to me and back again, several times.

Then she gets to her feet.

"Whatever," she says. "I'm already late. Make sure you talk to me before doing anything else stupid."

And she sweeps out of the room, in much the same manner as she entered.

*

For a few seconds no one speaks.

I am in a state of euphoria. It is all I can do not to punch the air. I am, at long, long last, safe. Councillor Lambert is not going to risk her political future by nodding through planning applications from the Church of England any time soon. I have secured the Rectory and its garden for my darling Helen.

This time I really have won.

289

Eventually the silence is broken by Ivy Boakye.

"Well," she says. "I think that went pretty well, don't you?"

I look at Doug. He is staring at me again.

"I don't know," he says. "How would you say it went, Ambrose?"

I meet his gaze with a smile. "I think I'd say, it went as well as could be expected."

Ivy Boakye gives a satisfied nod and leaves the room. I make to follow but then I feel Doug's hand on my shoulder. I turn to find his face inches from mine. His breath smells of black coffee.

"I'd say it's you that owes me one, now," he says. "Wouldn't you?"

30

It is Saturday evening. Time to pay the price. The price of saving my beloved Helen's Rectory.

I have arranged with Jane Gardner that she will arrive at seven. Everything is prepared, everything is ready.

I am ready.

At five past, the doorbell rings.

I open the door. "Hello, Miss Gardner," I say.

I hand her a glass of chilled white wine. It is much better than they serve at the Halfway House, but I do not know whether she will notice this.

She smiles from beneath lowered lids. "Hello, Mr Hillier."

She is wearing the same green dress as when we had dinner together. But tonight she is wearing less make-up and has done something different to her hair.

"You look nice," I say.

"Thank you," she says. Her eyes flick down. "You're looking none too shabby yourself."

She takes a sip of wine but says nothing. She has

not noticed.

She looks at me. I look at her. Her eyelids drop again and she moves closer and I realise that I am now to kiss her.

I take the wine from her and place it on the hall table then I put my arms around her, pulling her towards me. Our lips meet and part. She tastes of mint breath freshener, with just a hint of Chablis.

I allow my hand to drop to squeeze her buttock, then release myself from the kiss.

"Good to see you," I say.

She moves away, her hands jerkily smoothing her dress down, though it has not been creased by our embrace. "You too," she says.

She looks around her at the hallway. "So this is it – the famous Rectory."

I follow her gaze. "Indeed it is. A veritable paradise of Victoriana." A furrow creases her brow. She probably does not know what Victoriana is.

"But it's not really the house itself that's important. It's the garden," I continue. "Come on – grab your drink and I'll show you."

I lead her through the kitchen to the back door, and from there outside.

And there it is. Helen's pride and joy.

The garden always looks its best at this time of day. The evening sun is filtering through the trees, and a golden green glow suffuses everything. With its high, old brick walls and its secret glades among the chestnut trees and the rhododendrons, it looks truly magical. A priceless half-acre oasis of tranquillity, a unique refuge from the urban desolation beyond.

I do not know if Jane Gardner will be able to appreciate this. But I somehow feel the need to make her understand what all this has been for.

"Over here," I say. I lead her past the garage to the side of the house. "Look at this."

She stares at the huge lawn, nestling between the carefully nurtured flower beds, the occasional glimpse of brickwork visible between the surrounding shrubs. And she nods.

"I can see why you think it's special. It's enormous."

I stare at her, wondering if she does indeed understand. But all she sees is a big square of grass.

I am wasting my time.

"That's what all the girls say," I say.

She glances at me with a quick grin. "I guess I'll be checking that out later, Mr Hillier." Then her brow furrows.

"Listen, about the other day. I was probably out of order. It had all been a bit of a shock, and I was tired and stressed about it all. And..."

"And?"

This is her chance. Her chance to say, 'actually, you were right. We shouldn't do this thing.' Her chance to suggest that all we do is have a friendly drink, maybe some food, and then I drive her home. Her chance to save us both from the course that she has herself mapped out for us tonight.

"And I wanted to say sorry. But..." She moves towards me, her lips tilting into a smile. "I really do like you, you know. I couldn't let you get away that easily. Even if..." She shrugs. "Even if it's just this once, it's

293

worth a try. You do understand, don't you?"

I look down at her. For a moment I am depressed by her stupidity, her blindness.

But she has made her choice. And now I must make the best of the situation.

I smile.

"Of course I understand."

*

I put my arm around her waist and lead her back indoors.

"But since you're so stressed," I say as we walk. "How about this for a plan? I run us a long, relaxing bath, and then I give you an even longer, more relaxing massage?"

She puts her own arm around me and giggles. "Sounds good to me," she says.

We go upstairs. As we walk, hand in hand, everything, every plate on a table, every picture on the wall, every book on a shelf, reminds me of Helen. To my fevered mind the creaks of the stairs are the house protesting, why are you doing this, why?

But the answer is simple. I am doing it for her.

Once in the bedroom I go to run the bath while Jane Gardner begins to disrobe.

She calls out to me over the sound of the running water.

"I've got something for you. Don't let me forget to show it to you later."

"I bet you have," I call back.

She giggles again. She is in a giggly mood tonight. "Not that, silly," she says. "And don't bother to look for it. I've hidden it."

I return to the bedroom. She has removed the green dress and is now standing in just her bra and panties. They are a matched set, dark brown.

The bra is too small, her pale breasts are nearly spilling over. She suddenly looks very young, very vulnerable.

"You okay?" I ask.

She nods.

I am not okay. This is our bedroom, mine and Helen's. There should not be another woman undressing here. It is wrong.

For a moment the wrongness nearly overcomes me and I have to remind myself, forcibly, why this is happening. Also, that Helen will never know. That thought fortifies me.

I move to her and reach behind her back, unclasping her bra. It slips to the floor. I kneel down and pull her panties down. I step back and she kicks them away.

I inspect my conquest with curiosity. Her skin is almost white, smooth and unwrinkled. Her breasts are firm for their size, with large nipples, brown against the surrounding pallor. They point slightly outwards. Her stomach however is not firm, drooping downwards towards dark pubic hair that looks recently trimmed.

As my eyes survey her body I realise that Jane Gardner's face is her best feature.

"You're beautiful," I say.

She smiles.

I take her hand and lead her into the bathroom. The old, freestanding roll top bath is nearly full. I turn off the taps and gesture for her to get in.

I return to the bedroom and remove my own clothes. The sound of splashing tells me that Jane Gardner is now in the bath.

When I return she is lying with the water up to her chin. Her knees are bent and just visible above the water line, which pleases me.

She raises a hand and beckons me forwards with a crooked finger.

"Come on, room for a small one," she says. Then she drops her glance with a grin. "Or a large one."

I return the grin, then perch on the edge of the bath. "In a moment."

I gaze at her for a few moments, contemplating what I am about to do. I feel my pulse quicken as I think about her wet, white flesh writhing beneath me, imagining the sounds that will issue from that small, red mouth.

"I genuinely tried to avoid this, you know."

I expect some suitably sentimental, or perhaps coy, reply. Instead she leans forward and does her ridiculous nose-poking thing.

I stare at her, appalled. This woman simply does not know how to behave in, what is to her, supposed to be a romantic tryst.

"But I have to say, after that I feel less bad about it," I say.

She looks momentarily puzzled at my words. But the moment does not last long, as I have risen to my feet and grasped her firmly behind the knees, hauling them upwards and dragging her head beneath the water.

The beginnings of a shriek are cut off by the water entering her mouth. She flails, and tried to get a grip on the side of the bath with her hands, but I have the situation well under control. I lift her legs even higher so that her arms can get no purchase on the slippery enamel.

And I wait.

It takes longer than I thought, and is messier. Jane Gardner is not a small girl and her roiling body creates great waves that slosh over the sides of the bath. But eventually the struggling ceases, and what remains of the bath water lies placid around her still limbs.

It is over.

31

I sit on the edge of the bath and look down. Jane Gardner's face bobs just under the surface of the water, her hair swirling gently alongside.

It was interesting, this drowning thing. It was not as much fun as I had anticipated. Perhaps if I had toyed with her more, allowed her up for gulps of air a few times like I understand the Americans do with the terrorists at Guantanamo Bay. But that would have been cruel, and I am not a cruel person.

I feel no elation, no euphoria at this killing. It was just a job, something that had to be done. I would not say I regret it, but I would rather have not had to do it. It means I have broken the Rules, for starters.

But done it has been, and now I must deal with the consequences. I lean forward and remove the plug from the bath. Then I look around the room. There is a great deal of spillage, but no real harm has been done.

While the water drains away I go to fetch a mop

and a roll of black bin liners. I mop the floor as best as I can, then heave her still warm body out of the bath.

My plan is that Jane Gardner should appear to have drowned herself in the Thames. For this it does not matter that either her or her clothes are wet, but clearly she does have to be fully clothed.

I set about replacing the garments on the sprawling mass of flesh that used to be Jane Gardner. It is more difficult than I had imagined. She is not light, and her limbs have an irritating habit of falling back where I do not want them the moment I have positioned them. Also, her tight clothing does not slide easily over the still damp skin. But eventually it is done.

Next I wrap the whole body, mummy-style, with the roll of bin liners. Then I dry and dress myself.

I run downstairs and reverse the Skoda up to the back door. I open the boot and look around. As I had hoped, both I and the car are completely shielded from prying eyes by the overhanging trees. (This is yet another good reason to preserve the Rectory garden.)

I return to the bathroom and lug my package downstairs and dump it into the boot of the Skoda. I lock up the car and go back into the kitchen. I am panting from my exertions. The open bottle of Chablis sits on the table invitingly, and for a moment I am tempted.

But there is still much for me to do.

*

I return to the bedroom to check for any remaining traces of Jane Gardner. She and her clothes are now in the car, but her handbag is on the floor by the bed. I look under the bed to make sure nothing has fallen there, then in the bathroom.

All clear. I can now move to the next phase of my plan.

I take the handbag downstairs and remove her mobile.

I am not entirely clear how much information can be gleaned about the location of a mobile phone at any given time. Certainly if you believe everything you see on television (say on Spooks) it can be pinned down to within a few feet when it is being used. That may of course be science fiction, but it is not something I can leave to chance. If (as I do) I wish her phone to play a part in my plan, it will have to take place elsewhere. At least it is not a Smartphone.

So I lock up the house and get my bike out of the garage. It seems very strange to be leaving the house with a dead body in the boot of the car. But as with so many things in my life at the moment, I do not really have any alternative.

I have no particular destination in mind, just to get as far away as possible in the general direction of Jane Gardner's home as I can in fifteen minutes.

I find a quiet alley behind a row of shops. I take the phone out of my pocket and proceed to send a text message to 'Martin'.

'have got to see u, coming round now.'

I mute the phone, wipe it free of prints and hide it under a wheelie bin.

Then I return to the Rectory.

*

I go to my study and make myself comfortable in

300

an armchair. But then I change my mind. Surely one glass of Chablis cannot do any harm. And it will help steady my nerves. Though to any external observer (of which, thankfully, there are none) I will be looking calm and methodical, inside I am jangling like a peal of bells at one of Helen's weddings.

I fetch myself a glass of the wine, then settle in the armchair again and pick up the telephone.

It is time to catch up with a few friends and relations.

*

Two hours later and I have had a long conversation with my mother, shorter ones with my sister and Naomi, and left a message for James. I have also tried Helen's mobile but there is no reply. I do not anticipate having to provide an alibi for the time that Jane Gardner is supposedly spending with 'Martin', but if it is ever needed, it is now in place.

None of this has been easy. I am in the middle of perhaps the most complex and risky operation that I have ever undertaken, and I am too wired to have much interest in my nephew's ear infection or my parents' plans for Christmas. I have also managed to eat a portion of leftover lasagne, though this too was an effort. But all these things had to be done, so done they were.

Now it is time for the next phase. Once again I lock up the house and set off on my bike, aiming for the same back alley and the wheelie bin.

Jane Gardner's phone is still in its place, I am pleased to find. I put it in my pocket and head off on the bike again, this time in a direction that is away

301

from both her home and mine. I do not want any clever policemen drawing lines on maps and coming to any awkward conclusions about her last movements.

I find another quiet alley and take out the phone. Then I send what is to be her final text, again to Martin.

'cant believe u said those things. i loved u bastard, u lied to me all along. ull be sorry.'

I turn off Jane Gardner's phone and head home. Everything is now in place.

*

By now I am exhausted, both physically and mentally. But my night is far from over.

My own cheap little pay-as-you-go is now no longer required. I take the back off and remove the SIM card. I find a pair of kitchen scissors and cut the card into four pieces. I put the pieces and the handset in my trouser pocket. Then I replace Jane Gardner's phone in her hand bag.

All this time I have this nagging feeling that I have forgotten something. But though I rack my brains I cannot think what it is. I return to the bedroom and the bathroom and check for any last traces of Jane Gardner, but I find none. Nor are there any in the hall or the kitchen. It must be my nerves playing tricks with me.

I go back to the living and turn on the television. For the next little while all I have to do is wait.

*

I must have dozed off, as I wake with a start to hear the phone ringing. I mute the TV and pick up.

It is Helen.

"Ambrose? I didn't wake you did I?"

"No — I was just watching a late film." I glance at my watch. It is a quarter to midnight.

"Only I saw that you'd tried to call. I wanted to talk to you too."

My heart swells with love for my wife, who somehow is aware how much I need her right now. "That's nice. How's the conference?"

"Oh, you know. Like all these things. Basically just a talking shop. It's good to catch up with some old friends. What have you been up to?"

"Not a lot. I went for a bike ride this afternoon, just around town."

"Still. It sounds a lot more fun than where I am."

"I'm sure it is."

There is silence for a few seconds.

"I miss you," she says.

"I miss you, too. More than I can say."

"But I'll be back tomorrow."

"Yes. What time?"

"Early evening, I'd guess. Sevenish?"

"I'll look forward to it."

Another silence. "Well, I'd better get to bed," says Helen. "Sleep well."

"And you," I say.

I hear the dialling tone as she hangs up. I continue to hold the telephone, looking at it, thinking of her, until the tears well up in my eyes.

Sleep well, my darling Helen.

*

I take care not to fall asleep again.

At one thirty I turn off the television and haul

myself to my feet. It is time for the final phase.

I open the boot of the Skoda to throw Jane Gardner's handbag in with her. For a few seconds I gaze down at the shiny black bundle. Though I know it is stupid I half expect it to move. But of course it does not.

I shake myself. I am tired and I am stressed and have had too many hours unable to do anything other than think. It is no surprise that my imagination is in overdrive.

I shut the boot as quietly as possible and get in the driver's seat. I ease the Skoda out of the drive, noting with satisfaction that there are no other vehicles or any passing pedestrians to witness my departure. Then I set off for Battersea.

*

The roads are quiet at this time of night. Nevertheless I stick to the speed limit, and make sure I do not go through any red lights. I do not need any bored police officers taking an interest in the contents of my car.

Eventually I reach my destination, an old wharf by the Thames in Battersea. I discovered it on one of my cycle trips some months ago. Most of the wharves and warehouses on this stretch of the river have been replaced by fancy blocks of flats for people like James. This one is itself scheduled for demolition and lies empty, poorly secured and abandoned. It is not perfect. But it will do.

The old wharf is as I hoped, ill-lit and deserted. I am able to manoeuvre the Skoda into the shadows of a building about thirty yards from the riverbank.

304

I turn off the engine and spend a few moments standing and listening. At this time of night even London's constant dull roar of traffic has declined to a murmur. I hear sirens in the distance, but nothing else, nothing close to hand. On the opposite bank, I observe smart flats beyond the busy road. But the Thames is wide at this point, and their occupants will see little (and, I guess, care less) of what takes place a few hundred yards away across the muddy river.

I am on my own. I and Jane Gardner, that is.

I open the boot and pull the body into a sitting position on the sill so that I can remove the shroud of bin liners. I place the handbag over the body's shoulder, making sure it is securely in place. Then I heft it on to my shoulder and head for the river.

Thirty yards is not a long way, but when you are carrying a fat, dead body that you should not be, in the open, it feels a lot further. However, after what seems a long time, but is almost certainly less than a minute, I am standing in the same place as earlier, looking down onto the dark, gently rolling surface of the Thames.

I take one final glance around. The bank behind me and to my side. Nothing. The river in front, likewise. I check the boats moored across from me but they are motionless and in darkness.

I lower Jane Gardner's mortal remains to the ground and gently roll her into the water. The splash is louder than I would have liked, and, still crouching, I look around me again. But I remain alone.

I straighten. There is no light on the river here but I can just make out Jane Gardner drifting away from the bank, starting her last solitary journey. I raise my hand and wave a small farewell.

Though I shall not miss her.

I reach into my pocket and pull out the pieces of my SIM card and the pay-as-you-go phone. I throw the phone as far out into the river as I can, then, one by one, drop the remains of the SIM into the water. I cannot see if they sink or float but it does not matter. They will soon be far apart from each other, and this record of my contacts with Jane Gardner will itself be history.

It is done.

32

The next morning I am shattered.

Though I miss Helen when she is away, today I am grateful to be able to get up late, and slob around drinking coffee and reading the newspaper undisturbed.

Not that I am able to concentrate on the newspaper very much. I have the local radio station on, and every half hour I listen, nerves in tatters, to the news. But there is nothing about Jane Gardner, not yet.

The longer the better, I tell myself. The further she has drifted before being discovered the less chance there is that the authorities will be able to establish where she was dropped in. Or, as I hope they will imagine, jumped. With luck her handbag will have remained with her, so that she will be identified immediately. I am counting on those clever police scientists being able to resuscitate the drowned mobile they will find within the bag. They will then understand (they believe) from the texts why she jumped, even if they have no real clue as to how she spent her last evening.

That is the plan, anyway. There is now, again, nothing more for me to do but wait, and see if things work out.

I wish I were less tired, though. Wired as I was after my frenetic night's activities, I did not finally drift off to sleep until gone five o'clock. And when I am tired I am apt to be fractious and nervy. Perhaps this afternoon I should go for a cycle ride, then have a nap before Helen returns. Though annoyingly it has now started to rain.

I am sitting at the kitchen table, thinking along these lines. Suddenly the doorbell rings, making me jump half out of skin.

I glance at the clock, surprised and irritated. It is ten thirty.

I get up to answer the door, wondering who it can be. No one for Helen, surely. Even if they were not aware she was away this weekend, they would expect her to be at the church at this time, half way through the ten o'clock service. So it is either someone for me, or a stranger.

It is a stranger.

A man, about my age. Suntanned, hair cropped short. Hard little eyes. Dressed in jeans, open-necked white shirt and navy jacket, and jangling a set of car keys in one hand.

Not a tramp.

"Mr Hillier?" he asks. The voice is familiar, though I cannot place it. But I do not like the tone. It is polite, but there is an unpleasant edge to it, as if the stranger

308

would like to be aggressive but is restraining himself.

"Yes," I say.

"My name is Donald Dennis," he says. "I believe we've spoken on the phone?"

*

I stare at the man who has caused me so much trouble. So this is Mr Donald Dennis. And it is this of all mornings that he chooses to pay me a visit.

He gives a humourless twitch of the lips. "Though if I remember rightly you were calling yourself something else at the time," he continues. "I'd like to talk to you. Can I come in?"

"What do we have to talk about?" I ask.

He looks surprised. "There are a few matters of mutual interest, I think you'll find." The little eyes narrow. "I really think you'd better invite me inside."

I am tired and stressed at having spent the night drowning Jane Gardner and dumping her in the river and trying to conceal the fact, and I have no desire to spend time talking to the criminal vandal who wants to demolish Helen's Rectory. But I see from his face that Mr Donald Dennis is not minded to take no for an answer. He will only cause more trouble if that is what he gets.

I stand aside.

"That's better," he says. He enters the hallway and waits for me to shut the door.

I gesture towards the living room door. "Through here," I say.

He sits on the armchair uninvited, which is rude. I take the sofa, and wait.

"I had a chat with a mate of mine yesterday," he

309

says. "And oddly enough, your name came up."

"Let me guess," I say. "Alan Grant?"

He snorts. "Grant? He's no friend of mine. More like the hired help, I'd call him. And not very good at that, either. Flaky."

This is something that Mr Donald Dennis and I can agree on.

"No," he continues. "This was someone else. Charlotte Lambert."

He sits back. I see that he is watching for my reaction.

It takes me a moment to realise who he is talking about. I have never thought of Councillor Lambert by her first name, and if asked would have struggled to remember it. But now it is mentioned I recall that the first time I heard it I thought it bizarrely inappropriate. What image, after all, does the name Charlotte conjure up? Someone ladylike, genteel? A bit classy, perhaps? Not the phrases that normally spring to people's lips when talking of Councillor Lambert.

Who I now discover is a 'mate' of the thug sitting opposite me.

This is very interesting.

I maintain a neutral expression. "I didn't know you two were friends."

He shrugs. "Well, maybe not exactly friends as such. More that we help each other out from time to time."

"Okay, I didn't know that Councillor Lambert was corrupt," I say.

He smiles, properly this time, showing a lot of teeth with some gold at the back. "I suspect there are

310

a lot of things you don't know," he says.

This is probably true.

"Anyway," he continues. "Even though you tried to put the frighteners on to Grant, I was never that worried, as I thought I could rely on Charlotte. So you can imagine, when she tells me that you've nobbled her as well, I wasn't best pleased."

I think of telling him that I am still not interested in whether he is pleased or not, but decided not to provoke him further. I am getting the distinct impression that Mr Donald Dennis has the potential to be a quite dangerous person to have in the house.

"I'm sorry about that," I say. "But you must see my position. My wife and I are very fond of this Rectory. It's our home. Of course we're going to do everything we can to protect it."

He spreads his hands. "Absolutely. And credit where it's due. You've been very resourceful. In other circumstances you're the sort of chap I'd like to have working for me. But enough is enough. You've had your fun. Now it's time to stop."

I shake my head. "I don't understand. You're obviously a seriously successful developer. You must have loads of things on the go. Why can't you just accept that this is one that got away/"

He waggles a finger at me. "Because that's not the way it works."

He stares at me to emphasise his point. I stare back. Exhausted as I am, I will not be intimidated by Mr Donald Dennis in my own home.

I shrug. "I think it just has."

He frowns and gets to his feet. I watch as he

311

prowls around the room, examining things. He stops in front of the picture of Helen on the beach at Corfu, then picks it up.

"This your wife?" he asks.

I nod. "It is."

"She's a lovely looking girl. You'd never guess that she's a priest." He darts a glance at me. "I'm old-fashioned, me. Never really got used to the idea of women priests."

I say nothing. I am waiting for him to put the photo down and get back to the point.

"Yes, lovely girl," he repeats. "It would be an awful shame if anything – happened to her."

As he says the word 'happened' he turns his gaze back to me. And with a terrible, vulpine smile, he lets the photograph slide through his fingers onto the polished wood floor.

*

There is a crash, and the tinkle of broken glass, and then silence. Our eyes hold each other's gaze. Neither of us speak.

It is as in the moment that the telescope comes into focus, and all the blur and fuzziness disappear, leaving one sharp, unmistakeable image. A man, standing in front of me in my own living room, threatening Helen.

My Helen. The most precious being in the world, the person I have devoted my life to protecting. And this filth is prepared to hurt her, possibly kill her, simply so that he can make a few pounds out of building a miserable block of flats.

I have been sitting here, preoccupied with

312

thoughts of Jane Gardner, and worrying about whether I have forgotten anything important. I am also still trying to work through the implications of finding out that Councillor Lambert is corrupt. Above all I am wishing that Mr Donald Dennis would go away and leave me in peace.

But now this.

For a moment I am too shocked to be angry. Then the rage comes, singing, surging, sweeping through me. My whole being is consumed with the desire, no, the need, to tear and rip Mr Donald Dennis limb from limb, gouge out those horrible eyes, scrape every inch of that unnatural skin away from his skull with the shards of glass that he has so carelessly scattered over the floor.

Yet something holds me back, warns me from this natural instinct. That is not the answer. Now is not the time.

I do not know how I restrain myself. But I do.

The man who intends to hurt Helen continues to stare at me. The corners of his mouth flicker upwards for a moment. He has seen my reaction. But he mistakes it for fear.

"You do understand what I'm saying, don't you?"

"You're saying that unless I drop my opposition and allow you to knock down our home, you'll make sure that something unpleasant happens to my wife."

He gives a sharp nod, another ghost of a smile. "Good boy. Quick on the uptake. I like that. So..?"

As I look into Mr Donald Dennis's hard, grey eyes, I realise that he means what he says.

Alan Grant was right. Once again I have been

guilty of underestimating one of my foes.

Suddenly I am overcome with weariness. It is all too much for me, I feel as if I have the whole world ranged against me. Like those that offended the classical gods I am thwarted at every turn.

But I cannot allow this man to harm Helen. Not in any way or in any form. It is unthinkable, unimaginable. He must be stopped.

"Okay. I'll do what you want. But on one condition."

The eyes narrow. "What condition?"

"I want you to come out with me into the garden, now, and take a good long look at what you want to destroy. Then if you still want to go ahead, so be it."

He glances at the window, then down at his feet, at his highly polished brown loafers. Then back at me.

"It's pissing down."

"I'll lend you an umbrella."

I wait for his reply.

I am confident that he will agree to my request. He has gone to a lot of trouble to get to this point, and I do not believe that he will want further confrontation over something so trivial. Not when victory is so close.

Eventually he rolls his eyes. "All right. But this better not take long."

I get to my feet. "Don't worry," I say. "It won't."

*

I lead him out of the back door, as only a few hours previously I had led Jane Gardner. Then I had been wired, on edge, but at least I had been in control. Now I am simply exhausted, resigned to what must be done.

I have given him my large umbrella, and am using Helen's small folding one myself. He glances around.

"Is this it?"

"Over here."

He follows me round to the side of the house. I stop at the edge of the lawn.

"There," I say.

His eyes dismiss the vista in one sweep. "It's a lawn."

In the grey rain the lawn is not as impressive as in yesterday's warm evening glow. But even so I am disappointed (though not surprised) at his reaction.

"Okay," I say. "Just one more thing."

With an audible sigh he follows as I lead him back behind the house. I stop in front of the rhododendron shrubbery and stand aside.

"In there," I say. "Go on."

He gives me a puzzled look but does as he is asked.

As soon as his back is turned I stoop and pick up one of the stones lining the side of the gravel path. It is hard and cold in my grasp, and reassuringly heavy.

Mr Donald Dennis has to lower the umbrella to get under the trees. At that moment I raise my arm and bring the stone down as hard as I can on the back of his head.

He drops without a sound. I bend down and check his pulse. He is still alive, so I drag him into the middle of the cluster of rhododendrons. Once there I pound and I pound at his head, until the bone is shattered and his blood is everywhere, and there can be no doubt.

315

Mr Donald Dennis will now not be able to hurt Helen.

33

Another day, another body to dispose of.

But today I have no time to do anything fancy or clever. I must just cover my tracks quickly, and sort things out properly at a later date.

I go to the garage and fetch a shovel.

Digging a grave is harder than I had imagined. Even though the soil is softened by the rain, here in the middle of the shrubbery it is full of roots. If I was going to do it properly, the traditional six feet under, I would need all day. As it is, even the couple of feet I need for a temporary resting place for Mr Donald Dennis seems to take forever.

Though my anger gives me energy. Anger that I have been put in this position, I who take so much pride in my planning and perfect, untraceable execution of such matters. Forced to improvise, to take risks, to leave evidence quite literally in my own back yard. It is intolerable.

But I have no choice.

And all the while it continues to rain.

*

Eventually it is done. Using a handkerchief I remove the car keys from Mr Donald Dennis's now sodden jacket, as I will need them later. I also take his mobile phone, which I switch off.

I roll him into his new home. I scrape the surface soil from around his head where the blood has seeped in and toss that in after him. Then I refill the hole.

An adult male displaces quite a lot of soil, and there is still a large pile left over when I have finished. I spread it around the shrubbery, patting it down with the shovel. Finally, I spread dead leaves around the area, trying to make it as natural looking as possible.

I stand back and survey my handiwork. It is by no means perfect. Anyone looking closely would realise immediately that the ground had recently been disturbed, and in a major way. But unless they are deliberately searching, there is little reason why anyone should enter the middle of a clump of rhododendrons and start worrying about what is beneath their feet. That is my hope, anyway.

I return to the house. I have done what I can. My one remaining task is to dispose of Mr Donald Dennis's car, which is presumably parked nearby.

But I am filthy, and my back is aching from the digging. Before I can do anything else, I need a shower.

*

I stand in the shower, head bowed. It is set at its most powerful, and I will the hard jets to drive the exhaustion and tension from my muscles.

318

I cannot believe what is happening to me this weekend. Two killings within the space of twenty four hours, two totally different sets of tracks to cover. At least with Jane Gardner I had some time to prepare, some time to come up with a halfway decent plan. But this is awful. I thought I had done with all this panic and improvisation.

It is such a ridiculous situation to have got myself into. Killing people is supposed to be fun. Yet right now it just feels like a chore.

I remain in the shower so long that it starts to run cooler. Soon all the hot water will be gone. It is time to get out and get on.

My makeshift relaxation therapy works to an extent. At least I now feel clean, and able to face the world with some confidence. But inside I am far from calm. I am fighting a rearguard action, retaining control by a hairsbreadth. Just one more unlucky break and everything could suddenly spiral out of control, and the whole painstaking edifice of my campaign come crashing down quicker than a house of cards in a tornado.

I keep wondering, how, why, what did I do wrong? But there is no time now for self-recrimination. That can come later. That can wait until my task is complete.

But I do thank her God that Helen is away.

*

While in the shower I have formulated a plan for disposing of Mr Donald Dennis's car. Nothing very sophisticated, there is no time for that. It will just have to do.

I put on a dark blue, waterproof jacket, and a black baseball cap. I stuff a pale blue jacket and a white baseball cap and a grey backpack into my old brown backpack. Then I put on some gloves, and go to the front door.

I open it and nearly jump out of my skin.

There is a woman standing there, finger poised over the bell.

Joyce Burnside.

"What the hell are you doing, lurking there?" I say.

She bridles at this. I suppose my greeting is perhaps more aggressive than usual.

"I am not lurking. I came to see if you'd managed to find those plans for the church hall."

With all my other problems I had completely forgotten about this. I really do not need to be bothered by this sort of trivia today.

But I do need Joyce Burnside to go away.

"Sorry, it completely slipped my mind. I'll make sure I do it before this evening though."

She looks cross. "If you would. The man's coming round in the morning, so I'll come back for them then."

Then she seems to register my appearance for the first time. "Where are you off to in this weather?" she asks, peering at my backpack.

I do not have time to engage in small talk with this woman. Even if I did have the time I would much rather use it to despatch her to join Mr Donald Dennis in the shrubbery.

"Out," I say.

Her lips purse but she turns on her heel and sets

off back down the path.

I watch her go and give her a few more seconds. Then I lock up the house and set off down the path after her.

I am lucky in one respect. The rain is so hard now that there are few people on the pavements. Those that are there walk fast, heads down. No one takes any notice of the man who walks a little slower, keeping his hand in his pocket and pressing a remote control repeatedly until he sees a flash of lights on a BMW parked a few yards ahead.

I glance around to make sure that Joyce Burnside is now out of sight. Then I pull the brim of the baseball cap well down, get into the car and start driving.

*

My destination is Heathrow airport, but I am in no hurry. At first I take repeated diversions through residential areas, those that have little in the way of traffic cameras. But gradually I make my way west, and eventually I am on the M4.

I take the BMW to the long-term stay car park of Terminal 5. I leave it, with Mr Donald Dennis's mobile now safely replaced in the glove compartment, in an undistinguished corner, then make my way to the bus stop. After a short journey in the company of several sets of harassed parents and their overexcited children, all presumably off on their holidays, I am in the terminal itself.

Once there I keep my head down and make my way as quickly as possible to the underground station.

I know that I am being caught on CCTV, and there has to be a chance that when the BMW is discovered the authorities will be able to identify what time it was left and track the person who arrived in it, possibly all the way to the underground itself. This is not a problem as I shall be able to lose any trace later. But it does mean that for now I must at all costs keep my face shielded from the cameras.

I have a moment's panic as I nearly crash into an armed policeman who looms suddenly out from behind a pillar. He frowns at me as I mutter an apology and move on. Perhaps he will remember my face, but I doubt it. It is likely to be at least a day or two until he could even be asked to, and there are many, many faces at Heathrow Terminal 5.

I take the Piccadilly line as far as South Kensington and head on foot up Exhibition Road towards Hyde Park. My luck remains in, it is still raining. The park, which if this were a sunny Sunday afternoon would be rammed, is virtually deserted.

When I reach the middle of the park I veer off the path and head towards one of the areas where the trees are allowed to grow more densely. In effect they are small patches of woodland. I find a large tree near the centre and look around me carefully. Naturally there are no CCTV cameras here, that is why I have chosen this spot. But nor are there any prying eyes. None that I can see, anyway.

It is safe to make my final change of identity. I remove the dark jacket and hat and replace them with the lighter coloured models from my backpack. Then I put the old, wet clothing, together with the brown backpack, inside the grey backpack.

The result, a man in dark clothing with a brown

backpack walks into Hyde Park from the south. Half an hour later a man in light clothing with a grey backpack emerges at Marble Arch and gets onto the Central Line.

And half an hour after that, his work at last complete, a physically and emotionally drained Ambrose Hillier finally makes it home to the Rectory at St Nicholas, High End.

34

Despite my exhaustion I have a poor night's sleep. Unable to settle, my mind still whirls with images and crowds with unanswered questions. I cannot shake the notion that there is something that I have forgotten, but try as I might I cannot pin it down. Perhaps it is just my imagination. But it is troubling.

Helen expresses concern, and I have to make up a story about going down with a chill. Though I shall not be surprised if this turns out actually to be the case, given the amount of time I have spent in the rain recently.

The evening news carried a report of a young woman found in the Thames. The police were not revealing her name until the family had been told, the report said. This implied that, as I intended, Jane Gardner's bag was indeed found with her. It also said that it was too early to tell whether the death was suspicious. I suppose this is fair enough in the circumstances. But it does not exactly help a chap get a good night's rest.

Now it is Monday morning, and I have to face an entire new week's worth of problems and challenges. And I am even more shattered than I was yesterday.

At our weekly management meeting Doug's manner is sombre. It is immediately apparent to me that he has been told.

"I have some bad news," he says as soon as everyone is seated. "You may have heard on the news that the body of a young woman was found in the river yesterday. I regret to say that she was one of ours, Jane Gardner, who'd worked in the Planning Department for the last three and a half years. Andy Vine got a call from her family this morning."

A shocked silence greets these words. Death is ever present around us, yet for some reason it rarely seems to visit our workplace.

After a few moments someone finds their voice.

"Do we know what happened?"

Doug shakes his head. "Doesn't sound like it."

And that is that.

*

The meeting returns to its normal agenda of trivia, today rendered even more banal by what has preceded it. But it gives me time to think.

In fact I have spent much of the last few days thinking about this one matter, which is how I should play my involvement with Jane Gardner. The unfortunate fact is, that though there is nothing to indicate the full extent of our relationship (if something so dull and meaningless is deserving of the term), there does exist that brief, albeit non-incriminating email correspondence.

It is this that presents me with my dilemma. If the police come to a simple conclusion of accident or suicide, it is unlikely that this will ever surface. If however there is a full investigation for any reason, there is a good chance they will check her email to find out who was close to her and if there was anything untoward going on in her life. My name would crop up and questions would be asked as to why I did not come forward earlier. Once again I would be centre stage in a police enquiry, a position that I have been in before and which I did not enjoy.

I have therefore concluded that it is in my best interests to own up to having known Jane Gardner now. It is a tedious prospect, but short term pain for long term gain, that sort of thing. Or perhaps it is an insurance policy. I do not know. I am too tired to care.

After the meeting I join Doug as he is leaving the room.

"Bad business about that girl."

He nods, pulling a face. "She was only twenty three, you know."

I am surprised to realise that I did not know this. But then I was never very interested in the details of Jane Gardner's personal life.

I draw a deep breath. "Actually, I was only talking to her the other day."

He stops walking and turns to me. "Really? I didn't know you knew her. I had to look her up on the system. What were you talking about?" Then his expression narrows. "It didn't have anything to do with her working in the Planning Department, did it?"

I have noticed that Doug's attitude towards me

has changed on the few occasions that I have seen him since our meeting with Councillor Lambert. He looks at me strangely, and if I speak there is always a pause before he replies.

I frown at the inappropriateness of the suggestion. "Hardly. And I didn't really know her. I just bumped into her in the car park one evening. She asked if I had a few minutes, as she wanted to ask my advice."

"What about?"

"Her career. She thought she was due a promotion, but wasn't getting on with her bosses in Planning. But equally, she didn't want them to know she was looking around elsewhere."

Doug is still watching me with what I presume to be suspicion. "So what did you say to her?"

I shrug. "Same as you would. I just told her to look at the vacancies list on the intranet and keep an eye out for anything she fancied, and then if she wanted she could come and talk to me about it again. Then we met again the following week, she had a few more questions. But I never heard anything more after that."

"That was very noble of you. It's not exactly part of your job spec."

Again I shrug, more self-deprecatingly this time. "Doesn't do any harm to help people out from time to time."

Doug starts walking again. "What was she like?"
"Difficult to say. She was so shy, it was hard work getting out of her what she actually wanted. God knows how she ever summoned up the courage to even speak to me."

"Must be your reputation. A sympathetic shoulder to cry on."

"Maybe. But she seemed a decent enough kid."

We walk in silence for a little.

"So," I say after a while. "They've really no idea what happened yet?"

Doug frowns. "Officially, that's what they're saying." I catch my breath as he continues. "But when Andy spoke to her Dad this morning he said they'd been asking them all loads of questions about her private life, was she depressed, any money problems, boyfriend problems, that sort of thing. So it sounds like they're thinking it might be suicide."

"Suicide!" I repeat. I shake my head. "She didn't seem very suicidal when I spoke to her."

"Yes, well. Apparently they're going be coming round here interviewing people later on, and I've got to put together some background stuff for them. I'll mention that you knew her as well. I doubt they'll want to talk to you, but you'd better be prepared if they do."

Once again I shrug. "Sure. You know me. Always happy to help."

*

The police do indeed arrive that afternoon., interviewing Jane Gardner's colleagues in the Planning Department. The whole office is buzzing with it. But they do not seem interested in me. At least not yet.

But I am still on edge.

I sit at my desk, staring unseeing at my screen, reading emails that if asked afterwards I would have been unable to say even who they had been from. I am

328

utterly unable to concentrate. But today that is okay. Even though few people actually knew Jane Gardner personally, an event like this creates shockwaves throughout the whole building. They will die down within a day or two, but for now there is nothing out of the ordinary in appearing distracted.

I have plenty to be distracted about. I have to be prepared to persuade the police that my relationship with Jane Gardner was both fleeting and trivial. I have to work out a way of removing Mr Donald Dennis from my rhododendrons. And I still have to keep tabs on the planning situation. What Mr Donald Dennis told me yesterday adds a whole new dimension of uncertainty to a situation that I had thought was finally settled. Even with him out of the way I cannot afford to relax. From the little I know of her I suspect that Councillor Lambert may prove very unpredictable.

And I am very, very tired.

*

Around four o'clock my phone rings.

It is Doug.

"Ambrose? Just thought I ought to warn you. You've got a visitor on her way to see you."

His voice sounds odd, distant.   "Visitor?"   I say. "What sort of visitor?"

"You'll see," he says, and hangs up.

I replace the handset and lean back in my chair. I am puzzled, both as to who this mysterious visitor can be, and why Doug is being so coy about it. After our conversation this morning surely he would have said if it was the police. And he said 'her'. It is presumably therefore a woman.

It is very strange.

*

I wait for my visitor, trying to compose myself. If it is the police it will be just a routine conversation, one of many that they are conducting today. All I need to do is to stay calm and stick to my story. There is nothing to be afraid of.

It is not the police however. It is Councillor Lambert. (I do not think I will ever be able to think of her as 'Charlotte').

I am so shocked that for a few moments I forget my manners. Then I leap to my feet and gesture to the chair in front of my desk.

"Councillor Lambert," I say. What a pleasant surprise. Take a seat."

She plants her hands on the back of the chair but does not sit down. "This won't take long," she says. Dark, unreadable eyes pin mine. "Guess where I've been today?"

I am tired and stressed and completely thrown by having Councillor Lambert arrive in my office out of the blue. The combination of these things seems to produce a state of mild hysteria in me, and I find my mind filled with intrusive ideas for possible answers to this (probably rhetorical) question.

'Boots, as you've clearly run out of lip gloss?'

'Harley Street, to enquire about breast augmentation surgery?'

'The Cayman Island consulate, to ask about setting up an offshore bank account?'

Though I do not know if the Cayman Islands actually has a consulate in London.

330

Instead I settle for a look of polite interest as I retake my own seat.

She nods, as if this was the response she was expecting. "That's right, the Planning Department. And guess what? Surprise, surprise. There just happens to be an upcoming application for a redevelopment from the Church of England. For a Rectory."

She pauses, still staring at me, now from above (though not by very much, she is indeed very short).

"And still more amazing," she continues. "I find that it's got your name all over it."

She pauses again, and I understand that this time she does expect a reply.

"It's a terrible application," I say. "Pure vandalism. Destroying a unique green space. It's massively in the interests of the community at large for it to be blocked."

"That's for me and the rest of the committee to decide, wouldn't you say?"

I realise that Councillor Lambert does not know that I know of her involvement with Mr Donald Dennis. Perhaps he did not tell her he was planning on paying me a visit, or perhaps because he has not reported back afterwards (for obvious reasons) she is assuming that he has not done so yet. Or maybe it would never occur to her that he would implicate her in that way.

In any event, it can only be to my advantage to keep her in ignorance on this matter. It could be useful to me one day.

And, loth as I am to admit it, part of me is a little frightened of Councillor Lambert. At the moment I am a nuisance to her. If I were to be promoted to the level of full-blown threat I suspect this small creature in front of me could turn very nasty indeed.

I shrug. "Absolutely."

For a moment she says nothing. Then she leans forward across the desk. "I don't like being jerked around, Hillier. I don't like being played. Especially by a little no one like you." She spits these last words out with what sounds like contempt, which I find quite offensive. "Do you understand me, Hillier?"

I nod. She nods. All the while, those eyes, almost hypnotic in their intensity, never leave mine.

She straightens. "I won't forget this, Hillier. I'll be watching you."

When she has gone I look down at my hands.

To my surprise they are shaking.

*

In the evening Helen is late. I fret as I always do, and try her mobile as I always do. But as usual it is turned off.

I force myself to stay calm. She is probably only at the hospital. There is nothing to worry about.

So why do I always worry?

I put on some music to distract myself from her absence. Vivaldi's La Notte. The Night. It suits my mood.

Helen does not return until after ten thirty. I am now very sleepy but I did not wish to go to bed without seeing the local news. I have at least two items to listen out for.

My patience is rewarded in one regard. Jane Gardner's name has now been officially released, together with details of her life, her family and her job.

But there is nothing as yet regarding the unexplained disappearance of any dodgy property developers.

Helen joins me on the sofa and I put my arm around her.

"Anything interesting?" she asks.

I sigh. "Bad news, actually."

She looks round at me sharply. "What?"

"You know that girl I was talking about the other day? The one in Planning, who was giving me the heads up on the application? She died at the weekend. Drowned in the river."

Helen looks shocked. "But that's awful. Do they know what happened?"

I shake my head. "There's nothing official. But the vibe in the office is that it might have been suicide."

Helen's eyes widen still further. "Oh no! Poor girl."

That will always be Helen's reaction to news of this nature. Even if she knew what Jane Gardner had really done (or wanted to do, I should say) I suspect the reaction would still be 'poor girl'. Though I may be wrong there.

She is continuing. "When you talked to her, you didn't get any sense that she was... you know?"

I shake my head. "Not in the slightest. She seemed completely normal. Though ever since I heard about it, I can't help running over things in my mind, wondering if there was something I could have said, or done."

This is not strictly true, but it is the sort of reaction that Helen would expect, and she would be surprised if I did not display it.

In such ways lie begets lie, begets lie.

She leans across and snuggles her head against my shoulder. "You mustn't torture yourself," she says. "I'm sure you did everything you could."

I glance down at her with fondness, and raise my hand to stroke her hair.

"That is true," I say. "I did everything I could."

35

The police do visit me the next day. Around eleven, unannounced. I look up from my desk, and there they are. Two of them.

"Can I help you?" I say.

The elder, a man with a square, pockmarked face, stares down at me.

"Detective Inspector Jarvis," he says. He waves a grubby plastic rectangle at me. "And this is Detective Sergeant Mills."

The overweight woman with the sullen expression who is accompanying him also flashes her card.

Once again my night was troubled. I had thought that my exhaustion would finally win out and grant me a decent eight hours' sleep, but I reckoned without Councillor Lambert and her threats. My rational self knows all she was doing was warning me off. Since there is no reason for us to ever have any dealings with each other again this should not be a problem. But in my fevered state in the small hours, half awake, half in perpetual nightmare, her tiny, asexual frame loomed large and menacing.

So yet again I am sitting at my desk, my eyes dry and hollow, my mouth bitter from too many cups of coffee. I feel stupid (though I know this is not the case), unable to string two thoughts together. Every limb seems as though it has weights attached, and my nerves are so shredded I find myself jumping when the telephone rings.

But I must put that all to one side for now. I have to make an effort for the Metropolitan Police's finest.

"Do sit down," I say. I gesture towards the plastic chair in the corner. "There's another seat over, there, just push those files onto the floor."

They make themselves comfortable (or at least as comfortable as possible on local authority issue chairs) and Detective Inspector Jarvis clears his throat.

"We're investigating the death of Miss Jane Gardner," he says. "I understand that you knew her."

I nod. "Though I think 'knew' would be putting it a bit strongly. I think we actually met only twice."

He has opened a loose file and is studying a sheet of paper. "That would have been, what, four weeks ago?"

"If you say so."

He glances up sharply. "You knew we were in, talking to people who'd had dealings with her. Why didn't you come forward?"

I am momentarily taken aback by the aggression in his tone. But I have encountered it before, from other of his colleagues. I know that it is intended to do precisely that, to throw me off balance, force me to drop my guard.

In your dreams, Detective Inspector Jarvis.

I frown. "I mentioned it to my boss yesterday, and he said he was going to put it in the stuff he was sending over to you. So I assumed you'd come to me if you were interested. It's not as if I've actually got anything important to tell you."

The woman leans her beetling brows towards her boss. I hear her whisper.

"That's right, guv. He did."

He looks annoyed. "Yes, well, whatever. What did you talk about?"

"She wanted some careers advice. It wasn't a formal meeting. We just bumped into each other in the car park, she was aware that I was in HR and asked if I could spare her a few minutes. Normally I'd have said it was something that should be handled in the office, but she looked so nervous, poor kid, I thought why not."

Detective Inspector Jarvis is examining his sheet of paper again. "I've got a copy of your emails here. They don't sound very much like careers advice to me." He gives me a meaningful look.

"Like I told my boss yesterday, she didn't want anyone in her department knowing she was looking around."

He reads from the sheet of paper. "'Just wanted to say how much I enjoyed our conversation the other evening – as we said, it's good to be able to chill away from the office sometimes.' 'im good thx drink sounds fun. This eve?'"

He stares at me. Blank eyes, disbelieving everyone and everything.

Some people are so cynical.

"Listen, we agreed to make things sound social, just in case someone else in Planning saw it over her shoulder or something. It's no more than that."

Still the stare. The sidekick is attempting to do the same. But she just looks sulky.

"Some of her colleagues think there may have been a man in her life recently."

I shrug. "She was a young woman, single. It would hardly be surprising, would it?"

"But you knew nothing about it?"

"It didn't crop up in our conversation, if that's what you mean. We didn't discuss her personal life at all, any more than we did mine."

"So what did you talk about on the second occasion? It was you that suggested it, from the look of it."

"Only because I'd had to cut short the previous week. The whist evening, as you can see from the emails. And she just wanted to talk a bit more about what sort of thing might suit her."

"And were you able to help?"

I pull a face. "Not a great deal, to be honest. Like I said, she was a nice kid, but not exactly the sharpest knife in the block."

There is another long pause. Detective Inspector Jarvis looks thoughtful. His lips and cheeks are moving in a strange pattern, as if he is chewing his tongue.

I glance from one to another of the two detectives sitting in my office. I know they are watching my body language, looking for signs of stress or anxiety. I take care not to show any, keeping my

338

breathing level and my hands still and apart.

"So where were you on Saturday evening?"

"Saturday?" I pretend to think for a moment. "At home. On my own, before you ask. My wife was away."

His expression does not change, but I see the sidekick flick a glance in her boss's direction. I simply wait for the inevitable next question.

"Anyone able to back that up at all?"

I allow a touch of irritation to enter my voice. "Well, let's think. Since I was on my own, I did try to catch up on a few phone calls. Got hold of a couple of people, left messages for others. You can check with them if you want, though God knows why you would. I mean, are you trying to suggest that I spent the evening with her, or something? I've already told you, I hardly knew her."

"I'm not suggesting anything, Mr Hillier. These are just routine questions. But perhaps you could jot down the details for Sergeant Mills here anyway."

As I do this, he continues. "By the way, these phone calls. Did you make them on your mobile, or on the landline?"

"The landline. So feel free to check the records there, as well, if you want."

"I see."

I hand over the list of names. There is another pause, more tongue chewing.

Eventually he leans forward and starts gathering his papers together.

"Okay, that's it for now. Give me a call if you think of anything else." He hands me a card. "And I'll need your address in case we need to speak to you again."

He heaves himself out of his chair with difficulty (he must be close to retirement age). He now sounds bored, as if his mind is already moving on to the next thing. I hope this is indeed the case. The interview was more confrontational than I had been expecting, although that might just be his normal style. But in any event I feel that I have acquitted myself as well as could be expected.

I recite my address for Detective Sergeant Mills to take down.

Suddenly Detective Inspector Jarvis turns back to me. For the first time in our conversation his expression displays a flicker of interest.

"St Nicholas, High End? I grew up round there as a boy. How come you live there? Don't tell me they've sold the place off."

"No, my wife is the Rector there."

"Really? What a small world. Do you still hold the Children's Party?"

"Absolutely. It's this coming Saturday in fact."

He gazes at me, nodding slightly to himself. "Well there's a coincidence."

He turns again to leave, but stops in the doorway.

"Who knows," he says. "I may even drop in. Just for old times' sake."

I manage a smile.

"Please do," I say.

36

This evening I am meeting James.

I am looking forward to it. It was arranged some time ago but the timing is apt. I intend to treat it as a kind of celebration. Today's interview with Detective Inspector Jarvis should be the last major hurdle in what has been a much more protracted, and complicated process than I would ever have imagined possible. Now that is out of the way there should be little else that can go wrong (putting aside for a moment the little logistical issue of the disposal of Mr Donald Dennis).

Though it has all been vastly more stressful than I had expected. I find myself seriously contemplating reverting to the first Rule. (Never Again). It is possible that three killings in the space of little more than a week has finally exhausted my appetite for the blood of others (though that makes me sound like a vampire, which I am not). But perhaps it is just because I am so tired at the moment. We shall see.

But for tonight I shall not think of any of that.

Tonight I shall just enjoy the company of my successful friend, and for once be able to hold my head up and know that there is at least one thing that I do better. (Albeit one it is difficult to talk about).

*

We are meeting at his flat. Whether or not we are staying in or going out later I am not sure. James sounded a little vague and distracted on the phone about it earlier. Perhaps we will just 'wing it' as James puts it. James likes winging it.

I take the near-silent lift to the eighth floor, where James's penthouse is. He is waiting in the doorway for me.

"Ambrose!" He grabs my arm and hauls me into the flat. In his other hand he has a glass containing a clear liquid which he waves at me. "Hope you don't mind, I started without you."

His speech is a little slurred. I glance at my watch. It is, as I thought, just gone seven. Early even for James to be drunk.

I follow him into the cavernous living area, with its white spiral staircase leading to the bedrooms, its toning brown and cream furniture and the huge canvases of violent primary colours that James calls his art.

He heads for the shiny steel American fridge. "What'll you have, old man? Beer? Wine? G and T? Vodka? I'm on the vodka tonic myself."

I shrug. "That's fine by me."

I watch as he tops up his own glass and pours one for me.

"A bit more tonic in mine, please," I say.

He hands me the drink. "Long day?" I ask.

"Nah." He takes a swig from the glass. "I left early, in fact. You?"

I think back over my day. The police, the anxiety, the furtive checking of the news websites. "Felt like it," I say.

He claps an arm round my shoulder and leads me over to the living area.

"But here you are, and here I am. It's good to see you, buddy."

We settle ourselves on opposing cream leather armchairs. Because of the size of the room this makes us about five yards apart. I struggle to hear what he is saying over the too loud, over-maudlin music (the Smiths, I believe).

So, apparently, does he.

"Whaddya say?" he asks.

"I was asking how were things. You know, work and so on."

He frowns, and lunges for the remote control. Morrisey remains miserable, but is less noisy about it.

"Things" he says. "Are pretty damned shit, quite frankly. Absolutely fucked, even."

I feel a pang of concern. I am aware that James's business has been struggling, but I have never heard him speak of it in quite these terms. I do not like the thought that he may no longer be successful.

"What, worse than they were?" I ask. "I knew it was tough but I always got the impression you were confident you'd get through it."

He waves a dismissive hand. "Tough really ain't the word any more, Ambrose me old mate. It's now

343

completely screwed." He leans towards me, suddenly focussed. "Let's put it this way – if we survive the week, it'll be a miracle."

I stare at him. "That bad?"

He nods. "That bad."

That is indeed bad.

"So what happens then?" I ask.

There is a long silence while James swills the ice cubes around in his glass. He appears fascinated by them, peering into the glass from different angles.

I wonder why he does not answer my question.

I try again. "I mean, can you just set up again, or what?"

Eventually, still gazing into his glass, he speaks.

"Ambrose, old chum, I don't think you quite realise how bad this particular bad is. Or, more accurately, how long this bad has been."

This of course does not make sense, but I think I know what he is getting at.

"I've had to put everything into the business this last few months." He looks up at last and waves his glass at me for emphasis. "Everything. And more. I borrowed against the flat to shore things up. And now it's gone. Gone, gone, gone."

He subsides again into his ice-studying mode.

I cannot believe what I am hearing. James, the all-conquering master of the Universe, the man who has made more money than everyone else I know put together? James, who sailed through life like a carefree young God? James, the person I could have been (or so I have always told myself) if things had turned out differently?

And now, James the failure.

I feel my head spinning, though whether this is from his news or my tiredness or his ridiculously strong vodka and tonics I do not know. Perhaps a combination of all three.

"Jesus," I say.

He nods. "Indeed."

Then he struggles to his feet. "Come on – I need some fresh air."

*

I follow him out onto the broad terrace that is wrapped around three sides of the building. A great sweep of the Thames stretches out in front of me, glinting in the early evening sun. It is one of the best views in London, James once told me. I shall miss it when he is forced to sell the flat.

I go to the rail and stare down at the river below me. I wonder what it would have been like to be standing here and see Jane Gardner bobbing along. Quite exciting, I would imagine, certainly very interesting, particularly if you happened to have a pair of binoculars with you. I scan the water now, looking for any other bodies, but of course there are none. None that I can see, anyway.

I turn back to James, who has slumped into a chair.

"Perhaps you just need to get away from it all for a while," I say as I take a seat next to him. "Travel a bit, take a breather. Then when you get back you can make a fresh start. You've done it once, there's no reason you can't do it again."

He looks at me sideways, from beneath lowered

lids. "You know, it's a weird thing, but you've always had way more confidence in me than I have in myself. I can't think why. It's like you have this image of me, this illusion of the great financier."

"Aren't you?"

"No! I'm just a punter, man. I punt the markets, and for a while I got it right. But then I fucked it up."

There does not seem any good answer to this. James is obviously depressed about his financial problems, and the alcohol is making him worse. I am sure he is wrong about himself, but there is not much point in arguing with him when he is in this mood.

"The stupid thing is," he continues. "Is that I've always been jealous of you."

I turn to him, genuinely astonished.

"Jealous? Of me? Why the hell would you be jealous of me?"

"Because you were always so settled, so happy. You had Helen, you knew where you were going and why. There you were, two good-looking people, madly in love, neither of you having even the slightest interest in anyone else. You were secure. Sure, I've got loads more money than you, and there're the exotic holidays, and all the different girls. But the novelty of all that wears off, you know. And then all you want is to find your soul mate and settle down with her."

I stare at this man that is supposed to be my friend. And I wonder if everything I have ever thought about him is going to turn out to be wrong.

*

We are silent for a while. All the normal noises of London are present; the traffic, the aircraft overhead, the seagulls shrieking on the riverbank. But on this balcony nothing is normal.

"Talking of girls, how's Beccy?" I ask after a while.

He opens his eyes, looking disorientated. I wonder if he has actually passed out for a moment or two. It would be a very rude thing to do with a guest present, but it would not be surprising given how drunk he seems to be.

"Beccy?" he repeats.

"Australian girl, figure like a boy scout?"

"Oh, that Beccy." He smiles, then the smile fades. "Yeah, that broke up." He sighs. "Like they all seem to."

"You can say that again. Helen did wonder whether the problem was that you were actually secretly gay."

This comment takes a moment to register. But then for some reason he seems to find it enormously funny.

"Helen?" he repeats through great barks of laughter. "Helen thought I was gay! My God – that is hilarious. Absolutely hilarious."

I agree that it is amusing, but hilarious seems to be taking it a bit far.

"I think she was joking," I say. "But..."

"No," he interrupts me, still wheezing with laughter. "You don't understand. It's not the gay thing, though that is funny. But that Helen, of all people, should say so..."

Something icy and hard seems to materialise on the back of my neck.

"What does that mean?" I ask.

347

"Nothing," he splutters. "I'd have thought she'd have told you, but obviously not. It's just that she had pretty good evidence that I'm not, you know what I mean?"

I believe I do know what he means. The shock of understanding takes my breath away, and for a few moments I cannot speak. Then with the words comes the fury, and before I know what I am doing I am straddling him on the chair, my hands locked around his throat.

"What are you saying?" I hiss. "Did you make a pass at Helen? Did you touch her? When? Tell me. Tell me!"

I am shaking him and he stares up at me, his eyes boggling with fear.

"No!" he croaks. "No – I wouldn't – I'd never. You've got the wrong end of the stick. Let me go, Ambrose, and I'll tell you."

Like a flash tide, the fury recedes. I release him and return to my own chair.

"Go on then," I say.

He rubs his throat and eyes me, still fearful.

"It's nothing like that at all," he says. "It's just that – you remember that party that Adrian Carter had down at his place in Hampshire, must have been ten years ago?" I nod and he continues. "It was pretty wild, and we all got thoroughly rat-faced – well, I did, anyway. And so did Naomi. She and I took a couple of bottles of fizz down to the woods at the end of the garden, and – well, one thing led to another."

This is another surprise. I had thought that Naomi and Ben were, if not devoted to each other, at least

348

contented with their choices. But obviously not.

He is looking at me expectantly. Whether he is expecting admiration or disapproval, I do not know. But I do not care who he fucks. Just so long as he keeps his filthy groping hands away from Helen.

"And this has to do with my wife, what?" I ask.

"She barged in on us! Caught us completely in flagrante whotsit. She was just taking a bit of a break from the crowds she said, not looking for us at all, but then she more or less stepped on us. Of course Naomi was distraught, and was begging her not to tell Ben, and even pissed as I was, I could tell Helen was pretty upset too. But I never touched her, Ambrose, never even suggested anything. I wouldn't."

I look at him and I know that he is telling the truth. And I know that because I am tired and worried and feeling that my world has been turned completely upside down by all James's other revelations that I have behaved like an absolute imbecile.

I shake my head. "I'm sorry, James. I'm so sorry. I don't know what came over me."

He stands and claps me on the shoulder.

"It's okay," he says. "I know you and Helen..." He doesn't finish the sentence.

He seems a lot more sober now. Perhaps that is what happens when the person you believe to be your best friend tries to strangle you.

37

The next morning I am late for work. I also have a new dent in my car. And I have one more person on my list of those I would like to put to a slow, agonising death. Unfortunately, I do not know his name.

As now seems to be becoming a habit, I have slept poorly again. I am beginning to get resigned to spending the small hours in that living nightmare of semi-consciousness, eventually collapsing into an exhausted pre-dawn slumber only to be woken, what seems like a few seconds later hollow-eyed and weary beyond belief, by the Today programme. Just as I am becoming resigned to a week where every fresh day brings another jarring lurch towards calamity, another grinding twist of the knife in my gut.

I am beginning to feel that perhaps Ambrose is not immortal. He is cursed.

This is what happens. I am driving along my normal route. I was not going fast, so perhaps my tiredness has made me less attentive, or slowed my reflexes, I do not know. But when a moronic teenager with a mobile glued to its ear steps off the central island right in front of me I do not have time to brake, still less punch the horn in warning. Instead I instinctively pull the wheel to the left, away from the hazard.

And right into the path of the cyclist speeding up the cycle lane next to me.

The cycle also swerves. Its front wheel hits the curb. The cyclist flies off the bike, onto the pavement.

I stop the car and jump out. The cyclist is just standing up, dusting down his lycra leggings.

He looks, to my relief, unhurt. The last thing I need this morning is another police investigation, this time into a road traffic accident. Though Ben is right, the lycra leggings make him look gay.

"Are you all right?" I ask.

A snarling, feral face is turned towards me. "No thanks to you, tosser."

I do not expect him to be happy but this is not necessary.

"Yeah, well it wasn't exactly my fault," I say. After his response to my earlier question I speak with less friendliness, less concern. "That idiot walked straight out in front of me. I had no choice."

I turn to indicate the idiot teenager. But it has disappeared into the crowd, oblivious to the chaos it has caused.

"And anyway, you were going too fast."

"That right?" sneers Lycra Leggings. "Well, I can tell you... Christ!"

He is now looking at his bike, which has a large scratch down the black alloy of its front wheel.

"Look what you've done to my fucking bike!"

He pulls the machine upright and examines the rest of it. Then he turns to me, his face contorted into an ugly, threatening grimace.

"Wanker. This is your fault. You're going to fucking pay for this."

I have had enough. His words and attitude are completely out of proportion to the situation. It is people like him that give cyclists a bad name. It is unfortunate that his bike is damaged but it is not my fault and I shall not be paying for it.

I take a step towards him, fixing him with my eyes, matching him menace for menace.

"No I am fucking not."

By now there is a small crowd of onlookers gathered around, watching the entertainment from a safe distance. At my words I sense a small frisson go through them, as they anticipate the exchange getting more interesting.

But Lycra Leggings is more mouth than trousers. He steps back.

For a second he simply stands, the sneer still twisted across his pale, ugly face. Then to my horror, he raises his leg and crashes his heel into the rear door of the Skoda as hard as he can. Then he jumps onto the bike and is away into the traffic before I have even opened my mouth to speak.

The crowd begins to disperse, but I stare after him, trying to memorise his face, his clothing, his bike.

If I ever run into him again, a scratched wheel will be the least of his worries.

*

I am still fuming when I arrive at the office. As I go

through the entrance hall I see Alan Grant heading towards me.

He has not seen me. I am in no mood for small talk so I say nothing. But as he passes he suddenly looks up.

As he recognises me his eyes widen and his mouth drops open. It would be nice if this reaction conveyed fear of me, but it is more likely to be simple surprise.

But then his expression changes, becomes more calculating.

He gives a slight nod. "Hillier," he says. But it is almost more of a question than a greeting.

It is odd. But I am too tired, and too pissed off with the cyclist who has dented my car, to think any more of it.

*

It is later in the morning. I am sitting at my desk thinking again about Lycra Legs.

What is it about me that seems to attract all the most hideously foul, repulsive lowlifes? Wherever I turn they are there. On my doorstep, on my days out in the country, and now on my journey to work. And that is without counting all the criminals surrounding me, like Alan Grant and Mr Donald Dennis. It is as if I have some sort of invisible aura, drawing them to me.

Ambrose Hillier, scum magnet.

It is very tedious.

The phone rings. It is Ivy Boakye.

"Ambrose? Have you got a minute? There's something I want to bounce off you."

I wonder what new lunacies our Chief Diversity

Officer has dreamed up. It must be something quite impressively outrageous. She normally has zero interest in anyone else's opinion of her ideas.

"Sure," I say. "Come on over."

In fact I have a number of things that I should be doing, some quite urgent (though naturally, none actually important), but I find myself unable to concentrate on any of them. Instead I have been indulging in a little pet (unofficial) project of mine.

I have a spreadsheet covering the entire payroll of our local authority, and am working out what could be done if the council only did what it needed to do, using no more resources than necessary. In other words, we end the subsidy of the legions of skiving wastrels in our community, and stop poking our noses in where they are not required. For this purpose I have to assume there are no politicians, trade unions, or self-serving management. So far I have come up with a reduction in headcount of around 47 per cent, and a rather larger reduction in total payroll costs (reflecting the swathe of expensive middle management that would be the first against the proverbial wall.)

It will never happen. Even now that same management is busy cutting services to families and pensioners in order to protect their own bloated pension pots. But it is fun to imagine what life would be like if Ambrose ruled the world (or at least wore the mayoral chain).

And if I get really bored, I can always leak it to the press, with the suggestion that this is the council's proposed 'austerity package'.

*

354

Ivy Boakye arrives a few minutes later.

"I just wanted your advice," she begins. "I know you and Doug get concerned about the political sensitivity of things."

I hide my surprise. That Ivy Boakye wants my advice is novelty enough. But that she is also worrying about political sensitivities (or is even aware of them) is little short of miraculous.

"And I could tell that Councillor Lambert was a bit touchy about what we were talking about," she continues. "So I wondered what you thought about bouncing this off her before we circulate it." She pushes a document across the desk to me. "I could have just emailed it to her, of course, but I thought there might be some etiquette in these situations. And you're obviously much better at that sort of thing than me."

I did not know that Ivy Boakye possessed this degree of self-awareness. Perhaps, I think, there is hope for her yet. But then I look at the document she has passed me and I nearly choke.

"Ivy, what the hell is this?"

She frowns at my reaction. "It's a draft memo for what we were talking about last week. You know, the memorandum to the committees of the council, warning them against discrimination. You must remember."

"Of course I remember. I also remember that we agreed to put it on hold for a few months, to give the Planning Committee a chance to get its house in order."

She shrugs. "Well, yes. But that doesn't mean we

355

shouldn't start work on it now. These things are important – I don't want it to be a rushed job. But you and Doug seem to think it's important not to offend Councillor Lambert. Personally I couldn't give a toss."

I manage to restrain myself from screwing up her pompous little memorandum and stuffing it down her self-righteous little throat. But only with a great effort of will.

"Ivy, I don't know whether you are really stupid or just completely bloody-minded. In what way is sending this, a few days after we've agreed to leave things be a while, not going to offend Councillor Lambert? You saw how she reacted when we mentioned it even as a possibility. Do you not think she might consider you going ahead with it regardless just a little bit provocative? Jesus."

She has been staring at me open-mouthed while I speak. But now her expression tightens and she leans across the desk towards me.

"How dare you speak to me like that?"

I return the stare.

I know that she is trying to intimidate me. Ivy Boakye is used to intimidating people. But as I have said before, I am not intimidated by her. In fact, far from worrying about what she might do to me, my mind is running riot, thinking of the many and pleasurable ways I could remove this woman from my life once and for all. I should like to introduce a little irony into the process, perhaps something like immolating her on a pyre of her politically correct memoranda. The last thing she would see in this world would be the words 'equal opportunities' drifting past her in flames.

But right now I have many more pressing matters to worry about. The most vital of these is to stop her provoking Councillor Lambert from going back on what I think of as our deal. And I am also very tired. It would not be a good idea to get into a full-scale fight with Ivy Boakye at this time.

I force myself to adopt a reasonable tone. "Ivy, this memo is never going to be sent. Councillor Lambert has just discovered that there is a Church of England application coming up, a very unsuitable application, that in all likelihood will be turned down. So the problem will go away of its own accord. Do you understand?"

She draws herself up. "The problems of discrimination and injustice and oppression *never* go away of their own accord. Whatever may happen in this one instance changes nothing. Constant vigilance is necessary. That is my mission. Do *you* understand *that*?"

I look at her face, glowing with revolutionary fervour, secure in her absolute rightness, intent on imposing her own warped ideology on the rest of the universe. And I snap.

"You know nothing! There is no discrimination! It's all a nonsense. You really think that Councillor Lambert is pro some and anti other religions? I very much doubt if she cares a damn about any of them. It's all just politics, Ivy. Just bollocks. And you're either too stupid or too demented to see it."

There is a long silence after I have finished speaking. She is probably unsure how to reply. But I

357

observe her hands clenching and unclenching in front of her, as if itching to give a more physical response. I am perhaps fortunate that there are no heavy metal objects nearby.

Eventually she gets to her feet. I expect at the least another tirade, but all she says is, "I am the Chief Diversity Officer. I will not forget this conversation."

She marches out of the office.

I stare at her retreating back. I am still not quite able to believe how close this woman came to snatching defeat from the jaws of my victory. God knows what Councillor Lambert would have done if our Chief Diversity Officer's self-important little memo had suddenly popped into her Inbox. I shudder at the thought.

I realise that I have now made another enemy. Yet another person is not planning on forgetting me, there is yet another Christmas card I am unlikely to receive. But it does not matter. Ivy Boakye has served her purpose. All that I have to do now (or rather, once all my other issues are sorted out) is to work out the best way of dealing with her. On a permanent basis.

In Ivy Boakye's case, that would be a genuine Public Service.

*

It is a long day.

I am surrounded by idiots. Whenever I lift my head I see them, flitting along the corridors, filling their empty lives by creating difficulties for everyone else. It occurs to me how useful it would be to have one of those ray guns you used to get in sci-fi films (and probably still do in computer games, I do not

358

know as I do not play them). Then I could just sit at my desk and shoot them whenever they passed, and they would disappear in a puff of smoke. And when I run out of passersby I could go down to the main lobby area, and zap everyone coming into or out of the building.

It would be immensely satisfying.

I leave the office early, pleading a headache, which by now is true. Helen is not home yet. I decide that I shall treat myself to a long hot bath, with an ice cold gin and tonic to help me enjoy it.

As the bath runs I reflect that this is the first time that I shall have used it since Jane Gardner's short immersion (I usually have showers). I wonder if it will feel any different, which is silly really. It is just cast iron and enamel, and it has been very thoroughly cleaned. And I do not believe in ghosts.

I step into it, feeling the bubbles tingling against my skin, the warmth seeping into my aching muscles. I reach for my glass.

The phone in the bedroom rings.

I decide to ignore it. It will not be Helen, as she would not expect me home yet. And if it is important the caller can leave a message.

It stops ringing, and I take a long, delicious sip of my drink. I sink back so that my chin is at the water level and close my eyes.

The phone rings again.
I ignore it, but less than a minute later I hear the same insistent burr.

I cannot relax with this going on. Cursing, I get out of the bath and reach for my towel. I pick up the receiver, still dripping bath water over the bedroom carpet.

"Hello?"

A man's voice, deep and gravelly. Once again Scottish. "Is that Barry Frith?"

For a moment I am rendered speechless with rage. Not only do these people continue to pester me, but this time they have spoiled my bath.

Then I find my voice.

"No I am not fucking Barry Frith! I have not the faintest idea who Barry Frith is, or where he is. I had never heard of him before you morons started ringing up about him. He is not here! Can you understand that, cretin?"

I am shouting now, the hand holding the receiver trembling with fury. But the voice on the end of the line seems unfazed.

"Have you quite finished?" it says. "Because let me tell you, I don't believe a word of it. After your little pantomime with my colleagues the other day, I looked at our records. Very carefully, as this is my business. And I can tell you, we checked up on Mr Barry Frith very thoroughly before we lent him ten thousand pounds. The ten thousand pounds that is, incidentally, now very overdue for repayment. So I am absolutely certain that the person on the end of this phone either is Barry Frith, or knows where he is. So, can *you* understand *that*?"

At this moment all I understand is that I wish this man were in the room with me, and that I had a very large metal implement in my hands. Preferably with spikes on it. However, I do not. All I can do is let him

360

know exactly what I think of him and his pond life colleagues, in a tidal wave of coruscating verbal abuse that will leave him reeling and defeated.

But I do not do this. I do not even hang up. Because if this really is the boss of Southern Whatever Finance it is probably, loth as I am to waste my time, worth trying to sort this nonsense out once and for all.

"I understand that your records must be as substandard as your employees' mental processes, if that's what you mean. If they're all so bloody good why don't you have an address for this guy?"

There is a pause. "There's a problem with that. We have an address, but it looks like he managed to slip a false one past us. Needless to say, the employee who made that particular mistake has paid for it." There is a pause for emphasis. "Heavily."

"So he gave you a false phone number as well. Even you can't be so thick you can't work that out."

"Our records show that we spoke to him on this number."

"Well, they're wrong then. Where was this address, anyway?"

"It's for a convent. You know, nuns and stuff."

I laugh. "At least he's consistent then. This is a vicarage." I do not wish to use the word 'Rectory' as there are fewer of them. There would be a remote chance that this man would be able to find us from that information.

He too laughs, but not nicely. "Unlikely, I'd say, given the language you've been using."

"Fuck you," I say.

There is a short silence before he speaks again.

361

"Okay," he says. "But understand this. I'm going to find Barry Frith. I'm going to find him and get my money back, and the interest he owes me. And if I find that he is actually you..." Again he pauses for effect. "I'll be taking a little extra payback. Understand?"

He hangs up.

*

I return to my bath. But although the exchange has taken only a minute or two it seems less warm, even when I top it up with hot water.

My nameless Scottish caller has ruined even my bath.

I finish my drink and get out.

*

While I am drying myself I hear that Helen has arrived home.

I go downstairs to find her pottering in the kitchen. She looks at me and her face creases in a frown.

"Are you all right?" she asks. "You look terrible."

I peck her on the cheek. "Thank you very much, darling," I say.

But then I sigh. "Just a shit day at work. One thing after another. I don't know, people are such..."

I stop. I do not like troubling Helen with my petty woes. And obviously I cannot talk to her about my big woes.

She stands in front of me, gazing into my eyes. It is as if she is peering directly into my soul, examining my very being. But I do not fear this scrutiny. I know that she cannot enter the dark places, cannot see those things that would destroy us both if she knew of

362

them. Because Helen herself is pure light, all she sees is light.

Nor can her light lighten my darkness. The darkness is simply incomprehensible to it.

She puts her hands on my shoulders. "You're tired, and you're upset," she says.

I nod.

She looks at me gravely. "It's that girl, the one who died, isn't it?" she asks. "You're upset about it. It's natural. But you can't blame yourself. It's not your fault. You do see that, don't you?"

Once again I nod.

"I know. It's not my fault."

And for the second time in a week, I feel my eyes well with tears.

38

I am running through the woods. Above me, trees obscure the sky, to my sides, thick clumps of bushes hem me in. I recognise them, they are rhododendrons. It is raining hard, the narrow path beneath my feet is heavy with mud.

I hear Sir Dundridge's voice behind me, yelling at me to leave his woods, but I must keep going. I must reach Helen.

I know she is ahead of me, but I cannot see her. I call her name, over and over, but there is no reply, only the roars of Sir Dundridge and the drumming of the rain on the leaves.

The bushes are denser now, the path narrower. The mud is getting heavier, I am struggling to lift my feet. I force my aching, burning legs forward, but they move so slowly, slower and slower.

Ahead I see a clearing. Raised ground, dry. Helen is standing there. She looks lost, she hears my calls, but does not know what to do, where to turn.

Then I see faces, arms, bodies, clamber out of the

*mud and onto the raised ground. I recognise James, Ivy
Boakye. They are crawling towards Helen.*

"She is mine," cries James.

"No, she is mine!" answers Ivy Boakye.

*They are nearly on her now, their filthy hands
reaching for the hem of her white dress. But the mud
holds me, I cannot move. I cannot save her.*

I cry out, one last, desperate appeal.

"Helen!"

I wake with a start, the scream stillborn in my
throat. Once again I am drenched with sweat, once
more my pulse is pounding.

It is still dark, but in the dim light from the
window I see Helen lying beside me, and hear her
gentle, regular breathing.

At least I have not disturbed her rest.

*

In the afternoon I receive an unwelcome surprise.
I am sitting at my desk deleting emails when the door
is pushed open (without anyone knocking first).

It is Detective Inspector Jarvis, with his sidekick,
the ugly fat sergeant whose name I cannot remember.
They both sit down without being invited.

"Do you have a moment, Mr Hillier?" he asks.

I shrug. "I suppose so."

I sit back in my chair and wait, as calmly as I am
able) to be told what this about.

"We just have a couple more questions," he says.

This I have already deduced.

"Fire away," I say.

He consults his notebook. "When we last spoke
you said you and Miss Gardner had agreed to make

your email correspondence sound social so that her bosses wouldn't know she was after another job." He looks up. "Is that right."

"Broadly, yes."

"Whose idea was that then?"

I am taken aback by this question. It is so banal and pointless that I have not prepared an answer.

"I really can't remember," I say. "Does it matter?"

"Not especially. It's just that, with you being so much more senior than her, it might have come across a bit odd coming from you. Yet it seems out of character for her, from what I've been able to gather about her. So I wondered."

I give a slow nod. I am trying to give my weary, battered mind time to think on its feet, as it were.

"I see what you mean," I say. "Well, as far as I can remember, towards the end of the conversation, when I was saying I had to go but could meet her again if she wanted, she was very anxious that I didn't do anything that would give her boss the wrong, or rather, the right idea. So I think I suggested, more as a joke than anything else, that I should make it sound like I said, more social. And she took me literally and said that's what we should do. She was a bit like that."

"A bit like what?"

"You know, literal-minded. You make a joke, she doesn't quite get it."

"I see. Can you give me any more examples of that happening?"

Shit! I have just broken the first rule of lying. Do not embellish too much, keep things simple.

"Not really. It was more of a general impression, if

366

you know what I mean."

"I see."

I wait for him to add to this comment, but he simply sits, motionless, even his gaze almost unblinking, watching me.

"Was there anything else?" I ask.

He appears surprised at the question.

"Anything else? Oh yes. Oh yes indeed."

He glances down at the notebook again. "Some of the people we've spoken to seem to be under the impression that you were rather better acquainted with Miss Gardner than you've told us."

The words hit me like a hammer blow. I see the ugly fat sergeant observing me, studying me like some specimen in a laboratory and know that this whole conversation has been planned.

I strain, with every fibre of my being, not to react. I must maintain the demeanour of an innocent man.

I affect an expression of puzzlement. "Not quite sure what you mean by that. I told you, we only met that twice. Who's been saying otherwise?"

A dry smile. "I'm not at liberty to say that, sir. So let's just clarify, shall we? You last saw Miss Gardner..?"

"On the Monday evening, four weeks ago. Oh, and actually, yes, I forgot. Sometime after, I can't remember when, she dropped some files in that I needed. But we didn't really talk."

Detective Inspector Jarvis raises his brows at this.

In fact, I genuinely had forgotten the incident with the files, so irrelevant was it to everything that followed since. But Tom Bates may have mentioned that he had sent her over, and I do not wish to be caught out in a lie. Not over something so trivial.

"You called her up for these files?" he asks.

"No, I called someone else. Tom Bates. He must have asked her to bring them over."

"I see."   He makes a note in his pad. "Just one more thing, Mr Hillier. Do you have a mobile phone?"

I nod. "Of course."

"May I see it please?"

I pull the handset from my pocket and place it on the desk between us.

"And its number?"

As I recite this the ugly fat sergeant jots it down. Detective Inspector Jarvis punches it into his own mobile. He then hits the call button.

My phone rings and he ends the call.

He darts a glance at me, though I have not said anything. "Just checking. And this is your only mobile?"

"Yes."

He makes another note and gets to his feet.

"All right then, that will do for now...."

Then he breaks off, frowning.

"You know, the first time I saw you, I thought you looked familiar. Since then I've been racking my brains, but I can't pin it down. Have we met before?"

My stomach does another flip as I think of the photo fit picture issued by the Chilterns police. No ordinary person could ever recognise me from that. But Detective Inspector Jarvis is a trained detective. It is not impossible that someone like him might be able to see through the primitive lines of the drawing to the essence of the man beneath. I instinctively push my hair back, to make it as little as possible like the picture.

"Really?" I say. "I don't think so. But a number of people have said the same sort of thing. I think I must just have one of those faces, you know?"

"Maybe." He makes to leave.

I know I should simply let him go but I cannot resist. The stress of all this is too much. I have to know.

"So when do you think you'll find out for sure what happened?" Both he and the sidekick, as one, turn back to face me. "You know. Whether it was an accident, or suicide. Are you any nearer a conclusion?"

A slow smile has spread across Detective Inspector Jarvis's face.

"Hadn't you heard?"

I look at his expression and feel suddenly cold.

"Heard what?"

His expression is now almost pitying. "Perhaps the news hasn't reached here yet. We only announced it half an hour ago. But it's neither of those things. It's a murder enquiry now."

*

I wait until the detectives have disappeared completely down the corridor and I have heard the door slam shut at the end before I dare to relax. Then I let out the breath that I seem to have been holding for about twenty minutes, and allow my head to sink into my hands.

Those two words echo through my mind, bouncing around in my skull as if it were a pinball machine.

Murder
    Enquiry
        Murder
            Enquiry
Murder
    Enquiry
        Murder
            Enquiry

How the fucking hell had that happened?

After all my planning. The minute level of preparation that went into every detail of Jane Gardner's demise and disposal. All they had was a woman's body, drowned, floating down the river with her handbag. No marks of injury, no signs of a struggle, no (as far as I am aware) witnesses. How on earth had they come to the conclusion that it was murder?

At one level I know that this should not concern me unduly. My tracks are well covered, there is nothing to link me with this newly categorised crime. But it is disconcerting, to say the least. I do not know what is going on. And if I do not know what is driving events, I cannot control them.

I so, so hate that feeling.

*

I get myself a cup of tea. I know that more caffeine is the last thing I need in my jittery state, but I have to do something. I am going crazy, not knowing what it is that these clumping detectives have uncovered to make them so certain.

About one thing there is no mystery though. Their anonymous informant, the one that has told them that

Jane Gardner and I were more than just passing acquaintances. There is only one candidate for that.

Alan Grant.

I should have guessed from the expression on his face yesterday that he was up to something. I have always known that he was unreliable, not to be trusted.

Bastard.

There is a limit to the damage he himself can do. After all, he does not actually know that I had any involvement in the girl's death. He is just making mischief for me. And he cannot go too far down that route, or his own shady dealings will begin to emerge. But it is the sort of complication I could do without.

And it is not something I shall forget.

*

I arrive home just in time for the local London news on the television. It is read by the man with the annoying voice. Ordinarily I would find this irritating, but today I am too preoccupied by other matters to take much notice of such things.

Jane Gardner is the lead item.

"Police have confirmed that they are now treating the death of Jane Gardner, the young woman found dead in the river Thames at the weekend, as murder."

There is then a rehash of previous information. Where the body was found, where Jane Gardner lived and worked. But as to why the police had now decided it was murder, nothing. And nothing at all about which direction they are taking their enquiry, about possible motives, or suspects.

It is all most frustrating.

371

The item ends. I am in the process of getting up to fetch myself a drink when the screen is filled with a photograph. It is of a young man, in ill-fitting wedding attire, but with a familiar, rat-like face.

I sit down again.

"Buckinghamshire police have made a fresh appeal for anyone with any information about the death of Darren Little, who was killed twelve days ago while cycling in the Chiltern Hills. They have reissued the photo fit of this man," The screen shot changes to the abysmal non-likeness of me, "That they want to interview in connection with the crime."

Two in a row, I think as I get up again to fetch my gin and tonic. That surely must be a cause for some pride.

But the best (in a manner of speaking) is yet to come. As I return to the sofa with my drink I hear the following.

"Mystery still surrounds the disappearance last weekend of London businessman Donald Dennis. He was last in contact with friends on Saturday evening, but since then his whereabouts are unknown. However, police have now revealed that his car has been found at a long-term airport car park, leading to speculation that he may have left the country. While he is now a successful property developer, it has emerged that Mr Dennis has previous convictions for fraud and actual bodily harm. Police are asking anyone with any information regarding his disappearance to contact them."

I had not been aware that Mr Donald Dennis was an ex-con. It is not a surprise. But it is most fortunate from my point of view. If the police are imagining that he has fled the country, presumably as a result of one of his dodgy property deals going wrong, they will not be looking for him under my rhododendron bushes.

I switch off the television and sit back to reflect on what I have just heard. Three separate murders on one news programme. And every one of them mine.

A hat trick.

This is truly a great achievement. And though I have no way of proving it, I am absolutely convinced that it must be a record.

It is almost enough to cheer me up.

39

Somehow I get through Friday.

It shudders by, a series of caffeine-fuelled spurts of paranoia punctuated by long, drawn-out spells of treacly lethargy. I jump whenever someone walks down the corridor, and find myself staring at the phone as if it were a scorpion poised to strike. At other times I realise I have just spent five minutes gazing at the same email, unable to make sense of its laboured syntax and grinding argument. (Though of course this may be that there is no sense there to make). Throughout, I experience this burning need to know what is happening in the various police investigations in which I have an interest, coupled with a dread conviction that the only news for me can be bad news.

If I did not know myself better I would think I was going mad.

But I hear nothing from the police.

In fact it is a quiet day generally (which suits me very well). The only distraction of note comes from an email from Ivy Boakye, informing that I have been enrolled on one of her compulsory Diversity and Anti-Discrimination Training Days. (Doug is also on the list.)

But I do not care. I have more important things to worry about.

That is my fun day at the office.

*

I am home early again. Helen is out somewhere, presumably busy with last-minute preparations for tomorrow's Children's Party. But all I can think of is my relief that it is at last the weekend. The longest week of my life is over.

I take a long shower, then (uncharacteristically for me) decide to slob it by pulling on an old, loose track suit. It is not an elegant look. But I am on my own, in my own home. I can do what I want.

I fetch myself a gin and tonic and settle onto the sofa with a long sigh. The hot water has eased some of the tension in my muscles, though perversely this makes me feel more tired, not less. My eyes feel gritty and heavy, and I think that it is maybe not such a bad idea to have a doze before Helen appears.

At which point the doorbell rings.

I remain on the sofa for a few seconds. I am not expecting anyone. In all likelihood whoever it is at the door wants to discuss something to do with the Children's Party. It is equally likely that I will not be able to help.

The bell rings again, for longer this time. With another deep sigh (this time of resignation, not of contentment) I heave myself off the sofa and go to answer it. If it is Joyce Burnside, my one satisfaction will be the look of disapproval on her face when she

375

sees my tracksuit.

But it is not Joyce Burnside. It is Detective Inspector Jarvis.

*

His square face cracks in what I believe may be intended to be a friendly smile.

"Mr Hillier? They told me at your office that you'd come home early and as I was passing this way anyway I thought I'd drop by. I've just another couple of questions for you."

For a moment the combination of exhaustion and shock renders me speechless. All I am able to do is stand and blink at him stupidly.

Then I recover myself.

"Sorry," I say. "I was just having a lie down. Come on in."

"A bit under the weather, are we sir?" he asks as he follows me down the hallway.

"Just a headache. I get them."

I seat him on the armchair and myself on the sofa.

"So," I say. "How can I help you?"

Once more that friendly smile (which I do not trust one inch). "I'd like you to think back to your conversations with Miss Gardner, sir. Did she ever talk about a 'Martin' to you?"

I have to suppress a start at the mention of the name. It means that some information has indeed been gleaned from Jane Gardner's mobile.

At least something is going to plan.

I frown and look into the middle distance, as a person might do when he is trying very hard to be helpful and remember something.

"Martin," I repeat. "No, I can't say that it sounds familiar. What would the context have been? Family, friends? Work?"

"We think he may have been a boyfriend of sorts. But there's also a suggestion that they may have worked together."

"Ah." I raise my eyebrows at this, as any self-respecting HR executive would. "I see. Well, obviously we have a few Martins on the payroll, but off the top of my head I can't think of any in Planning. And of course if she were dating a colleague she might well have been a bit wary of mentioning it to me, We do have policies on that sort of thing, and if they were... Well, you know."

"Indeed." He looks disappointed.

"Sorry," I say.

He says nothing else so I continue.

"So is he a suspect, then, this Martin?"

He appears to consider for a moment.

"Let's just say that we would like very much to talk to him. From what we can make out from her mobile – which is not everything, of course, it had been in the water quite a while – it seems that she may have seen him on the evening of her death."

"I see," I say. "I can well imagine that you would like to talk to him then."

I have answered his questions but Detective Inspector Jarvis still seems in no hurry to leave. I wonder if this new (apparent) amiability is down to him having checked my alibi and reassured himself that I cannot after all be 'Martin', and can therefore be trusted.

I decide to test this theory.

377

"There's one thing puzzling me," I say. "You're obviously treating this as murder now, but originally you said she drowned. Have you changed your minds on that?"

The question seems to surprise him. "Changed our minds? No. Why would you think that?"

"Then how..? I mean, do you think she was pushed in, or something?"

He gives a crafty smile. "I'm sure she was pushed in. But not until after she was dead."

For a second, maybe more, I cannot tell, time seems suspended. I try to swallow, but discover that my mouth is too dry.

"I'm not sure I quite understand."

He stares at me. Once again I am struck by how flat and unblinking his gaze is. It is like that of a snake, cold, unreadable, inscrutable in the truest sense of the word.

"Well," he says slowly. "I shouldn't really tell you, it's not in the public domain yet. But it'll come out soon enough. We analysed the water in her lungs. If she'd drowned in the river, it would have been river water. But it wasn't. It was good old London tap water."

"You're kidding!"

"I know! Amazing, isn't it? I mean, how could anyone be so stupid as to think that we wouldn't spot that? Any idiot who watches any of those rubbish detective programmes on telly would know we could do that, wouldn't they?"

"Well, obviously. Jeez. What a schoolboy error."

In fact I had no idea the police could analyse the

378

water in someone's lungs and find out where it came from (though I suppose it is obvious now it is pointed out to me). I do not watch those rubbish detective programmes, only Poirots and Miss Marples. But I certainly cannot have Detective Inspector Jarvis believing that I am even more stupid than the idiots that do.

"Jeez," I repeat. I shake my head at the ignorance of others.

"So," he says. "Now you know why we're so sure it's murder." He pulls himself out of the armchair. "Anyway, have a think about this Martin character, and if anything occurs to you, give me a call, yes?"

"Absolutely," I say. I also rise from my chair.

We go out into the hall and I open the front door.

Suddenly he stops and turns back to me.

"Did you say it was the Children's Party tomorrow?"

"That's right. It's already set up for it outside."

He glances out through the door.

"I've got such memories of those parties. I'd love a look round the garden again. Would you mind?"

I think of the garden, and what is out there in addition to the trestle tables and games. And I think how little I want this detective wandering through my rhododendrons.

"Of course not," I say.

*

I lead him round to the back of the house and the great lawn. It is lined with tables and stalls, in one corner the improvised stage for the band. Silent and empty for now, but ready and waiting for tomorrow's

379

crowds.

Detective Inspector Jarvis smiles.

"It's strange," he says. "In some ways it's just how I remember it. But in others – I don't know. Some of it seems bigger, some of it smaller. Does that make sense?"

I very much wish that he would go and leave me in peace, but despite this I feel that I should play the polite host. This is also despite the fact that I know very well that if Detective Inspector Jarvis knew half what I know he would clap me in the proverbial irons without a second thought. He would not feel the need to be polite.

"I suppose you were much smaller then, so all the things like the lawn would have seemed much bigger. But obviously it's been some years and quite a lot of other things really would be bigger, because they've grown. The trees, for example."

He nods. "That must be it."

He turns away from the lawn and starts heading around the house. "I remember me and my brother used to sneak off round here..."

He stops dead in front of the open garage door and stares inside.

"That's a nice bike you've got there. Keen cyclist, are you?"

I do not wish to discuss my cycling habits with Detective Inspector Jarvis. Still less do I wish him to examine the bike (though thankfully long since washed clean of Chilterns mud), or any number of other items stored in the garage.

"Not as much as I'd like. It's not enormous fun on

380

these roads."

He gestures towards the Skoda. "You should bung it into the back of that, take it out into the country. Much more relaxing out there. Healthier, too."

I adopt what I hope is the expression of a person to whom this has not occurred before.

"That's not a bad idea. I should think about that."

*

I keep waiting for Detective Inspector Jarvis to express his farewells (again) and leave. But again I am disappointed. He continues along the path.

"No, as I was saying, my brother and I used to sneak off round here to the bushes and roll up a cigarette with baccy we'd nicked from our dad." He stops in front of the rhododendrons. "Right here."

His manner is now positively genial. He is smiling and looking around him and talking to me as if I had the slightest iota of interest in what he and his scabby brother got up to in their prehistoric youth.

Though I am beginning to wonder if there is more to his little performance than meets the eye. Perhaps he is just taunting me, pretending to believe that I may care about these things (which may all be made up anyway, for all I know), while all the while taking me on a mute tour of my own past misdeeds. 'This is the bike that you took to the country to kill Darren Little, this is the car that you used to dispose of Jane Gardner, this is where you put Mr Donald Dennis into temporary storage'. Yet he cannot be aware of any of these things. Can he? Surely I am just being paranoid?

I do not know. I am too tired.

He is now bending down, peering into the gloom

381

amid the rhododendron bushes. While his back is turned I pull my handkerchief from my pocket and quickly mop my brow and upper lip.

"These are bigger as well," he says. Then he looks down at the disturbed earth and leaves. "Hallo. Looks like somebody's been up to something in here."

My heart nearly stops, and I feel suddenly faint. I do not know how much longer I can continue like this.

Then he straightens. "Probably foxes."

I am glad he is not watching me. He does not see my silent exhalation of breath, the relieved slump of my shoulders as my body starts to function again.

"Yes," I say. "It's probably foxes."

40

Saturday. The day of the St Nicholas, High End Children's Party.

Helen is bustling around in a state of high excitement. I, however, feel strangely calm.

This is mainly because I have had my first decent night's sleep in a week. The visit of Detective Inspector Jarvis yesterday evening seems to have had a cathartic effect on me. It is as if Fate has led me right to the brink, but then gently released my hand and faded away, leaving me free and unscathed. The searching beam of the police investigation has turned on me, but finding nothing, has moved on. I am safe. Ambrose is once again invincible.

This may of course all be hideously premature. But it is how I feel.

*

We are in our bedroom. We are in danger of being late, but Helen is flapping around. She cannot find an earring.

"It can't be far," she is saying. "The other one is exactly where it should have been, on the dressing table."

"Where did you take them off?" I ask. I gaze around the room, not knowing where to start looking. Helen may be perfect in almost every way, but she is not the tidiest of persons.

"I don't know," she says. She disappears into the bathroom. "It was ages ago – I can't remember."

She has already searched the dressing table so I start looking on her bedside table. It is quite cluttered. As well as her clock alarm and the lamp there are several books, a number of magazines, and a box of tissues. It is difficult to see where an earring could have hidden itself.

Without any great expectation I lift the top magazine to look underneath. There is a folded slip of paper there. It is pink, which surprises me. Helen does not like the colour pink very much.

Curious, I pick it up and open it up.

Without exaggeration, I think I can say that what I read there nearly causes me a heart attack.

'I met you in the car park,
Handsome, you were, and tall and dark.
It was raining, I was wet,
So into your car you asked me to get.
We drank, we talked, you made me laugh.
At the Way House that was only Half.
After, at home, I lay alone,
And dreamt of your body, hard and toned.
Weeks it's been, only four,

But with every one I want you more.
And now at last, today's the day.
I finally in your arms will lay.'

I recognise the writing, the childish, curly lettering. As a special feature in the poem, however, all the small 'i's are topped with a heart.

All week I have had the feeling that there was something I had forgotten, some detail I had overlooked. And now I remember, that fragment of conversation that generated a moment's curiosity before being swept out of my consciousness by the enormity of what I was about to do.

"I've got something for you. Don't let me forget to show it to you later."

"I bet you have."

"Not that, silly. And don't bother to look for it. I've hidden it."

So this maudlin, illiterate piece of doggerel was 'it'.

And it was hidden on Helen's bedside table.

Suddenly I feel unsteady on my feet. I sit back on the bed, the hateful document hanging between my fingers.

Helen reappears. "Found it," she says. "It was behind my hairbrush." Then she notices the slip of paper in my hand. "What's that?"

I glance down. "That? Oh, just a flier for mobile phones or something. Must have got caught up in one of the magazines."

I crumple the paper in my hand.

"Well, we need to go in a moment. Are you

ready?"

"Almost."

*

I go down to my study.

I am like a man sleepwalking. This must be what shellshock feels like, one part of my brain is thinking. The final trauma that pushes a person over the edge, the disaster that is avoided by a fraction of a hairsbreadth. The person survives, but he can never be the same again.

I block out the thought of what would have happened if Helen had picked up that sheet of paper rather than me. The look on her face, the realisation of betrayal, my inability ever to explain the real situation to her. I would have lost her, permanently, irreconcilably. Forever.

It is, quite literally, unthinkable.

I unfold the paper and feed what might possibly be Jane Gardner's last written words into my shredder. As I do so I wonder if this is not also part of my message from Fate. Yes, you have got away with this, with these things, but enough is enough. No more. You have risked the love of your life, gambled with the very meaning of your existence, and you have won. But you are playing Russian Roulette, and next time I, Fate, will not be so kind. It has to end.

The grinding of the shredder ceases, and I hear Helen's voice.

"Are you ready?"

I call back.

"Yes, my love. I'm ready."

*

Together we make our way outside. The garden is already bustling, some familiar faces, many more strange to me. Toddlers with their mothers, older children skittering around in twos and threes, members of our congregation behind the stalls and issuing directions. We are greeted with smiles and nods as we walk across the grass.

It is a perfect day for the Children's Party. Not a breath of wind, light, fluffy clouds drifting across a deep blue sky. Not too hot and not too cold. Our garden is an oasis of joy, a tableau of eternal summer.

"Can I have your attention please."

All heads turn to the far end of the garden, where Karen Eady, the curate, is standing on the stage that will later be used by Helen's young band. She is clutching a microphone.

"It is my great pleasure, on behalf of all of us at St Nicholas High End, to welcome you here today, and to declare this, our Children's Party, officially open."

There is a roar of applause and cheers. But all I can think is, it should be Helen welcoming people to our garden, not Karen Eady.

The curate raises her hand for silence before continuing.

"And I know that I speak for everyone when I say that today's party is being dedicated to the memory of someone who over the years has given so much to these occasions..."

No!

I turn to Helen. But she just shakes her head.

"...and who I know would have so loved to have been here today..."

387

No! Do not say it. Do not say those words!

I stretch out my arms.

"Don't go," I beseech her. "You can't leave me."

But she is starting to fade. A sad smile on her lips, she fades. Fades away...

In desperation I scan the crowd, looking for her. I see faces, faces, faces, some familiar, some unknown. Dimly I become aware that one of them belongs to Detective Inspector Jarvis. He advances towards me, seeming to glide through the crowds, flanked by a pair of uniformed police. He wears a grim smile, they are blank-faced and purposeful, but the gaze of all three is fixed unwavering on me.

And all the while those hateful words continue.

"...our own dear Rector, Helen Hillier, who passed away so tragically after a short illness two months ago."

I am aware that I have fallen to the ground. My eyes are tight closed, and my hands cover my ears. All I hear is a man screaming. Over and over and over he screams. There are no other sounds, nothing else at all. Just the screaming.

Just the screaming.

The screaming that will now never end.

THE END

Acknowledgements

Many people have helped me with my writing career over the years, but I would particularly like to mention Elena Forbes, Richard Holt, Cass Bonner, Gerry O'Donovan, Kathryn Skoyles, Margaret Kinsman and Broo Doherty - and most of all, my wife, Pui Kei.

About the author

Keith Mullins spent over two decades working in the financial markets before deciding that there must be more to life than watching small numbers flickering over a screen all day. His love of crime fiction led him to try his hand at writing, and 'The Rector's Husband' is his first published novel. He lives in Surrey.

2924200R00210

Printed in Great Britain
by Amazon.co.uk, Ltd.,
Marston Gate.